PRAISE FOR WILLIAM DIETRICH'S FICTION

ICE REICH: "Rousing, Indiana Jones–style debut thriller… rivals the page–turners of Alistair MacLean."
— *Kirkus Reviews.*

GETTING BACK: "An engaging read with considerable depth and twists."
— *Christian Science Monitor.*

DARK WINTER: "Tightly constructed, fast and very real… will send chills through you."
— *Austin Statesman–Journal.*

HADRIAN'S WALL: "Page–turning historical fiction seething with action, adventure, and passion."
— *Booklist.*

THE SCOURGE OF GOD: "A wonderful book… the battle-field descriptions are so vivid that one can almost taste the dust in the air… excellent and highly recommended."
— *Library Journal.*

NAPOLEON'S PYRAMIDS: "Superb… As in previous novels, Dietrich combines a likeable hero surrounded by a cast of fascinating historical characters. Riveting battle scenes, scantily clad women, mathematical puzzles, mysteries of the pharaohs, reckless heroism, hairsbreadth escapes, and undaunted courage add up to unbeatable adventure… Readers will cheer."
— *Publisher's Weekly starred review.*

THE ROSETTA KEY: "Historical fiction meets thriller here, with plenty to interest fans of both genres. The action is nearly nonstop, the humor is plentiful, and the intrigue is more than enough to keep the pages turning."

– School Library Journal.

THE DAKOTA CIPHER: "Fast, fun, and full of surprises."

– Publisher's Weekly starred review.

THE BARBARY PIRATES: "Dietrich is an excellent writer... An action–filled romp that's both historically accurate and great fun."

– Library Journal.

BLOOD OF THE REICH: "A barnstorming novel that sets its sights high and never fails to deliver... It would make one hell of a great film."

– New York Journal of Books.

THE EMERALD STORM: "A breathlessly exciting adventure, as fast paced as an Indiana Jones movie and just about as entertaining."

– Booklist starred review.

THE BARBED CROWN: "Readers will be treated to Dietrich's fascinating touches of historical detail and Gage's infectious personality, one part humble global servant and two parts self–directed opportunist who simply has to be where the action is."

– Publisher's Weekly.

THE THREE EMPERORS: "Historically accurate with an especially interesting underlying tension of mysticism and science. A fast–paced and engaging read."

– Historical Novels Review.

THE MURDER OF
ADAM AND EVE

THE MURDER OF ADAM AND EVE

BY WILLIAM DIETRICH

September 2014
ISBN 978–0–9906621–0–5
Burrows Publishing
www.Burrowspublishing.com

To inspiring teachers:
Leonard Lukin, English
Velma Smith, Creative Writing
Don McLeod, Writing
Robert Keller, History
Ted Stannard, Journalism
Howard Simons, Life

TABLE OF CONTENTS

Chapter 1

THE FORT

GOAT ISLAND IS forbidden.
As in, "No Trespassing." Hands off. Keep out.
Get lost, kid.

Which is why I paddled like a madman toward the island's abandoned Fort Whitman when hidden by fog. I'm your typical troubled teen doing my best to keep out of trouble, which meant I needed to get on and off the island before anyone spotted me.

Skagit Bay was flat as a game board this windless autumn day, my kayak cutting like a spear towards the shrouded isle. I startled at a gull's cry, and tensed at the far–off drone of an outboard. Otherwise, the world was muffled in cotton.

Which meant I could hear the lilt of the paddles and my heart in my ears. I was pretending to be stealthy as a Ninja and chill as a Navy SEAL, but I didn't want my quest for a scholarship to land me in Juvy.

I'd paddled ten miles from my hometown of

Anacortes the day before to spend the night alone at a state park closer to Goat Island, timing ocean fog. I supped on an energy bar, banana, and cold pea soup from a can. Because the trek was for a History Day scholarship, Mom tolerated my overnight – or, more accurately, was too tired to worry. She's a bookkeeper who pulls barmaid at The Brown four nights a week, and it's still not enough. Accordingly, boy wonder Nick Brynner – that's me – scrapes hamburger grills after school.

Since my Dad died of cancer I've grown up, and Mom's grown old, faster than either of us wants to. I'm sixteen in calendar years, about ten in social skills, and twenty in taking care of myself. If you think that's somehow good, you haven't missed a good chunk of your childhood. Responsibility sucks.

Morning brought the predicted pall from the Strait of Juan de Fuca. I rode the flood tide through Deception Pass at a jogger's pace, dark kelp undulating and saltwater at a boil. The famous canyon–like cleft reared into mist like a craggy castle, and two hundred feet above, the bottommost green girders of a highway bridge were faint and fuzzy in the fog.

There's a plaque up there to a teenager who jumped, the water hard as concrete and chill as the grave. Just the thought gives me the creeps. Did he regret his decision those long seconds down?

So I paddled faster, the current spitting me into the broader bay, and made a jump of a different sort. As I coasted the final yards toward Goat Island, red–and–white *No Trespassing* signs materialized out of the mist. They warned me from a place that the U.S. Army had hastily abandoned a hundred years before.

Why?

"Federal biologists made it a no–humans–allowed wildlife refuge so they don't have to worry about people breaking their neck in the abandoned fort," theorized Peter Faunus, my biology teacher and, no contest, the most awesome adult at Anacortes High. "You must never, ever, go there, Nick. Rules, right? But if you *did*, in the fog, when nobody could see you, the GPS on a cell phone would help you navigate." He'd laid his own phone on a lab bench. "You'd hide your kayak in the trees and get back off the island before the fog lifted. *If* you went there. Which of course you won't."

This was classic Mr. Faunus. He'd be in trouble if I got caught on Goat Island at his suggestion, but he was as curious about forbidden isles as me. Faunus was a sudden, eccentric, long–term substitute for Mr. Quinn, who was recovering from a fall. For some weird reason Quinn's replacement took a liking to me, which never happens. Two outsiders, I guess. The temp and the geek.

Here's the problem, or should I say opportunity? My History Day project is a report on four 1900–era forts that once protected Puget Sound. Trouble is, Fort Whitman is a blank in the records. Almost completely forgotten. In fact, *so* forgotten that it seems *purposely* forgotten. Suspicious, right? History's mystery. And Mr.

Faunus seems more fascinated by secrets than cranky Mrs. Riley, the American History teacher who actually runs the contest with lemon–pucker mouth and steel wool hair. But then Faunus is fascinated by *everything*, and by Goat Island precisely *because* you aren't supposed to go there.

"There's no rare seabird colony. No endangered species. So when government says 'Beware' without reason, a good citizen asks 'Why?'"

Mr. Faunus pushes us to question things. He loves to talk about our prehistoric origins. Sometimes he even drags God into discussions of evolution, and if parents complain on either side he doesn't back down. He says that's because he's a substitute and single: So what if they fire him? I say he cares about truth. In high school, that's the Red Badge of Courage.

In fact, Mr. Faunus is sort of like the dad I'd have liked if my own dad hadn't died of blood cancer, back when I was ten. That is, if Mr. Faunus could ever be a dad in the regular way. Kids figure he's gay since he's not married, plays opera and musical tunes in biology class, and baffles the pep crowd by having interests beyond football. He wears bowties, bright socks, and every day tells his classes about the latest book he's excited about. Which means he's about a thousand IQ points ahead of Carl, Mom's refinery janitor boyfriend whose intellect stops at cheap 12–packs of beer and redneck opinion.

"The guy's a fruit, Nick. He likes you for a reason."

Carl's a tool.

Mom's boyfriend even smokes, as if he didn't pick up enough carcinogens at work. She insists he do it outside but I know he cheats, since our couch stinks of tobacco and beer. So he's giving everyone else cancer, too, but Mom won't say anything because who else wants a wrung–out woman with an underachieving teen as dependent?

Mom thinks Carl is the best she can do. I say, sometimes something is worse than nothing.

So I paddled alone, navigating in the fog with my cheap cell phone and calling my habitual solitude self–reliance. I wore a faded red baseball cap, backpack with the Ten Essentials, and pricey trail boots bought with money I told Mom I was saving for college. All to pretend that loneliness is cool.

Too bad I can't fool myself.

My kayak grounded in the shallows, the scrape of barnacles no big deal since I'd salvaged the boat as a wreck. I saved up from work at Fidalgo Drive–In and bought epoxy and fiberglass from West Marine for a crude patch.

Carl took one look, announced, "It looks like crap," and didn't offer to help make it better.

Mom was simply grateful the boat was cheaper than a car and more wholesome than drugs. She'd helped me carry a hull the color of paste down to saltwater. "Don't get bumped by a whale."

My kayak is escape. I hide the boat in a hollow cedar log at a university marine research reserve where no one goes, and launch it to leave teenage wasteland behind. *Hooah*, a Marine might grunt.

I once mentioned to Mr. Faunus that Marines shout "hooah," and he cocked his head, thought a moment, and said, "Given their circumstances, that's an entirely appropriate thing to say."

Faunus said I restored his faith in the youth of America because I preferred paddling to screen time. I didn't tell him our computer is six years old and we have a crappy tube TV.

Anyway, I've thought about enlisting as a jarhead someday, except I'm not too keen about taking orders from people who call themselves jarheads. Or doing pushups. I didn't even like the jolly jockdom of Boy Scouts, except the campout skills. I'm not much of a joiner, schmoozer, leader, or follower. I'm just me.

Now I heaved myself onto thickly forested Goat Island, boots soaked, and dragged the craft into the bushes. A heron shrieked in protest, flapping away into the fog.

Which way? Logic dictated where the guns must have pointed, so I shouldered my pack and bush-whacked uphill through fir and hemlock, feeling the press of time. *Get in, get out.*

Fort Whitman was completed in 1911, a strategic afterthought for enemy ships that tried to sneak the back way into Puget Sound by squeezing through Deception Pass. When they ran by Goat Island its cannon would blast them to pieces.

Accordingly, concrete was laboriously barged, batteries built, guns hoisted. But before firing a practice shot, the Army took its cannons and left.

Historians explain the fort had become obsolete, but that's bogus because the other forts were used through World War II. So the military had gone to enormous trouble putting a gun battery on a remote island and then walked away. If I could explain why, my project might have a shot at a History Day scholarship.

I'd found old clippings. "People go out there and don't come back," the county sheriff said ominously, way back in 1922. A soldier named Ruben Dunbar was recorded AWOL, but the truth was that he'd simply disappeared. Poof!

"Police state propaganda," Mr. Faunus called the sheriff's warning. "Also, quotable in the extreme."

So I planned to put that sinister little sheriff sentiment on a poster presentation with some clever new theory.

That was the strategy. Not courage, but desperation.

Look: No money for car or college. Grades that bump unexceptionally at 3.0; I'd rather read my own library books than tedious texts. My after–school activity is changing fryer fat, and my tryout at second–string football ended with bench boredom. I need a scholarship if I'm ever going to do what I want to do, and a fat History Day prize might help. Ms. Riley didn't offer much encouragement, but Mr. Faunus said I could win

$5,000 at State, which might get me notice from other financial aid sources.

Of course, I don't know yet what I *do* want to do, except not be like Carl.

And, explore old forts.

A game trail led toward the likeliest bluff, the forest light murky as an aquarium. Mist hung like smoke. Trees dripped. I broke into a clearing with blocky concrete buildings the color of snot, their window holes empty of glass. Moss and fern fuzzed every roof like pyramids in the jungle. What was so bad about this place that people stayed away? Peaceful as a graveyard, it seemed to me.

An eagle shrieked, and I jumped. Then laughed at myself.

History Day, dude! Document, and depart.

I held the cell phone out and snapped a selfie.

"Should have brought a pith helmet."

CHAPTER 2

THE LOCKED GATE

THE BUNKERS *WERE* eerie, matted and gloomy. Four huge circular concrete platters marked where the cannons once pivoted, and half–wrapped around each of these circles was a protective bunker that had held shells, supplies, primitive telephones, and men. Now the concrete rooms were as featureless as the inside of an empty cereal box.

I hesitated, wishing Zach or Jonas had come. But my kayak only holds one, I'm trespassing, and my nerdy friends are incapable of keeping a secret. Besides, they just want to play Xbox, another toy I can't afford and therefore suck at. Fifty bucks a game to blow away zombies? "When I win the lottery, buddy," Mom likes to say.

Grandma is even worse. "Wish in one hand, spit in the other, and see which gets full the first." She has a million sayings like that.

So I took a breath and went inside alone. Footsteps echoed and water plopped. Rodents and insects skittered from my flashlight beam. There were puddles, the stink of mold, and little pimples of limestone that had leached from the concrete ceiling like tiny stalactites. Extreme fixer–upper.

I used a notebook to sketch the fort's plan and snapped pictures wherever light glimmered enough to make my cell phone focus. The darkest places squeezed, but I told myself that this was an adventure I'd later savor.

Ha.

What would really be sweet would be bringing Andrea Martinez here, because I could imagine her clinging tight. Of course, I've never had the nerve to ask Andrea *anywhere*. I was pathetically relieved when I heard she was going to the prom with Shane Wagner, because it meant I didn't have to risk asking her myself, even though we were science class lab partners. Yes, lame. But with her glossy hair, astonishing female architecture, teen queen smile, and 3.9 smarts, Andrea seems as unobtainable as car, college, Xbox, or popularity. You goddess, me mortal.

At first I hardly noticed the iron slab on the bunker floor that rested in the middle of the fort's magazine like the lid on a tomb. But when I worked my way back, scribbling, I tripped on it and swore.

Talk about stumbling on destiny. I shined my light. The slab was crooked.

Not crooked, but slightly *ajar*. Four–feet–square

and askew enough to show a cavity underneath. The slab was a locked hatch, but a hatch that had shifted.

Or maybe a lid to seal something *in*.

I looked closer. There was a chain to secure the thing, and an old padlock, rusty as a shipwreck, to keep me out. Message received. Except – and this was the weird part – the chain itself had broken at a link, as if struck or pulled by some immense force.

Had someone been here before me?

I had a sense of being watched. But when my flashlight danced over blank walls there was nothing and nobody to solve the mystery of the fort's abandonment except good ol' Nick. Was there a clue below?

Let's see what kind of a man you are, Brynner.

I tugged the broken chain through the hasp and heaved to get the hatch open. Stale air wafted up. It had the smell of a well, a sewer, or the kind of basement you don't want to go down in.

A concrete shaft descended straight into the earth, an iron ladder on one side. The other side had two embedded rails. Descent looked about as prudent as cliff diving at Deception Pass.

No way was I going down there.

Except.

Very faintly, the cavity glowed.

The ladder rungs were flaky with rust and cold as ice. I played the flashlight and saw nothing but another wet concrete floor far below, so I jammed the light in my belt and climbed down, cautiously testing each rung before putting my full weight on it. If I fell, there was no one to rescue me.

The shaft was deeper than I'd guessed, and as I climbed down the exit at the top looked increasingly remote. I imagined something sliding the hatch back in place, like closing the lid on a casket.

There's nobody here, dude.

The bottom was a puddle of black water. I examined the two vertical iron tracks opposite the ladder and wondered if they were rails to hoist artillery shells. It would make sense to have an ammunition magazine down here, safe from enemy gunfire. I dutifully made notes, just to have an excuse to hesitate. A corridor led off horizontally, so I painted it with my flashlight until I worked up the courage to follow, splashing to dry pavement.

Hope the batteries don't go out.

There were empty rooms on each side, peeling paint the only thing left. Then stairs, smooth concrete leading down to a rock fissure. Had the Army accidentally burrowed its way to a natural cave? I felt entombed. I also had that feeling of being watched again, and thought I heard something prowl. I shined the flashlight back the way I'd come.

Don't want rats.

This rustle sounded bigger than a rat.

Imagination, Brynner. Shut it down.

I beamed my flashlight down the stairs and it played off the bars of an iron gate on a landing below.

Unfortunately, that was interesting.

Faunus wouldn't quit.

So I gingerly went down the old concrete stairs, feeling the massive weight of all that earth above. Why the heck did this fort delve so deep? Weird, weird, weird.

The gate was a grill like a jail cell door, secured with a second and newer padlock. There was a faded and rusty metal sign. *"Danger. Do Not Open."* Alongside was a cobwebbed skull and crossbones.

On the opposite wall was a corroded steel slab with a metal ring to pull on, except this door's edges were welded shut.

Got it. Don't go this way. Don't go that way.

New theory: the Army found a cave that undermined their foundations so they left before cannon recoil caused a collapse. Geology doomed the enterprise. I'd never heard of caves around here, but it was plausible enough for History Day – and reason enough to turn around. I set down the flashlight to shine on the gate and took another picture.

Odd. When I checked the cell phone camera roll, the image had whited out.

I stood a minute, listening to nothing but dripping water, and finally got up the nerve to turn off my light. An avalanche of blackness. Except... Yep. There definitely was a faint glow beyond that grilled door.

"Hello?" My voice echoed, scaring myself.

I turned the flashlight back on. The lock on the bars gave me an excuse to retreat. *If I broke a leg down here, I'd never be found.* I gave the gate a farewell shake and turned to go. Then I heard a tinkle and realized the locked padlock had a key that swung on a fine chain. That seemed to defeat the lock's purpose, but...

The padlock had no keyhole.

The bottom of the lock was solid metal. There was a metal door covering the face of the lock, but when I pried with my fingernail this cover wouldn't budge. Why a key with no purpose?

It's a puzzle, Nick.

I looked closer. Old–fashioned skeleton key.

Time was ticking. *Get off the island!* But curiosity nagged.

I twisted and tapped the padlock. Stumped.

Except... my flashlight showed the tiniest of shadows, a hole near the edge of the padlock's metal door. It was a fissure impossible to see unless the padlock was held to the light in precisely the right way.

Far too small for the key to fit.

So I'd give up again! Yet even as I dropped the key I finally registered what my finger had unconsciously felt, a tiny protuberance on the key's end. There was a blunt spike an eighth–inch long, just the right size to fit the hole.

Tab A into Slot B.

The chain let me twist the key around just enough to insert the bump into the padlock.

Bingo. With a spring the metal door on the face flew open, revealing a big fat keyhole for the big fat key. But why a lock? Why a key? Why a puzzle? Why a solution?

I inserted the skeleton key, gave it a hard twist, and the padlock snapped open. The door squealed invitation and clanged against the cave wall.

Do you ever think that what happens is *supposed* to happen?

I do, now.

More stairs leading downward, toward that glow.

The surface seemed a million miles away. But I knew I was near the solution to Fort Whitman's mystery. The Army hadn't just found a geologic fault.

People who go out there don't come back.

I counted the steps as I walked down, the air so heavy it felt as if I were descending into a pool. Was there a hum, or did I imagine it?

Thirteen steps. Then a stone tunnel that twisted like a worm.

I realized I could see without my flashlight. The strange glow had grown stronger.

Radiation. Nerve gas. Killer fog. Except I didn't feel dread.

The cave burrowed toward light and as it grew brighter my fear floated away. I explored as if in a dream. And there *was* a hum, or was it a whisper of voices? A strange lilt of song?

Nick, get out of there! But my warning thought called from a great distance, and I fell *horizontally* toward the light, the stone dissolving into a crackle of pure energy. No, a white tunnel, sucking me *up!*

Am I dead? I felt pulled, *stretched.*

And then all illumination winked out and I was in the blackest blackness I'd ever experienced. There was no *there* there.

*S*omething was sadly, irrevocably, misplaced.

Me. And History Day was history.

Chapter 3

DESERTED

Birdcall. Shrill, piping.

It penetrated my unconsciousness like annoying pricks of sound, lilting yet insistent. *Chirpadee–chirp–chirp–chirp.* I wanted to sleep, but it kept getting louder. Shut up! And now *glare* again. I squeezed my eyes, and then peeked. Golden sunlight, scratchy vines. I shifted, stiff and cold.

I'm outside, I dimly realized. How?

I was sprawled in brush as if tossed like a ragdoll, the morning's fog lifting like steam. Groaning, I sat up, pounded as a punching bag. Every muscle ached.

What had happened?

Nothing, it seemed. I lay on Goat Island after fainting or falling asleep. Had I gone into Fort Whitman at all? And where was my pack? Flashlight? Cell phone?

The light grew as the mist burned.

Go or risk getting caught. Not supposed to be here, remember? I stumbled toward shore.

The kayak was where I left it, so only my brain was missing in action. I dragged the boat to the water and stopped to listen. Any boats? Any authorities looking for me? Silence. A distant fog bank was a wall. I boarded awkwardly, almost tipping until I used the paddle to balance.

Around me the sea boiled as if it had come alive. I looked over the side. There were thousands of herring churning the shallows, in shifting shoals of silver. Why so many? Seagulls were splashing down to feed, shrieking excitedly.

Paddle, Brynner. You've got to get out of here.

I stroked a hundred yards and glided. No shouts of outrage, no patrol boats, no police helicopters. In fact, no boat or airplane anywhere. I'd visited Forbidden Isle and no one seemed to care. All I could hear was birds. I was relieved, but the lack of drama was almost disappointing. Had I cut and run too soon?

Worse, the tide was still flooding, pushing me away from escape through Deception Pass and pushing me toward Swinomish Channel. The current should have turned, but hadn't. I was drifting the wrong way.

I glanced at my watch. Despite a recent battery this new one had stopped at six minutes past eleven, about the time I'd been in the old fort's bunkers – if I'd really been there.

Terrific. Another repair we couldn't afford.

I stroked in place against the current. How was I going to paddle home?

The hazed afternoon sun was low. Surprisingly low. Disturbingly low. How long had I been asleep? Why hadn't the tide turned?

Okay, Plan B. Swinomish Channel led to La Conner, a fishing-and-farming village turned touristy. Its oddball name came from its founder combining last name Conner with his wife's first two initials, a romantic gesture equaled by my own Anacortes, a corruption of the founder's wife maiden name, Anna Curtis. The pioneers must have been running out of ideas by the time they crossed the continent, because my stomping grounds also included names like Sedro Woolley, Concrete, Acme, Oso, Diablo, Hoogdal, and Chuckanut.

If I had the world to name, what would I pick? It seems important, like naming a child.

Kandahar. Tahiti. Masada. Kamchatka. I like maps.

Focus, Nick. I'd paddle to La Conner and call Mom. She'd be annoyed to make the half-hour drive, but no way could I fight the tide.

That strange white light! Maybe Mr. Faunus could explain it. Or Rudnick, from physics.

I'd need another fog to sneak back to Goat Island to find my phone and gear. Meanwhile my confusion had essentially left a business card for federal wildlife agents: "Nick Brynner, trespasser, was here."

Cool move.

I shook my sluggish head. I've only been drunk once, at Whistle Lake with Zach, Jonas, and a bottle of whiskey that Zach lifted from his parents. It made us all puke. Didn't enjoy it, which is just as well since I don't get invited to keggers, smoke–outs, or anything else where you're supposed to bring a personality. My not–so–secret life as dweeb, worried about past, present, and future, keeps me shy and running near empty in the self–esteem department. Still, I remembered feeling after Whistle Lake what I felt now: hung over.

Had I really been in that tunnel?

The current carried me. There was no other boat traffic. Ritzy homes lined the water, but I saw no lights or movement. I passed under orange–colored Rainbow Bridge and past tribal gillnetters docked like landing craft at the Swinomish Indian Reservation. The pioneer town of La Conner was on the eastern shore, a mosaic of clapboard and brick with bright false fronts and Victorian trim. It's all very charming and precious, filled with knickknacks Mom says we can't afford.

I tied up on La Conner Pier, lifted myself out, and stretched, trying to figure out why everything felt wrong.

It was quiet, I finally realized. Too quiet. No other boat moved on the Channel. There was no hiss and rumble from cars. No drone from airplanes. Just the splash of fish in the channel, salmon jumping to smack like beaver tails. There were so many that they were popping like popcorn.

That never happened.

It was when I walked up First Street that things got really weird. There were no people *anywhere*.

As in nada. Zero. Except me.

The town's main drag was entirely empty, littered with leaves and fir needles. Cars were parked but they were still and filthy, their windshields coated with grime. Storefronts were dark. Power poles marched down the main drag as they were supposed to, black cables drooping, but there was no electricity.

No voices. No music. No hammering.

I could hear the *wind,* and how often do you listen to that?

I looked in the window of Calico Cupboard. Unpeopled and dark. Had there been some kind of evacuation?

Wood Merchant: Empty.

Art galleries: Empty.

Sweet Shoppe: Empty.

There was one payphone left downtown, a blue antique. I picked it up. Dead. A coin didn't help.

A thousand possibilities flashed through my mind. Nearby refineries had leaked. A dirty bomb in Seattle. Terrorist plague here in Cute and Cozy. An eruption of Mount Baker. Zombies, vampires, or a neutron bomb.

I heard the clop of hooves and turned to what I thought would be horse and rider. Trotting by instead was a deer with a five–point rack that a guy like Carl would give his left ear for, not to mention his left something else. The buck was magnificent, and as out of place as a Pamplona bull in Nordstrom. It eyed me with serene unconcern, as if it had never heard the crack of a gun in its life.

Now other movement caught my eye. A raccoon waddling out of sight by a pub. A family of quail making a dash across pavement. And on the hill behind an art gallery, a rustle in the bushes between buildings that I first thought was a dog.

That's one humungous dog, Mr. Brynner. Can you spell b–e–a–r? A black bear, scary as a tank, was working its merry way uphill toward a church above.

Oh.

My.

God.

I broke into a trot, jogging down the street. "Anyone here?" My shouted question echoed back at me.

Windows were dark mirrors. Cars were still as boulders.

A barn–red building with a twin gable roof had a kitchen store called the Ginger Grater. I sensed movement up high and stopped, hoping to spy another refugee like me. I surveyed the roofline.

Yes! Something crawled on the silver metal as quick as a child.

Except it wasn't a child. It was a monkey, or an ape.

I was going nuts.

The ape stopped midway along the roof peak. Its sentry gaze swept to survey the town.

Then its snout twitched and it peered down, fixing me like a riflescope. It sniffed.

I stumbled back, terrified.

Because the creature up there was definitely *not* an ape, nor a child, nor anything else I'd seen before. Its eyes were as black and pitiless as a shark's, its muzzle set in a permanent frown, its ears pointed, its back hunched. Its forelegs, or arms, wrapped the roof peak with claws like a devil.

The being was a freakin' *gargoyle*, the kind of monster they put on medieval churches and old New York skyscrapers. Except this one was alive.

Please wake up.

And then there was a shout, the girl's voice urgent.

"Run *this* way!"

Running was the most sensible suggestion I'd heard in some time, so I bolted in her direction. Another human! I got a glimpse of blond ponytail bouncing like a squirrel tail as she sprinted up First Street toward the city's marina. I chased after with a jolt of adrenaline, still not sure I'd really seen what I'd just seen.

But *something* descended the downspout of the Ginger Grater with the fluid moves of an animal.

Or monster.

I was fast – my stupor had evaporated from fear – but barely gained on a girl who sprinted like an antelope. I dared not look back but I heard something big thud heavily to the ground, and a *whuff* like an animal snort. I ran faster.

The girl led me a couple blocks further from my kayak and swerved through Gilkey Square, dashing to reach a dock ramp and float. I followed and saw her clamber into a speedboat on Swinomish Channel. She turned a key and the outboard roared to life.

Behind me there was the pound of pursuing... feet? Hooves? Paws? Coming on fast, with a *whuff, whuff, whuff.*

"Hurry!" she yelled, as if I needed encouragement. She tossed off lines. The boat began drifting.

I sprinted like a track star, boards barking, and felt the quake of that thing landing on the float behind me. It smelled like a refrigerator when the food has spoiled. The float rocked crazily, threatening to pitch me in, and there was a three–foot wide gap of water between the speedboat and me. A girl my age grasped its wheel and throttle, not even bothering – or daring – to look back. I didn't jump so much as dove, arms outstretched, and hit the side of the craft hard. My feet dragged in the water. I grunted.

She jammed the throttle.

The outboard roared and the boat reared like a stallion. I barely hauled myself aboard as the propeller dug. Then we surged forward, starting to plane on flat water. The speedboat leveled and we raced back past La Conner, our steep wake radiating in a large V.

I looked back. Something squat and dark had stopped at the end of float and was angrily lashing the water with long, sinewy arms, eyes red, teeth yellow. Were those *horns?*

I heard, over the whine of the engine, an unworldly shriek more hideous than anything I'd ever imagined.

Message received. Officially a nightmare.

The creature rapidly shrank as we shot down the channel at more than thirty miles per hour, bouncing my moored kayak with our waves. Rainbow Bridge flashed overhead.

"What the hell was *that?*"

"Not hell, Nick. The heavens. You just saw a Consequence."

I looked at my savior, who somehow knew my name. She peered resolutely down channel to avoid logs or rocks, wind levitating her ponytail from underneath a blue cap. A pretty girl in designer jeans, white T–shirt, and light hiking boots, spiffy as a model for an outdoor catalog.

"I'm having a bad day," I managed.

"Of course you are." She skimmed through a group of black cormorants, sending them flying. "You trespassed."

CHAPTER 4

THE PIT

WHEN I ASKED where we were going she said, "To the time we're supposed to be," and arrowed toward Goat Island. I tried to tell her the place was bad news but she slid in fast, ramming the boat up a cobbled beach. The outboard kicked out of the water and howled, until she killed it.

Must not be her boat.

She hopped over the bow and disappeared into the woods without waiting. What could I do but follow?

Her slim legs threaded brush as gracefully as a deer, my savior having a clearer idea of direction to the old bunkers than I did. We were panting too hard for any questions. At Fort Whitman she glanced back just once, not for me but past me for any pursuit, and then made a beeline for the chamber where I'd descended. She felt her way in the dark to the open shaft and its peculiar underground glow.

"Down the hatch," she said. "Or maybe I should say down the rabbit hole, like Alice into Wonderland."

I caught my breath. "Not."

"Don't you want your things?" She dropped onto the rusty rungs, stopping when her head was just below the lip. "Get down here beside me, Nick. We have to pull the lid back over."

"I'm not going down there again."

"It's the only way. Or do you want to wait for the gort?"

That creature had a name? "It's still chasing us? Can it swim?"

"It never stops when things leak through."

"Leak through *what?*"

"The warp and weave of existence. Trolls, pixies, unicorns, dinosaurs mistaken for dragons, and people like you and me. The gorts retrieve them, or rather dispose of them, like a dogcatcher or litter collector. It keeps the worlds in order. Sometimes gorts pop into our time track, which is how gargoyles came into the imaginations of medieval sculptors. Do you understand we weren't supposed to be there and see that?""See *what?*"

"A Consequence. It's not real, except as an illustration of what might happen if we don't act. Or maybe if we do."

I groaned. "Please make sense."

"Get down here before it's too late." The blue of her eyes was electric, pleading, commanding. "I've risked a lot to fetch you. I need a hand."

C'mon, macho man, this can't be real. So I clambered down next to her, our hips and shoulders touching. Like I said, she was pretty. I'm a guy.

There was an iron ring hanging on the bottom of the lid. We heaved until the hatch sealed us in.

"I feel buried alive."

"It's worse than that." She was already climbing down toward the faint glow. I followed, too disoriented to try anything else.

When we descended to the cave I started to go through the grilled gate again, but she stopped me. "That just takes you back to the gort. Wait here a moment." She trotted toward the glow but came back quickly with my pack, flashlight, and cell phone.

"Good thinking. The cops might find it."

"You'll wish there were cops." She held out my belongings. "We're going to need these because it's primitive where we're going."

"Where's that?"

"Somewhere important." While I put on my pack the girl slammed and locked the gate, clicking the cover back over to hide the keyhole. "Fortunately, gorts are stupid and lack fine motor skills. Chewing is not a problem."

"Should we take the key just in case?" I yanked it from its chain and put it in my pocket.

She nodded approvingly. "You learn fast."

"But now we're trapped, right?"

"When one door closes, another opens. Look behind you."

I turned. The solid steel door that had been welded shut last time was now flung wide, revealing a dark cave. There was no glow, just a cold draft. "Who opened this?"

"We did, by choosing to come back."

The edges were bare raw metal, as if the steel had been wrenched by a sudden blast. "That's some choosing."

"It's the only way home." She seized my hand, her palm radiating tension. "Ready?" She faced the black tunnel.

"No! What *is* this?"

She looked impatient. "A wormhole through time and space, a scientist might say. Except there's not really time or space in the way we think. It's a corridor."

"A corridor *where?*"

"Don't you mean a corridor *when?* The Xu understand it. We don't. You and I are ants at an astronomy lecture."

"The Zoo?"

"Yes, Xu. X–U, they spelled it to me. The overseers of the Judgment." She pulled, her tug urgent. "All we can do is harness their technology to do what you're destined to do."

"Which is?"

"Find Adam and Eve."

"Oh Jeez. You're absolutely nuts."

"Am I? Stealing a boat? Dragging you here? Your

job is to rescue us, Nick. Save your own life and that of everyone you know. In that deserted town you saw a Consequence of what happens if you fail. In that monster, you saw how bad things could become."

She dragged me into the dark.

"Wait, I'll use the flashlight." I turned it on. The beam illuminated nothing.

"Useless," the girl said. "Batteries are a waste."

She yanked my arm, hard, and we fell forward into nothingness. It was just like pitching off a bridge, except there was no bottom. We plunged, my brain screaming, into the darkest of darks once more.

CHAPTER 5

GARGOYLES AND ANGELS

I STOOD ON STARS. No, stood on something solid, except it was nothing I could see. A galaxy of stars was underneath my feet. They were overhead and all around, thicker and brighter than any night sky I'd ever seen. We were near a galactic center lit with the blaze of a hundred thousand suns. They were not just white but red, yellow, blue, and green, glimmering amid clouds of luminescent gas. Christmas, squared.

I stood in outer space on something firm as a gym floor, as cozily warm as a kitchen, and breathable as a park. Which meant I couldn't be in space at all, could I? Was it some kind of projection in an ordinary room? Were the walls and floor mirrors, endlessly reflecting starlight at each other? I couldn't tell.

The girl was six feet away, wary as a rabbit. Movement tripped the edge of my vision and she whispered. "Rock still."

The monster materialized from the shimmer of

stars, hunched and sinister. Yes indeedy there were horns, claws, and all the other impalers of a choicest midnight movie. It knuckle–walked like an ape but had talon fingers, and made that *whuff, whuff, whuff* as it swung along. I froze, waiting to be eaten. But the gort, or whatever it was, never turned its head of scales and filthy fur. It ambled on until it seemed to dematerialize into space as eerily as it had appeared.

My companion relaxed slightly. "They react to movement. They're stupid, I think. They still haven't hurt me, but they will if we try to escape, and fail. Or if we trespass. You saw a Consequence by paddling to that town, Nick, which meant you blew the normal time circuits and went onto the wrong track. Now we're back in what Gabe calls the Roundhouse, and we've been chosen to find the *right* track."

Oh. My. God. Next this girl would be baying at the moon. I shut my eyes and opened them. Same spangle of galactic sky. I realized I still had my backpack on my back, my cap on my head, and my boots on my feet. Those trappings were my only hold on reality.

"This is a dream, right? A hallucination? I've gone crazy? Been drugged?"

"I wish, because that would mean it's a dream to me, too. But if it is, it's one I can't wake up from, and believe me I've tried. I'm afraid it's as real as that stuff I used to call reality."

"Who is Gabe?"

"I am," said a deep, fluidic voice, the kind you hear

in a PBS documentary or school DVDs. Which made what I encountered next even weirder.

Shimmering against the stars, having materialized like the gort, was an angel. Or what might be mistaken for one, the way you could mistake a gort for a gargoyle. I saw a handsome man with curly dark hair and of indeterminate age in a glowing white gown, with Greek–god looks and Jesus–wise eyes. Elegant. Dignified. Kind. As fantastically perfect as a centerfold, solemn and yet kindly, with wings of mist that materialized in and out. Sometimes they looked like those of a dove, and sometimes like those of a butterfly.

All was clear now. "I'm dead."

"Not yet," the angel said matter of factly. "You've been recruited, Nick Brynner, to what I realize seems a very strange place for a very strange mission. But you're alive, and your challenge will be to stay that way. Survival, in fact, is one of the points of the Judgment. I've been assigned as your mentor. I'll explain what I can."

When you have a million questions, sometimes you blurt out the dumbest that comes to mind. "How do you guys know my name?"

"Peter Faunus told us you were coming."

My mouth was open as a mailbox. "Mr. Faunus?"

"He said you had the curiosity and perhaps the character."

My teacher was part of this? "And 'Gabe'?"

"Ellie gave me that name." He nodded at the girl.

"Short for Gabriel. I understand he's a famous angel. She's instructed me as I've instructed her."

"About what?"

"Earth. While she's been studying, too."

I turned to her. "Studying what?"

The girl looked at me guiltily. "The place of Judgment, which is a kind of game. You've been chosen, Nick. Or rather you chose yourself when you trespassed and stepped into that glowing tunnel. It was resourceful, by the way. Brave."

"Faunus thought you'd be prepared," the angel added. "Boy Scout prepared."

Fear was beginning to give way to frustration. "Brave, or dumb?"

"I've been waiting for someone like you to help me," Ellie said. "I saved you by dashing ahead to commandeer that speedboat, but you're saving me, too. It was fate and it was choice.""Chosen by what? Who?"

"The Xu," Gabe said.

This was as bad as calculus class. I actually like math, but in that one I sweated to get my 'B.' "Where are we? What are we standing on?"

"I call it the Roundhouse," the angel–creature said with professorial patience and an upper–crust English accent straight out of Hollywood casting. "Like the place to turn train locomotives around to go on a different track. Or, a terminal, an airport, a turnstile. But I guess most people would call it a spaceship. It isn't made of metal and plastic like the spaceships you're familiar with, Nick. It's made up of force, but then we Xu would say energy and matter are simply sides of the same coin. A life force, so it's also as if we're inside flesh, swallowed by a whale. There are forms of energy and matter your species hasn't detected yet. We manipulate them as you manipulate electricity or steam. But what you're experiencing is very much a part of the real living world, not of whatever comes in the afterlife. This... panorama... is as concrete as that army bunker you explored, and as tangible as your bed at home."

I closed my eyes and opened them again. Same stars. "Let me get this straight. You're the Xu? An angel who looks like a movie star and talks like a British lord? Called Gabe?"

He smiled. "I'm flattered if the illusion is successful. It's a disguise we plucked from Eleanor's subconscious, because the way we truly appear would be upsetting. Not horrible, but completely strange, because evolution and genetic engineering set us on a different path from yours. Our kind is very much older, and we roam the stars. We came to your planet in the year you call 1947, after detecting the heat register of the first atomic explosions. A bomb is several million degrees at the core, and several thousand on the face of the expanding fireball. Civilizations only produce this when they're on the brink. We've been investigating since."

"The UFO craze," I said. "Except the crazies weren't crazy."

"Most *were* ordinary lights in the sky, mistaken for

flying saucers. But not all. We've tried communicating with our real appearance but most can't handle that. Some went insane. Now we're more careful."

"So you choose an angel as your disguise?" He was the one who was crazy. "You're reaching, spaceman." I'm not a smart ass, but this wackiness was six impossible things before breakfast, as the Alice book put it.

Gabriel looked at the girl he called Ellie.

She shrugged. "You plucked it, not me."

"Maybe next time I'll be a wizard," the angel said, mimicking her shrug as if still practicing. Creepy.

I fell down a mountain once and broke my leg, kind of a graceless tumble after stepping on a slick snow bank when hiking. Now the sick realization of having made an irrevocable mistake was repeated. Somehow I had slipped.

"We took the details from art in your civilization," the creature went on. "Your species seems reassured by it."

"Trust me, we aren't. Most of us want to postpone angels as long as possible."

"You have a sense of humor." Gabe said this without smiling. Which implied he didn't. Bad sign.

Maybe this was a hallucination. But the weirdest thing was that it didn't feel weird, it felt real. And I didn't get it. "You guys aren't making any sense. I'm chosen, or chose myself... which is it?"

"With time travel, all those things get jumbled up together," Ellie said. "It was your decision to go to the fort, but it was destined, too. You have free will, but it shuttled you onto a track of fate. We're stuck in history, but it can still be altered."

I groaned. "And I'm in a spaceship?""Yes," Gabe said. "But this spaceship is so *different* that it could hover over Manhattan and no one could see it. We're standing on what existence is really made of. Since you can't detect that with your limited senses and technology, we provide this Hubble Telescope illusion."

None of their answers were real answers. "Instead of just going with wood paneling and a fifty–inch TV."

Gabe cocked his head. My mouth had puzzled him, which was reassuring. He wasn't God, wasn't an angel, and wasn't all knowing. He was some kind of damned disguised alien, he said, mining images in Ellie's brain and practicing disguises. But he also didn't share smart–ass humor, and that wasn't good either. What if I grabbed and shook him? Would something awful pop out?

"We reassure as best we can," he finally said. "Until the Judgment begins."

"*What* judgment?"

"This is the hard part," Ellie said. "You and I have been picked – drafted, if you will – to be in a game. A contest. A test. An exam. A trial. Gabe has explained to me that the Xu are custodians. Angels, demons, intergalactic police, shepherds, take your pick. They represent some kind of galactic fellowship. Planets with intelligent species are candidates to join, or to be obliterated if they threaten evolution and the environment. The Xu check how planets are doing. Earth, Gabe says, isn't doing so good."

"Polluted, over–populated, exploited, and in decline," the angel summed up.

"Humans are on probation," Ellie said. "We invented nuclear weapons, are deep–frying the planet, and driving plants and animals to extinction. Now we're being expelled. Unless you and I save us."

"Us?"

"Humankind. Our species."

Was *she* even real? I stepped toward her as cautiously as if I were on an ice rink. But no, I didn't fall through to infinity. She looked substantial enough. Smelled real, sounded real. I could *feel* her humanity. A girl. "Who are *you?*"

"My name is Eleanor Terrell." She bit her lip. "I'm sixteen years old and until recently was a high school kid just like you. I live in California. Or at least I lived there; so far I can't get back."

This sounded very bad.

"We were having a picnic at the reservoir. My friends went off swimming and I fell asleep. When I woke up these greenies were all around me."

"Greenies?"

"Little green men, but they aren't really. They're not the Xu. The greenies and the gorts are worker bees. The critters that abducted me are actually kind of slug colored and have big black eyes like squid. They're short like E.T., except stronger and more frightening. If they have mouths, it's a fold on their head – they never smile. Think of rubber pulled over a face, or the snout of a snail."

"You're claiming they kidnapped you.""I felt paralyzed, unable to move or talk. They picked me up somehow – levitated me. I would have screamed except I couldn't speak. It was like being on an operating table, waiting for doctors to cut you open, *watching* them, and being absolutely helpless. Or being trapped in the dentist's chair. And then I was in this room. I didn't know where, or why. Gabe came, looking like an angel to keep me from going crazy. I thought I was dead too, but he insisted I'm not."

"I hadn't entirely thought through my appearance," the angel conceded.

"He told me I'd been chosen to help them make a difficult decision," Ellie went on.

"What decision?"

She looked grim. "Whether to eliminate our species, or at least humanity as we've progressed so far."

"Regressed," Gabriel said.

"It's called a Reset and it's supposed to produce a better, purer planet."

"You're crazier than a loon, aren't you?"

"Am I, Nick? After what just happened to you?"Score one for Eleanor.

She gripped my hand again, her grasp confirming her reality. She was fierce, desperate, urgent, her eyes as blue as Tanzanite. "Crazy like a fox. You triggered a Consequence, and I knew enough to save you before the gort got you. Now we're back in the Roundhouse, and Gabe is giving us – giving everyone on earth – one last chance. You and I can save mankind. Prove us worthy."

"Save mankind how?" She might be crazy, but she was holding my hand.

"I told you, by rescuing Adam and Eve. By time-jumping to prehistoric Africa, where it all began. Do you love your mother, Nick?"

"What?"

"This is your only chance to save her. We're being tested, and it's the biggest exam of your life. Worse than trig, worse than the SAT, worse than boot camp."

"So brace yourselves," Gabe said. "Because the game is about to start."

CHAPTER 6

THE GAME

I T DIDN'T HELP that Ellie was scared too. Flushed with sweat, taut as a bowstring, and her voice catching with emotion as she babbled her crazy talk.

"But time travel is impossible," I stalled. "Isn't it?"

"Time loops and winds like a snarl of fishing reel line," Gabe said. "You can cross from one time to another where the lines cross and touch. It's like a game of Chutes and Ladders."

"You know Chutes and Ladders?" I looked about for escape, but stars were all there were. How do you escape from infinity?

"Ellie suggested that analogy."

"So, can't you go to the future and just change it?"

"We can only travel into the past. The future hasn't happened yet. Do you know what a mousetrap is, Nick? How it's baited with cheese?"

"Stop talking like I'm a moron."

"Fort Whitman is our mousetrap. We went back

in time and installed a time wormhole where the fort would be constructed, so their excavation would connect. The Judgment requires only a select player or two, so we needed the tunnel to be in a remote place. We counted on mystery to draw someone curious."

"A soldier."

"A private stumbled in, didn't come back, and the same was true of a dog sent in after him. No one else would volunteer. The phenomenon was declared secret and the military gated the tunnel and evacuated. We later added a special padlock to keep out the casual, the timid, and the stupid."

"What happened to the soldier?"

"This was almost a century before your time. Ruben Dunbar didn't react well, and provoked the creatures he encountered." Gabe shook his head. "He didn't survive."

"Your time tunnel killed him."

"No, his panic and mistakes killed him. You might do better." There was no pity in that upper–crust voice for Ruben Dunbar, or me. "We waited for someone with initiative to find our tunnel, but decades went by. Meanwhile, we decided it would be preferable to have someone young without the adult prejudices of a Private Dunbar. Someone open–minded. Fair. With energy."

"A better lab rat, you mean."

"Mr. Faunus was dispatched to a nearby school to encourage exploration. You intrigued him." He peered at me. "You will have to demonstrate why that is."

That pissed me off. The angel–alien had that same

annoying condescension you get from too many adults who like to grade and sort the young. "This is completely unfair. How can I absorb all this? Swallow this? It's nuts."

"It's life. It's reality, truth, the fact of where and when you are. As I'm sure you've heard, life is unfair." Yep, annoying as hell.

Ellie winced. "Gabe explained existence isn't what we think, Nick. Imagine being able to hear but not see. That's the analogy the Xu use. We humans are blind to entire spectrums. There are more dimensions than we're aware of, different energies, and strange forms of matter. Because of this, things could have turned out differently."

"Things?"

"History. The Xu have decided on what they call a Reset, made by an Erasure." She clasped my shoulder and shivered slightly, eyes wide. She was one of those girls who like to touch, apparently. What was the word? Tactile. Blue pupils so bright they looked electrified, pursed lips, skin and swan neck reminiscent of polished marble, ears shell delicate. Pierced with small pearls, I noticed.

Focus, Brynner. You're in a nightmare, remember?

"They want to wipe out the beginning of the human species and everything we've ever known," she said. "Maybe by getting rid of people entirely, like that town we just escaped from. Except that was just an echo of a Consequence you could have triggered by trespassing. It was an illustration of what could be. In a real Reset the town wouldn't exist either, because there never would have been anyone to build it. No us, Nick. No past, no future."

"Extreme." I was struggling to maintain the obligatory dry cool.

"The Xu think humans are destroying our planet. Now, as custodians, they *could* get rid of the pestilence – us – by attacking Earth as we know it, lasers blazing like *War of the Worlds*. But that would blow up *everything,* including a lot of innocent species. It would cause a lot of pain and suffering by killing people who already exist. Much cleaner is alighting like a dragonfly on that snarl of fishing line at the very beginning. Why blast the whole planet when they can simply eliminate our ancestors?"

"You mean my grandparents and stuff?"

"Everyone's grandparents, at the beginning of human history. They want to murder Adam and Eve."

Whoa, whoa, whoa. "But Adam and Eve are just a story, aren't they?"

"The Xu don't think so. Neither do anthropologists."

Now I remembered. When Mr. Faunus taught about this, some religious parents complained and others thought it just confirmed the Bible. In every generation some people don't have kids, he explained. So their genes die with them. Now take that backward. As you march back in time there are fewer and fewer individuals in the past whose genetic code will survive all the countless generations to the present, because sooner or later their descendants die out. But some lineages do survive, more and more rarely as you go back older and older. And eventually you get to one man, and one woman, who are the lucky lottery winners, the two individuals whose DNA has never disappeared. A fraction of their genetic code, a fraction of *them,* is still in all of us. They're the original ancestors of us all.

When we asked Faunus how scientists could possibly know that, he explained that men have a Y chromosome, and women have genes in their cells' mitochondria, that don't change when a couple has sex and fertilize an egg. It's like a social security number that never alters. So scientists have traced back this permanent boy and girl DNA and calculated when and where this biological Adam and Eve might have first existed. If you sample present–day people, plot them on maps, and do the math, it turns out that we all originated in Africa from a very small band of humans about fifty thousand years ago.

This annoyed kids who preferred their Sunday–school picture of two naked white people in a garden with an apple. Even Miles Spinetti, who was always high on one thing or another, managed to focus for *that* classroom debate. We argued, Faunus explained, parents complained, and I thought the outrage was pretty awesome.

Also, irrelevant. Sure, somebody was the ultimate ancestor, but they never knew it. And we don't know them. So who cares if some caveman can claim to be the ultimate grandpappy? Well, wacko Eleanor Terrell does, apparently. "So you're saying that if they annihilate this one tribe, everything disappears?"

"All present–day humans. No wars. No pollution. No climate change."

"Man, that's *cold.*"

She sighed, glancing at the regal Gabriel. "To the Xu, it's… humane. By eliminating two humans the rest of us don't have to be eliminated, because we'll never exist in the first place. Maybe Homo sapiens will start over with another couple, another Adam and another Eve. Or maybe our species dies out entirely. They Reset and let history run again and see if things turn out better. And if not, Reset, Reset, Reset. Run the tape again and again."

"That's insane."

"We're bugs to them, Nick."

"Not bugs, Ellie," Gabriel put in. "Disappointments. Not by intention, but by instinct and evolution. By how your civilization developed. Many other galactic species have had the same problems. Some reform. Some don't. In the case of humans, perhaps a different lineage will do better."

"And if not, you squash us like cockroaches and take over the earth," I said.

"*Make* over the earth," he said calmly. "A Reset would let your planet be itself, instead of corrupted. And if a new line is less barbaric, it can be welcomed into a galactic fraternity that works together on moral development and universal knowledge. We believe the purpose of existence is to evolve together toward higher perfection. Everyone chips in. Homo sapiens contribute, or disappear."

Ellie squeezed my shoulder. "But we care about our fellow bugs, right Nick? Care about saving ourselves and everyone we know? If we have the guts for it, we prove our worth by saving our ancestors and winning this game. We make the Judgment. We're the test. The only people who can time–jump, and save everyone and everything, are the Chosen. Which happens to be you and me."

"I don't want to be the Chosen."

"I didn't say you volunteered. I said we were drafted. Although by deciding to enter that glowing tunnel you kind of drafted yourself."

"No I didn't."

She dropped her grip to my arm and pulled, urgent, pleading. "I haven't been able to get anywhere alone. Come through the door and help find our way."

"Back?"

"Eventually. Don't you want go home someday?"

"I was trying to go home when this all started." Yes, I was falling down a mountain, plunging down a rabbit hole, or plummeting mentally screaming into a yawning black hole. *Wake up, wake up, wake up.*

I looked hopelessly at Gabe. "I don't understand what you want us to do."

"I want you to try to save yourselves," he said.

"What about what *I* want?"

Now his look was stern, like a lecturing father, and I saw the angel get–up was indeed a disguise. A cloud came over his features, and what had seemed benevolent seemed darker and more menacing than I would have guessed possible. It was a glimpse of determined power, possibly majestic, possibly pitiless, or possibly so entirely alien that I could never understand it. His voice deepened and roughened, like a soundtrack from hell. "What choice does anyone have, Nick? To exist? To choose their parents? To get childhood cancer? To be paralyzed in a football accident? The only certainty life promises is death, and the only freedom is your reaction to whatever life throws your way."

"But why me?" It was plaintive, and I was embarrassed.

"Because you're ordinary." Gabe was beginning to fade back into the stars like a damned Cheshire cat, as if escaping my questions. It was maddening. "The Judgment demands the player be an average representative of his species. You, Nick Brynner, are utterly unremarkable."

Yep, the guy was an asshole, English accent or no.

Ellie yanked. "Come *on.* This is the way we have to go."

She jerked me across the stars. Walking on that invisible floor was incredibly eerie – like walking out over the Grand Canyon. I felt dizzy with vertigo, but didn't fall. Then something new materialized. A thin pencil of blue light formed an upright rectangle against the sky.

"What's that?"

"A door. What's beyond is a gantlet, or obstacle course. It functions as a test to keep failures away from the controls. We have to demonstrate we're worthy by getting through."

"Worthy of what?"

"Risking everything to save everything."

I looked back. Gabe the annoying angel was almost gone. And materializing from another wall was a snuffling gort, its nose up, making that *whuff whuff whuff* sound as if it sensed we were trying to go where we shouldn't. It saw the door, bunched, and got ready to spring.

That's called encouragement.

Chapter 7

STRENGTH

S O WE STEPPED through, like Alice stepping through a mirror, or the Narnia kids stepping through that wardrobe.

The stars vanished. We were in a dimly lit sterile cell.

I turned around. The "door" we'd come through had vanished. So had Gabe and gort. In its place was a blank gray wall.

"Shazzam." It was bitter. I felt like a puppet.

"This is the chamber that taught me I needed your help," Ellie said.

"Terrific." I looked around. What I saw was actually momentarily reassuring, given the terror of boundless space. There was a metal floor, ceiling, and walls colored battleship gray, completely blank. Probably an illusion, but an illusion I could handle. I could see how prison comforts people at the end of their rope. No more choices, no more failures. Just confinement.

I felt trapped and safe at the same time.

"Look," Ellie said, pointing.

On the opposite wall, near the ceiling, was an enigmatic message in faint yellow light. It read, *Through This Door Is Choice.*

What the devil did that mean?

"Here's what I discovered." She walked a couple steps and stopped at an unmarked spot on the featureless gray floor. Suddenly, on the wall below the lettering, another pencil–thin blue line outlined an exit opposite of where we entered. A door abruptly slid up like the raised portcullis on a castle gate. Another blank gray room was beyond.

"Doesn't look like an improvement."

"It's the way we have to go. Watch." Ellie bolted for the opening. But as soon as she left whatever she had stood on, the door dropped like a guillotine. The boom of its slam made me jump, the sound echoing like thunder. The blue line faded and the wall was blank again.

"I've tried to run through a hundred times and I'm never fast enough," she said. "Again and again and again. I cried for days in frustration. Finally I realized the message. I needed help. A partner."

"Me."

"Whoever trespassed. It sounds like you were encouraged to."

"By Mr. Faunus."

"Is he your teacher?"

"I thought so. Now…" What *was* he? Devil? Savior? Alien? "So what does the wording mean?"

"Just that we need to go that way, I assume. Now. When I stand on that spot to open the door, you have to hold it up until we both get through."

I was dubious. "Then what?"

"I don't know. I've never gotten that far. Gabe says this is the first part of the test."

"The *first* part?"

"It's an obstacle course, to prove us worthy so we have a real chance where we're really going. We clear each room or we're trapped forever. I was going crazy until I asked for a helper. Are you ready?"

"That door just fell like a cleaver!"

"Just hold it for a couple seconds while I run through. Then let go and jump. Look around; there's no other way. No tool, no doors, no switches, no instructions, no levers, no supplies, no tricks. Trust me, I've searched. Stand and get ready, please." She brushed hair from her face, impatient and tense.

That door had sounded heavy as a piano. "Ellie, I don't know."

"You had courage. You explored the fort tunnels."

"Stupidity, you mean."

"Courage, stupidity." Her look was wry. "It's a fine line."

"Ordinary, I believe he described me." But you want a guy to do something? Have a girl expect him to. So I stood like the condemned by the blank wall that had been a door and waited to prove manly. Idiotic, I know. Predictable.

"Ready?"

"Anything to be unremarkable."

She stepped again on that spot on the floor. Sure enough, the wall lit with the blue line of a door and slid upward, as slick and quiet as the portal of a super–villain. Neat bit of magic. I stepped underneath and held its lower edge with my upraised arms, braced like Samson.

Ellie charged.

As soon as she left the spot where she'd been stand-ing, the door pressed heavy as a refrigerator. I yelled, buckled under its weight, and fell to my knees. Ellie was running hard, only a second had ticked by, but the door pushed so powerfully that my legs slid out from under me and back into our blank room. I was flat on my back, arms screaming as I involuntarily bench–pressed what felt like the whole world. My arms shook and my elbows bent, leaving two feet of clearance. Ellie dived like a runner into home plate and slid past into the room beyond. Now what?

I couldn't hold, I couldn't turn, and I couldn't crawl. I let go, curled in a ball to get out of the way, and the door crashed down and disappeared.

I was stuck in the room where we started.

I trembled with exhaustion, my arms rubber bands. The message seemed taunting. *Through This Door Is Choice.* Except I was trapped without a choice. Eleanor

Terrell was somewhere beyond and I had no way to follow her. Had she used me? Shakily, I stood.

"Ellie!" My cry bounced off blank walls.

"Ellie!" I was panicked.

Now what? Condemned in a cube of hell?

Then the blue outline appeared again, the door that had nearly cut me in two calmly slid open, and my companion beckoned.

"Come on through, Nick. There's a switch on this side."

CHAPTER 8

AGILITY

DÉJÀ VU ALL over again. We were in another blank gray room, this one with a higher ceiling, and as soon as I stepped into it the door behind vanished. I tried the switch and it no longer worked. Apparently we could go forward but not backward. And someone, I guessed, was watching us rats in the maze.

"This is foul."

"No, look." Ellie pointed. "There's a hole."

I looked up. On the opposite wall was an opening to a tunnel three feet in diameter. Encouraging. Except the exit hole was more than a dozen feet high. Written nearby, in glowing letters, was another epigram.

Choice Is Freedom.

"It sounds like a fortune cookie."

"Gabriel said the game is for our own good. It makes sure players can really compete."

"Why do you keep calling this torture a game?"

As if to answer there was a bang, a clunk, a whining

of gears, and the wall we'd just come through began to close inward like a vise. I stared in disbelief. Inch by inch, our new room was shrinking like a trash compactor.

"Test. Race. Scramble. Gabe warned we don't have much time. We need to reach that tunnel quickly to escape."

I muttered an obscenity. Then I stepped back, took a running leap, hit the wall, and slid back down like a drop of water. The round exit hole was an out–of–reach mouth laughing at us. *Think, think!* The other wall ground inward.

I turned to Ellie. "Okay, climb on top of me and I'll give you a boost. Then you give me a hand up."

I leaned against the wall, cupped my hands to take her boot, and heaved the girl upward. I could hear her hands slapping for purchase as she balanced on my shoulders. "I've got a handhold inside! Push me higher!"

The opposite wall continued closing. Ten feet had shrunk to eight.

I got a hand on each boot and pushed upward. Thank goodness she was a lot lighter than that door! Her shoulders disappeared into the hole and she wriggled the rest of the way. Would she disappear again? No, Ellie twisted around.

The room had squeezed to seven feet.

She lay flat and extended her arm. "Jump!"

I crouched, leaped, and missed by six inches. So I backed to the steadily closing wall, pushed off to give a boost, and sprang like the basketball player I never was.

I soared, hit her forearm, slid down to her wrist, and clung.

Ellie shrieked. "You're too heavy! I can't hold you!" I was dangling helplessly, my weight beginning to drag her out of the tube. "You're dislocating my shoulder!"

I let go, sprawled backward on the floor, and looked up. She regarded me with horror.

Six feet. I was going to be crushed into syrup.

"It's not going to work," I said. "You go ahead. I'll keep jumping."

"No! Gabe said we had to do this together."

"Ellie, there is no together. You're up there, I'm down here. When the wall is closer, maybe I can scramble up. Just go."

"What if the walls slam shut like that door?"

"Go, go!"

She fiercely shook her head, twisted to go backward, and dropped back out of the tube, landing lightly beside me.

"Are you nuts? I just got you up there!"

"I won't go alone. You climb on me."

Our space had shrunk to five feet. Our cube of a room had become a corridor. No. A claustrophobic tomb.

"I outweigh you by fifty pounds."

"I'll brace myself like a tree. Then you pull *me* up."

"Ellie, I'll break you."

"I'm not made of glass. Hurry!" She stood, feet apart, determined and rigid.

There was no alternative. "Okay. Shove one hip out. I'm going to step there, and then up on your shoulder. It's going to hurt."

"Stop talking and do it!"

Four feet.

So I climbed her like a root. My own boot on her hip, my arms on her shoulder, and then I heaved myself upward as she cried out, me frantically thrashing against the wall to gain altitude and balance.

"Ouch!" she protested.

I precariously stood on her shoulders. She stooped, whimpered, summoned furious strength, and her whole body straightened and elevated me precious inches. I jumped off from her shoulders, praying not to fall back on top of her. The fingers of my right hand barely grasped the edge of the hole.

I hung there, my toes a few inches above her head.

"Go Nick go!"

I cursed again.

Then I managed to slap and grip the tube edge with my other fingers and did a pull–up. There was a slot in the tube wall that I seized. Thrashing like a fish, I kicked, grunted, and heaved to get myself into the exit tube. Then I hurriedly twisted around and looked down.

The room had narrowed to less than three feet. "Ellie!"

She was flat on her back. Had she fainted?

"Ellie!" I roared it. My sharp shout seemed to snap

her back to consciousness. She looked up at me, remote as the moon.

"You've got to jump!" I hung my arms down, fingers splayed. "I'll pull you up, I promise."

"It's too far." She sounded dazed.

"Brace against the other wall. Walk your feet up so I can grab you."

She looked confused and then saw what I meant. The vise wall had made the gap so narrow that she could shimmy like wriggling up a chimney. She put her back against the wall we'd climbed, planted her feet against its vise–like opposite, and crab–walked upward.

The gap kept narrowing. Two feet. Her knees were in her face. "Nick!"

"Keep coming! You're close."

"Please," she gasped, stretching toward me. I seized one wrist and hauled. Her feet slid out and she dangled. The room clenched like a closing crevasse. She sobbed. "Pull!"

The gap was down to one foot and saving her was like pulling a cork. She twisted around backward to let her knees bend and I retreated to drag her into the tube, her hair tangled in mine, her breath against my ear. Her legs popped out of the gap and into the tunnel.

The vise wall collided with the tunnel mouth with a resounding boom. Light snuffed out.

CHAPTER 9

TIME JUMP

WE LAY HORIZONTALLY for a moment, her feet pointed back the way we'd come, mine toward where we were presumably going. We clasped each other's arms, panting, sweaty, and afraid.

"This is horrible."

"Some game," I muttered back. "What next, Indiana? Arrows shooting from slits in the wall?"

She managed an exhausted wheeze. "We did it. You nearly crushed me when you climbed on top. I feel like hamburger."

I squeezed her shoulder. "Better than that." It was a joke she didn't reject, but she didn't return, either. So it was quiet.

Way to kill the moment, Nick.

We rested. Then I realized it wasn't completely dark. There was a glow behind me in the direction we must go. It was too tight to easily turn around, so I told

Ellie I was going to push along backwards. She nodded and followed on her belly.

Light grew. In fifty feet the tube we'd escaped to opened to another gray room. I let my body slide out of the tunnel, hung, and then dropped to a floor that had the same gray blandness as the last one. Ellie followed head first, looking as if she was emerging from a cocoon. She somewhat gracefully somersaulted forward so that I could catch her. Then, muscles throbbing, we took in our new torture chamber.

This time the doors weren't hidden. In fact there were three of them, each with a button in its center.

Above was another message. *Freedom Means Responsibility.*

I don't like messages, slogans, banners, posters, commercials, public service messages, intercom harangues from the principal, or tests of the emergency broadcast system. I'd be a grumpy old man if I were old.

Ellie walked close to inspect each door, like a cat sniffing its food. Then she stepped back. "I think the Xu want us to choose the correct exit. It's some kind of brain test. First strength, then agility, now smarts."

"If there's one thing I don't feel right now, it's smart." I had a ferocious headache. "Don't they want to exterminate us because we're dumb? What's the point?"

"To prove we can survive somewhere worse. But this one is like a quiz show, Nick, where there are possible prizes behind each door. We need to choose the correct door. I'm betting the prize is escape to the time–jump room. We have a one in three chance of winning."

"Choosing is luck, not smarts."

"Is it? Or some kind of logic puzzle?" She studied the doors with interest.

I sighed. "So which is the magic door, Ms. Einstein?"

She considered. "The middle seems safest."

"Why? There's a two–thirds chance you're wrong."

"Do you want to pick?"

"No." I was doing my best to think, and I was thinking that thinking under this kind of pressure did not encourage thinking. "Middle seems too obvious. But I can't see a reason to try left or right, either."

"Think carefully."

"Like I'm going to think uncarefully?" I didn't try to keep the resentment out of my voice. "The other two rooms made us work together. How do we work together here?"

"We think together."

With that there was a thump, a hiss, and an ominous rumble of rushing water. Vent covers popped open on the base of the wall we'd just dropped down and jets of water shot out with fire hose force. The spray hit our calves and knocked us down, the foamy tumult tumbling us like a washing machine and pushing us to the doors. We fought upright, drenched and alarmed. The water had already mounded to our knees, swirling and tugging like the universe's worst Jacuzzi.

"It's cold!" Ellie protested.

"The Xu don't give much time to ponder, do they?" I waded, and, before she could object, punched the middle door's button. Choice over! But instead of the middle door opening, the left one slid upward instead. What the hell?

To say it opened was, unfortunately, an exaggeration. The door slid up and away, all right, but the water didn't pour through. We couldn't get through, either. I could see the sky of stars beyond, but some kind of force field kept the water and us in place like an aquarium wall. When I leaned forward to try to see behind the other doors, I got a nasty electric shock.

The water climbed to our thighs.

I backed off. "I don't get it."

Ellie was shivering. "Game show, Nick. I've seen this on TV. We choose a door, but instead of opening the one we chose, the host reveals only that one of the doors we *didn't* pick was *not* the right choice. So then a new challenge comes. Do we stick with our first choice, the middle door, or switch to the right–hand one?"

Sure enough, the buttons on the other two doors were alternately flashing, suggesting we had to choose one or the other if we wanted to escape.

"This is stupid." The water was up to my waist.

"Fiendish." The flood was even higher on Ellie. Soon we'd be swimming. If the chamber filled we'd float to the ceiling, the air would be gone, and we'd drown. That's called Game Over.

She looked at the flashing buttons, eyes darting. "Fifty–fifty chance."

"No." Now I was trying to actually think it through. There had to be a point to this challenge. "It's not fifty–fifty, even though it seems like it." Why not? *Logic, Nick, logic.*

The water kept rising, chilling my brain and making a mockery of my attempt to use it. If we didn't pick soon, we'd die. The Xu, who could apparently obliterate the entire human race without losing much sleep over it, seemed to have a wicked sense of gamesmanship. Some angel! So I had to outwit the bastards despite myself, because I'd be damned if I'd let them win. *Think!* I thought and thought and thought, my mind a riot.

"I don't know which one," Ellie moaned. The buttons were already submerged. The water was to her shoulders. "Nick, I'm afraid. We have to choose!"

I fought down my own panic. "Here's how I see it." I sounded more certain than I really was. "There's a one–third chance the middle door we already picked is the right door, correct?"

"Yes!" She glanced around. The light was dimming as the water rose. We'd drown in cold blackness. "Hurry!"

"And therefore there's a two–thirds chance that one of the other two doors we *didn't* pick is the correct one. Right?"

"You're reciting the obvious, Nick."

"Except we already know the left is *not* correct. So

64

that means the right–hand door now has a two–thirds chance of being right, and the middle one only one–third." It sounded like common sense, except it didn't.

"What? Why?" She could sense my own doubt. Water was to her chin.

"It's math, Ellie," I insisted. "Logic. Another way to look at it is by combining the left and right door in your mind. Before we started, there was a two–in–three chance that one of those two doors was the right one. Now we know the left door was *not*. So that means the right door *still* has a two–in–three chance. You can stick with the middle one if you want, but probability says the right–hand door is the better choice."

"And if you're wrong, we're dead." Our feet had left the floor as we treaded water. We were floating toward the ceiling, but by optical illusion it seemed to be squeezing down. "Can I trust you?"

"Exactly. Can you?" It was a challenge.

So she studied me fearfully, gave a nod, sucked air, plunged her head, dived downward, and fatalistically pushed the flashing button on the right–hand door.

We poured through.

It was like being sucked down the drain, rats in a sewer. Instead of a view of stars we flooded into a grim gray corridor, bouncing like flotsam. We had to hold our breath for a fearful minute, but then the water level dropped, the current slowed, and we got a gasp of air. Our feet grounded on a grate that served as a floor. The water was pouring away through the grate, and the door we'd chosen had slammed shut behind us. There was a click as it locked, and then – of course – it disappeared.

Ellie was coughing, bedraggled as a wet kitten. Yet there was triumph in her eyes as well, and she looked at me with new respect.

"I *did* trust you. And you did it, Nick."

"*We* did it. You pushed the button. And this game of yours is going to kill us, I think."

"It's the Xu's game. And no, we have to survive to win. We've won so far. Gabe told me there were three challenges to get to the time–jump room, and we did three." She grasped my hands in hers, her grin crooked. "There's only one catch." Then her eyes widened.

"What's that?"

Her gaze had been drawn over my shoulder to something materializing behind me. "Never mind," she hissed. "Gort."

I heard a *whuff*.

"Run!"

We fled, boots squishing, my pack leaking water, clothes soaked. I was half–frozen, exhilarated to be alive, frightened of gargoyle monsters, and dreading whatever came next.

We burst into a very different chamber, this one dry, warm, and hushed, its dark walls spangled with stars. I pulled up in wonder. There was a giant floating hologram in the middle of the room, a three–dimensional movie ten feet in diameter. It was a picture of good old planet Earth, rotating in the chamber's middle like a serene balloon. The continents were easily recognizable but their shorelines were distorted. There was more land and less water. The planet's top and bottom were shrouded with a thick cap of ice.

"Ice Age," Ellie whispered.

On one wall was yet another message. *Responsibility Requires Faith.*

Whatever.

I looked back. Had we lost the gort?

Not likely. I heard an angry bellow. We were trespassing, and the stupid sentry monster sensed something was amiss.

"Gabe brought me here before so that I could follow you to the Consequence," Ellie said hurriedly. "The planet looked regular then, present–day. Now, look at those polar caps! It's beautiful, isn't it?" Despite the horrors we'd just endured, she retained a sense of wonder.

"Ellie, that grungy gargoyle is coming."

"The past is our future, Nick."

"No slogans, please. Is this floating ball an illusion? A satellite picture?"

"It's a control panel. Look. Africa!"

Now there was a rattle of claws. I turned. The gort was creeping into the control room with a sneer of suspicion. Ellie reached toward the globe. The monster spied movement. It bunched on its hind legs, eyes of a cat, claws of a bear, scales of a lizard. It looked bred in hell to me.

I braced for its spring.

Ellie's finger touched the hologram.

The monster snarled, and leaped.

Then a flash of white and we were whirling through the blackest of blacks again. We fell through a worm-hole in space, a door in time, or back into our time–track destiny. We'd "jumped."

And left the gort behind.

I managed a last question as we tumbled. "You said there's a catch?"

Her voice echoed. "Yes! That the Judgment is just beginning!"

CHAPTER 10

AFRICA

I WAS SPRAWLED ON my back, blinking against brilliant outdoor light very different from the misty Pacific Northwest. There was a great arc of sky, high hot sun, and puffy white clouds thick as a sundae, glopping from horizon to horizon. The grass crinkled.

I sat up. Ellie lay still beside me, not yet awake, cap aside and ponytail half–undone. She was still damp from our soaking. I stole a peek at her unstudied grace. Yep, I'm astounded by how girls look, and nature conspired to put this one together so nicely that normally she'd be out of my league. But I was the only guy here.

A bug lit on her forehead and I waved to brush it off. The fan of breeze switched open her eyes, transparently blue like stained glass.

"We jumped." She sat up, groped for her baseball cap, and jammed it securely on her head. Her instant alertness made me check that I still had my own hat and pack. The sun was intense.

"Africa?" I asked.

"If it worked."

On cue, an animal drifted into view.

We were in a shallow fold of grassy savanna. The critter had horns, big head, and humped shoulders like a bison, as if pumped on steroids. Shaggy beard like an old man, mane like a horse, and skinny hindquarters with a donkey's tail. It seemed like the black–colored creature had been assembled from animal leftovers. It moved gracefully, however, with the easy rock of a hobbyhorse, and grazed as methodically as a machine.

"Wildebeest," Ellie said. "A big antelope. Odd looking, aren't they? They migrate in the millions to follow the rains."

"You're an expert?"

"Gabriel gave me holograms to study."

"They kidnap you and then prep you?"

"The Xu don't like to be sole judge, jury and executioner of a problem species." She stood to see. "Before they pull the trigger, they want one of the doomed to concur, or to prove instead that our kind is worth saving. Maybe it salves their conscience."

"How sporting of them." I got up too. "If they have a conscience."

"I think it's like a dictator wanting his enemies to confess imaginary crimes to justify their execution. The game player for the condemned has to agree to an Erasure. A Reset."

"This 'Reset' being the assassination of our ancestors."

"So they reviewed for me our gruesome history, with holograms showing wars, slaughters, rainforest burning, extinctions, and oil spills. We look wasteful and mean. It's embarrassing, to tell you the truth."

"But why you? Why me? We're kids, Ellie."

"It's like Gabe said. They look for game players old enough to survive but young enough not to have fossilized opinions. So I said yep, maybe earthlings should go down the garbage disposal."

"You voted for our extinction?"

"I agreed to play their game to get out of that spaceship prison. I saw a chance of survival by agreeing to be their potential permission slip. What option did I have? Their Judgment, their rules. I realized in the first chamber than I needed a partner to proceed. When you trespassed and short–circuited the system, I drafted you."

She saw my look.

"Sorry," she said. "I didn't have a choice."

"I didn't either."

"Except you trespassed. Anyway, basic training was getting through those three spaceship chambers. So, hello Soldier." She glanced around, squaring her shoulders. "Now we have to move faster than the other team."

"*What* other team?"

"At some point the Xu follow us and start hunting for Adam and Eve. We get a head start to find the pair and hide our ancestral cavemen, if we think they're worthy of hiding. If Homo sapiens are worthy. Then we win."

"How do we do that?"

"How do we do what?"

"Any of it!"

"Back at the fort, I slipped a scanner in your back-pack to screen DNA. To confirm Adam and Eve. As for the rest, Gabe said we figure it out as we go along. He said we humans are cruel, but clever."

"Gabe is a dick."

"Yes."

"Ellie, this is ridiculous. It's not a game, it's *our* execution. What do we know about Africa? They make all the rules. They probably change all the rules."

"Yes." She rotated completely around, unable to offer hope. Her look was sad, or maybe wistful, or regretful, and that was the most frightening thing yet. "We landed on the savanna, I think."

Okay, Brynner. Suck it up. Absorb. And when in doubt, show bravado. "I haven't even been to Disneyland."

Her grim smile acknowledged my lousy humor.

Another wildebeest ambled into view, and another, and another. They focused on their feed, paying us no attention.

Some kids love animals. Some fear them. Since I'd never been allowed to have a pet I was mildly indif-ferent, or rather mildly interested, but not in that pas-sionate *Animal Planet* kind of way. Animals are hard to scope. These had dark, dumb, unreadable eyes – not hostile, but not cartoon cute either. Just wild.

They also looked *big,* so I stood taller. Ellie did too. The herd was filling our vale's short horizon and there wasn't a single strand of barbed wire between them and us. The wind was blowing our way, meaning they hadn't caught our scent. Conversely we got a nose full of them, a smell of dust, musk, and manure. What would happen when they saw us?

As if to answer, they bolted.

One minute we were looking at peacefully chewing animals as placid as dairy cows, and the next a regiment of wildebeest was panicked and charging straight at us, ground quaking, horns lowered, and clods flying.

I swore again, grabbed Ellie, and galloped, though I'd no idea where to go. We sprinted up the gentle slope, looking for a tree or rock. I spied a curious dirt mound that looked as if a giant child had scooped mud into a slumped sand castle six feet high. We darted for that.

There was a closing thunder of hooves behind, the whole world in motion, and the wind blew gritty dust ahead of the stampede and over us. I could hear the pound of heavy muscle and their labored snorts. I imagined myself tossed on their horns like a bullfighter.

We tagged the dirt pile and scrambled to its narrow top. "Balance!" As we clutched each other the stampeding herd broke around our perch like a black flood. We looked down at a storm of heaving backs and pitching horns.

Ellie clung, and I clung right back. "How'd we spook them?" I wondered.

"It wasn't us. It was *that*." She nodded with her chin.

A streak of tan hurtled through the dust, fast as a rocket, and then a young wildebeest somersaulted, something bigger and quicker rolling with it. I heard a snarl. Hooves kicked frantically in the air as the streak writhed on top of its prey, and then there was an awful strangled keen of sound as the antelope strangled. I heard a crack of bone.

"No way!" I was watching a lion kill.

"Way." Her tone was solemn.

I gaped, heart pounding. The victim's narrow legs stuck straight up in the air and trembled, its throat crushed, and then the legs fell over like pencils. Life left like flicking off a light switch.

As the dying animal went still, so did the herd. Predator had found prey, and now the other wildebeest were safe until the next meal. The lion killed only what it needed. The stampeding animals slowed, stopped, and gradually went back to grazing, heads drooped to feed.

Several other lions, including cubs, trotted through the grass to join the first at the kill's corpse, clustering like detectives around a murder victim. The cats growled and snapped as they knotted themselves to feast. Their muzzles turned crimson.

That could be us, I realized. Not the eaters. The eaten.

"It's really Africa," I said.

"Nature red in tooth and claw," Ellie recited.

"What?"

"Lord Tennyson. Tenth grade English."

"Damn. This is our rescue plan, coming here?"

"This is where Adam and Eve are. We have to warn them."

"We need help, Ellie. Starting with a gun."

She looked across the savanna. "Available in a mere fifty thousand years."

"Please don't say that." I sounded more pathetically stupid than I intended.

"We haven't just jumped in space, Nick. We've jumped in time. We've come to Africa at the height of the last Ice Age, when humans are about to leave and spread around the world."

"Fifty thousand BC?"

"Roughly. BP, scientists now say, or Before Present, because they don't assume everyone in the world dates things from Christ. Or, BCE. Before Current Era. Science is global."

"We're back in prehistoric times?"

"Barely. There're no dinosaurs. By that standard it's almost yesterday, because the dinosaurs died off sixty-five million years ago."

"What are you, a museum guide?"

"I told you, Gabe made me study. There are still mammoths and mastodons far to the north, just as there are elephants here. Maybe saber tooth tigers."

"Terrific."

"I'm not sure when everything disappeared, but I'm pretty sure there are still Neanderthal cavemen as well as human cavemen."

"What's the difference?"

"Neanderthals were stronger but maybe dumber, and died out. There could be other groups too, like Homo erectus. Tall, but extinct. The fossil record is pretty spotty. So there are no settlements, no guns, and no 911. Right now, right here, just us."

It felt so hopeless. From our precarious perch the grassy prairie stretched in all directions. On it were grazing animals, thousands of them, tens of thousands, gazillions, in a throng that stretched until they were mere specks. There was a sprinkling of salt and pepper, and I realized zebra were roaming too. I carefully rotated. It was the same every direction. Epic, but I couldn't enjoy it.

I like nature behind bars.

"I think we're standing on a termite mound," she said. "I hologrammed them. The insects eat grass instead of wood and build up fantastic mud colonies."

So we were perched on bug city, watching lions. Enormous birds had come to orbit the kill. Vultures. They looked big as hang gliders, and as capable of carrying us off as winged monkeys.

Not a road, not a house, not a fence, not a power pole, nor a single glint of anything metallic.

My voice was half–strangled. "So our mission, should we choose to accept it?"

"First, staying alive. Then finding our ancestors before the Xu." She grasped my pack and undid a flap. "I'm thirsty. Do you have any water?"

I had one liter and Ellie had nothing: no water, no food, no pack, and not much of a plan, beyond punching through three chambers of hell to dump us in pre-historic Africa.

"You didn't bring any gear?"

"I told you, I was kidnapped. I brought the gene scanner. The Xu hoped whoever your teacher encouraged would come equipped."

So I gave her a swallow, both of us fastidiously wiping the bottleneck. The primness would seem comic in days to come. We still had no clue.

"I don't see a water fountain," I noted. "Or a Burger King." I looked down at our clay perch. "Are there really termites in there?"

"Let's find out." She skidded down to the base, took a grass stem, and poked into one of the holes that per-forated the dirt mound. When she drew it out, termites clamped like squirming beads. "People eat these."

"Not this people."

"You're not hungry enough yet."

Not promising. "We're a snack ourselves if the lions don't fill up. We need to move, Ellie." I looked around. The land rolled on and on, animals thick as the Old West buffalo herds, way out to hazed horizons. The only interruption was a clump of gray rocks a few miles away. They erupted from a swollen gum of grass like jagged teeth, making a natural Stonehenge. "Maybe we can hide in those boulders before it gets dark." We needed a goal.

She mentally measured the distance. "Do you think the wildebeest will stampede again?"

"I can't even guarantee the lions won't come over for a sniff. I just know I can't balance on a termite mound for the rest of my life."

So we set off through the grass, feeling as exposed as flies on paper. The browsing herds were skittish but not really afraid, animals moving away from us and then closing back around as if I was Moses parting the Red Sea. They weren't afraid of us, but not hostile either. Just indifferent, because nature didn't give a hoot. The cats stayed clustered around their supper.

I took the lead, setting a brisk pace, and Ellie kept up. We were on high alert while acting cool, using the type of anxious energy it takes to cross a bad neighborhood. You know that prick of sweat you get, where every new sound makes you twitch? It's tiring.

The sun bonged my head like a cymbal, but a breeze kept us ventilated. There weren't many insects. It wasn't much worse than striding across a golf course, except for millions of animals, piles of dried manure, and grass that was knee–high.

I tried to think of something besides big cats.

Everything I thought of was worse. "Are these Xu watching us?"

"I don't know. I don't think so, because it's not much of a contest if they do.""And they're assassins, coming after caveman Adam and Eve?"

"They call themselves mentors, or shepherds. They try to make planets evolve correctly so intelligent species can join Gabe's galactic fellowship. But before achieving membership, a lot of civilizations destroy themselves with idiocies like nuclear war. When they do, they take their entire planet down with them."

"And you think humans are doing that to Earth?"

"The Xu think so. So they want to try a different gene line, or wipe us out entirely and try a different species. Maybe dolphins would do better. If we want everyone we know to someday exist, we have to judge us worthy despite our nukes, and keep our flawed ancestors out of their sights."

"How?"

"I'm not sure. Maybe just by migrating. The weird thing is, by the very fact of being here, maybe we succeed. You know?"

"What do you mean?"

"If we save caveman Adam and Eve, everyone in subsequent history is born on schedule, including us. We're here, so therefore we must have succeeded. Right?"

That was heartening.

"But, maybe not," she went on. "We fail and suddenly disappear: we exist only up to that moment. Or maybe we get stuck here if we fail; our time destiny was to come back and be marooned. Time jumps are confusing."

"Thanks for sharing."

"I think we're destined to be here and yet we can change destiny. Gabe said life is always a combination of fate and free will."

"Some free will. I'm here because I trespassed. But why you? All you did was take a nap."

She sighed. "Maybe because I'm a biology nerd who likes animals."

"What, you won the science fair or something?"I'm afraid so. For all of California, 10th Grade."

Another Andrea Martinez. Pretty, smart, no doubt popular, unobtainable. Stuck up? Not yet. But the cute ones do intimidate Nick Brynner, boy loser. "And you're a cheerleader," I guessed pessimistically.

"No." She was puzzled at my question. "Debate club, yearbook, class secretary. Wonk, I said."

Okay, not the stereotypical flick of flaxen–headed fluff. For survival, that was good. I needed Tomb Raider, not Barbie. "That's how you know this DNA stuff?"

"Nick, I'm as confused as you. Me as judge and jury? No way. Yes, I know about DNA, but I'm not quick at logic, as you could tell. I have to work at things. And right now I don't know where the aliens are, or the cave-men are, or where water is. I just stabbed at the globe where Gabe told me. For all I know, we're bugs in their microscope. Or about to get zapped by space lasers."

I stopped and turned, wind blowing the green–gold grass into waves like the sea. "I'm about to be slain by a light–sword?"

She gestured toward the lions. "I think devoured is more likely. Or killed by malaria. Rabies. Gangrene."

"Ellie, I'm struggling not to scream here."

"Sometimes you don't get to scream. You do what you have to do."

I looked at her. Cute. Grim. Determined. Expectant. Here's another thing about girls: They make you honest about yourself. *Suck it up, Brynner.* So I did my best to look resolute. *You're not dead yet.* "Okay. What we have to do is find shelter before nightfall." I offered her the water again. "One swallow. No more."

She nodded, her eyes betraying worry.

The savanna began to climb toward the beckoning fortress of boulders. It was odd geology, a rumple of rocks protruding like pimples. There were trees growing in the crevices. A few outlier trees on the grassy plain looked as prim and planted as a park, with that flat-topped acacia look like pictures I'd seen of Africa. They had pretty yellow bark, their branches as graceful as the track of a sable watercolor brush that Ms. Perkins had shown in art class. Their twigs were thorny, however. The trees cast dry shade as the day waned, but we didn't pause because the rocks offered more security.

"Maybe we can find a cave," I said. "Now that we're cavemen."

Near the base of the rocks there was a jumble of

white in the grass. At first I thought it was weathered sticks or branches, but when we stooped, reality rang our bell. They were bones.

A wildebeest skull, horns still attached, eye sockets empty, nestled in the soil. Nearby ribs curved upward like a gigantic comb. Leg bones were tumbled like chopsticks.

And when I reached to pick up a bone a snake undulated, revealing its perfect camouflage, and slithered away. I jumped back. The serpent was as long as my arm and lethal as a power cable. Fortunately, it wanted to get away from me as much as I wanted to get away from it, and disappeared into the grass.

I looked at Ellie, who had instinctively grabbed my elbow, eyes wide. *Don't scream, don't scream, don't scream…*

"Vote me off the island."

Chapter 11

LONG STARRY NIGHT

"WE NEED WEAPONS," Ellie said, picking up a bone to probe the grass and rocks. "The wildlife here is scary."

"Ya think?"

We ascended the ridge. When we reached the boulders I saw they were speckled granite, the surface sandpapery enough to give traction. We scrambled up, my companion probing occasional clumps of brush. Sure enough, another snake wound away with an irritated hiss. *Watch your step, Brynner.*

I also learned to be careful grabbing shrubs for handholds, because thorns and nettles were everywhere. My fingers felt on fire.

To top it off, I spied a scorpion scuttling into a crevice, black stinger twitching as it hid. I had the good manners not to share this discovery.

But Africa, in my considered opinion, sucked.

We gained the domed top of a boulder that was

as big as a roof and perched on its sun–warmed stone, looking back the way we'd come. I felt safer isolated on our island of rock, but the wind blew harder up high and the sun was setting to the west. The sky was pretty, silver and gold, but the emptiness was dispiriting. Nothing as far as the eye could see except prehistoric planet.

I turned into the wind, looking to what must be the east, and the savanna seemed just as infinite in that direction. Except there was a shadow in the dying light, a smear on the horizon that must represent mountains. There was also a dark green crease on the plain a dozen miles away. Between it and us, vast herds browsed in serene stillness.

"Beautiful," Ellie said.

"That's one way to look at it."

"I didn't know so many animals could be in one place."

"Steak everywhere, and not a bite to eat." My stomach growled so I took off my pack. "I've got two granola bars. One tonight, one tomorrow."

"And then?"

"We'll be eaten ourselves, probably."

"Don't joke like that. It's bad luck."

"Who's joking?" I broke the bar in two and gave her half. "You're not finding me very funny."

"Kids say I'm too serious." Ellie chewed slowly, trying to make it last. "Make jokes if it helps, but don't expect me to laugh. I'm stressed."

"Agreed."

"But we stay alive so our species stays alive."

"Sounds like a motto."

"Is that your only food and water?"

"Yep. I packed for lunch, not time travel. I do have compass, sunscreen, raingear, an extra T–shirt, fishing line, a flashlight, some Band–Aids, and matches. Plus a multipurpose tool with knife blade, screwdrivers and corkscrew."

"Thank goodness we can open wine."

"Hey, you made a joke! And I've got a cell phone. E.T. phone home." I turned it on. "Dead, probably from water in the drowning chamber. We can use it as a paperweight, if we invent paper."

"How about the flashlight?"

I tried it. "Toast. We can't read under the covers, and we can't signal for help."

"It's still more than a caveman would have. They survived."

"Some of them, anyway."

She huddled close. "It's getting cold. I thought Africa would be warmer."

"Ice Age, you said."

"Yes. Even near the equator the climate's cooler."

"We're near the equator?" I hadn't digested that. Pretty exotic.

"South of it, I'm guessing. We might also be high up, because Africa has plateaus. The air seems thin. The air is very clear."

"And clean. We can see a long way."

"It must have always been like this before pollution. Do you know we're breathing different air? Less carbon dioxide. Back when we came from, the dirty old twenty–first century, we've changed the atmosphere with greenhouse gases."

"And the Xu don't approve."

"They just predict it's going to spiral into catastrophe."

"I feel pretty catastrophic right here, and right now I'd rather have a smelly car. A Jeep, maybe. One of those army Hummers."

"Or a pizza delivery truck."

"Yum!" It hurt so much to think of food that I tried to unthink it. "Do you have your license?"

"I was taking driver's ed. How about you?"

"License, but no car, so not a lot of practice."

"That's another thing that's different," she said as we watched the sun go down. "No licenses. No rules."

"No law, no order."

"No alarm clocks, no sirens, and no buzzers to mark class periods."

"No church bells, no music, and no laugh track."

We stopped a moment, both recognizing the enormity of what we'd jumped to. I reached in my backpack. Ellie sat staring over the savanna, and then stiffened at something she spotted.

"If you're cold, you can put on my raingear," I offered. I pulled it out for her. It seemed the manly thing to do.

"Thanks." She put on the Gore–Tex. "The clothes are good, but fire would be better." She pointed. "I think we need to leave the lights on."

Tawny shapes were trotting toward us through the grass. Uh–oh. Our lion pals looked like they'd decided on the same rock motel we had. Of course! We could watch wildebeest from here; they could watch wildebeest from here. Great minds think alike. The cats were going for high ground.

What would they think of new neighbors?

I stood, peered, and pointed. "That cleft in the rock there. It's narrow, with shrubs nearby. We keep our backs to the rock, and use wood for a fire to keep them away."

Did these animals even know to be afraid of fire?

We scampered like monkeys, skipping across rock pitches and risking a bad fall. Then we wormed into a narrow spot where one of the titanic rocks seemed to have been split with a cosmic ax. The cleft was almost closed at one end. The broader opening on the other had a screen of bushes. I crawled into them, heedless of thorns and snakes, and snatched all the broken and dry wood I could find. Ellie wedged herself up high to keep watch.

"I think they've smelled us," she warned. "A lioness is looking our way." "How do you know it's a girl?"

"No mane."

"That's good, right?"

"Not really. The females do the hunting. The males just take it away from them."

"Not just carnivorous, but sexist." Lame joke, again.

"Hungry, lazy, and he gets to pick the movie." So she *could* tease, which we needed.

"Listen, we don't have enough wood for a long fire. Tell me if she comes this way and I'll light it."

But the day was fading rapidly. Ellie soon dropped down. "Sorry, Nick. I can't see a thing. You'd better start."

I was afraid to look for more wood, afraid to burn what we had, and afraid not to. Our only hope was that the cats were stuffed with wildebeest.

Something moved in the brush below.

I struck a match. Now I only had a dozen left.

Luckily, Africa seemed tinder dry. My kindling of dried grass, dead leaves and twigs caught easily and in moments we had a small fire, its light flickering off the rocks. Relief came with the heat.

"Feed it as slowly as you can," she cautioned.

The animal padded experimentally towards us, and from the fire we saw the gleam of cat eyes. Her smell mingled with the smoke, a musk made of blood and meat. I heard a low rumble. Like she was thinking it over.

"Maybe she doesn't know what people are," Ellie ventured, barely breathing.

"Or maybe she does. Dessert." The lion's muscles rippled with every twitch, and the guttural growl revealed an armory of teeth. She could snap a leg like a matchstick. My heart hammered as I tried to decide what to do. More wood and the flames might encourage her to back off. But the faster I fed the fire, the faster it would go out.

The lioness shifted, tail flicking. She seemed absolutely massive. Were lions bigger in prehistoric times? They sure didn't seem this big in the zoo.

I put on more wood and the flames flared up.

The lion's eyes disappeared. I was almost faint with relief.

Not enough wood to last, though.

I worked up my courage to belly crawl downhill to fetch a little more, wary of sudden attack. It was a relief to retreat again with an armful. Then we nursed the flames for a couple hours until I was out of fuel again and down to coals. The lioness hadn't come back. Was she just waiting? It was getting colder, and I didn't know what to do.

"Try to get some sleep," I finally told Ellie.

Amazingly, she did. She curled into a notch in the rocks and winked out. The girl was as exhausted as I felt.

Guess you're the sentry, Brynner. And first snack.

I glanced at the female who had dragged – make that "jumped" – me into this. Cute, but she hadn't brought a damn thing. Now she was curled up in my emergency raingear and snoozing while I worried.

You offered, dude.

I resented her. I wanted to protect her.

The lions started calling like a pack of wolves,

except they didn't sound like wolves. They'd moved farther away – a good thing – and they made deep, guttural roars that churned my guts – a bad thing. The noise wasn't as classy as the MGM movie lion, but instead a higher call, almost plaintive, dropping off to a muttery growl, and then huffs like a badly tuned engine or a prowling gort. I didn't know if the beasts were talking, announcing their territory, or belching with indigestion, but the rumble ate into your bones. Yet the feline bray was almost funny, too, because the noise seemed a safe several hundred yards away.

Unfortunately, they wouldn't shut up. Was this a nightly chorus?

I clenched my multipurpose pocketknife.

I was hungry, thirsty, cold, and scared. I'd been dropped into a wilderness with no hope of rescue. In fact, I was supposed to rescue someone else. No real weapons, no skills, no chance. It was easily the worst night of my life, and I was angry with Ellie for being able to sleep through it. I swayed from exhaustion, determined to keep watch.

So I looked up, trying to stay awake. The sky was an incredible spangle of stars, far more brilliant than home. It wasn't as intense as the view on that spaceship, but here in Africa were far more stars than I'd ever seen on earth. Not hundreds of stars you could count, but thousands. The Milky Way was so distinct it looked as if it had been put on by a paint roller. There was no moon but the silver glow was bright enough that I could actually see out over the savanna, where a speckling of dark granules presumably represented grazing animals doing whatever grazing animals do at night. It was beautiful, and chilling.

The real star count, Faunus had told us in one of our rambling classroom discussions, was maybe four hundred billion stars in the Milky Way galaxy alone, or more stars than every human who had ever lived. You could name a star after every one of us, and still have billions and billions left over.

And that was just one galaxy in a universe of maybe a trillion galaxies, which was only the tiny wedge of the universe that we could physically observe through the best telescopes. And our universe might be just one of an infinity of universes, with more exploding into being all the time. "We didn't evolve to get our mind around those kinds of numbers and distances," the teacher said. "What we did evolve is a sense of wonder."

And fear. I gazed up at infinity from the ashes of my cold fire, while listening to furtive scratching from little creatures I couldn't even imagine, much less see. I shivered, and you can bet it was from a lot more than cold. Man, I felt *small,* a pimple on this savanna, a speck in time, confronted with a dark glory that was impressive, yes, but also indifferent and implacable. It was as if my impression of prehistoric Africa had been lifted into the sky.

I even had a sense of vertigo, of falling *upward* into outer space, and actually gripped the granite to steady myself. What reassurance could I really hang onto? My mind reeled, and I almost panicked enough to wake Ellie. I held onto my soul, my inner core, since it was the most real thing in all the strangeness around me. The stars stopped receding. I could clock their slow nightly rotation as they brushed the black silhouette of the high boulder, and even though the constellations looked strange from my new vantage point, I managed to calm down. *I'm part of that. I belong here.*

Another thought occurred too, one of those really cool ideas that slide off before you can seize it. It was something important, something fundamental to the entire reason we were here in Africa.

What, what, what? The infinite cosmos…

And then I woke with a start, stiff and confused. Sometime in the night I'd fallen asleep. The stars were gone, the sky lightening. I felt sluggish, wrung out from worry, but had a new calm as well.

I'm still alive.

The lion roaring had stopped. I heard and saw birds flitting about our village of rocks. The heaped boulders were pearl in the gray light of dawn.

Miraculously, we still weren't eaten.

The ashes were stone cold, but the sun was cresting the eastern horizon. Yes, some kind of mountains rose in that direction.

I inwardly groaned at another day of this.

Stop the pity, Brynner. Make a plan.

There was no Mr. Faunus, whoever or whatever the

charismatic teacher was. No Mom. No Gabe, the spooky angel. Not even Carl the dopey boyfriend. Just me, and a sixteen–year–old girl who had both rescued and condemned me, and who I now had to help. Oh yes. And Adam and Eve, with only an entire prehistoric planet to hunt for them in, dodging space aliens in the process.

What could I do but accept it?

You took the first step. And then another.

Doing what you had to while making other plans.

I stamped to get warm and woke my companion up. She blinked sleepily, and then her eyes went wide with remembrance of where we were.

"We have to find water," I told her.

CHAPTER 12

THIRST

I T WAS COLD, we were sore from the challenges on the spaceship, and we moved stiffly. The grass and brush were wet with dew, reminding us how thirsty we were. We shared the last of my liter bottle and the other granola bar. That took the edge off but didn't satisfy, and it was clear our bodies would soon be in trouble. I was a teen boy used to running on premium and plenty of it, as Mom would say. I already felt hollow.

Ellie climbed up to her perch in the cleft for a look– see. "I think the lions are moving back onto the savanna to hunt," she said, dropping back down. "We need to go the other way, toward the rising sun."

"We need to think." Fear could be paralyzing, I was realizing. However crazy our situation was, we weren't going to survive unless we got command of our situa- tion. I'd read that the best Navy SEALs weren't the big- gest guys. They were the mentally toughest, the quiet ones who didn't panic. "We need a plan."

"I'm listening." She looked at me with interest. The insane challenges and long night under the stars had changed me. My voice was different, even to me.

"We're going to need food and water," I said. "And we're going to have to find your cavemen quickly. They know how to survive here, and they have to save us before we can save them. But they need food and water, too. And animals need water. So, we find water, we find animals. We find animals and we have food, if we can catch some. We find both of those, and we find other people finding the same thing. Solving one problem helps solve the next."

She slowly nodded. "So how do we find water?"

I ran my hand along some grasses and dew came off. I licked it. "I've got some ideas. The prairie slopes downward in the east to a line of deeper green. I'm guessing it marks a river or waterhole. That's our first goal. Eventually we need a better fire to make a signal for wandering cavemen. Why not have them find us, instead of us finding them? That's assuming the Xu have really given us a head start."

"How many matches do you have?"

"A dozen. Not enough, unless we find someone who knows how to make fire. And we need weapons if we're going to hunt. We need spears. We need to keep an eye out for fruits and berries."

"Hunt what? Wildebeest? They'll gore us."

"We'll start small." I pointed. In the dawn light, something furry and furtive was scrambling up a rock.

It looked like a woodchuck or giant hamster. It looked, I thought optimistically, like dinner. "I don't know what those are, but I'm hoping they're easier to catch than an antelope or a lion. I don't know how, yet, but I do know we don't have spears to stab, rocks to throw, or traps to spring. So we look for tools."

"I think it's a hyrax," Ellie said. "They look like rodents but they're related to elephants, believe it or not." She *was* a biology nerd. "The Xu briefed me on animals," she explained to my questioning look.

"The hyrax must need water. Maybe from dew, or maybe they found a seep here. We watch them. If cavemen really exist here, survival is possible."

"I'm impressed, Nick. I think the Xu – or this mysterious Mr. Faunus – sent a good partner my way." She pointed. "You know, birds need water too, and I've watched some flying to that crevice in the rock. Maybe it has water or seeds."

Bright blue birds were landing at a horizontal split in the stone and darting their beaks into the crack. "Smart girl. We'll make a team, Ellie."

"We already do."

We worked our way to a spot below the crevice and I boosted her up, the birds fluttering away. She found a small ledge to balance on and put her head to the crack. "I can't see anything, but I smell water. Funny how you can smell it when you don't have any."

"I see dark streaks marking where water runs down into those cracks when it rains." I was surprised at my own perception, but my brain had never felt so focused. "Reading nature is like reading a book, isn't it?"

"The opening is too small to drink from. I can't even get my tongue in there."

So near and yet so far! We needed a bird beak. Ellie started to climb down, but I thought of something. "Wait." I reached in my pack and took out the granola wrapper. I'd stuck it away unconsciously, trying not to litter – ludicrous in 50,000 BP, I suppose, but a good habit – and maybe there was an advantage in not throwing anything away. I carefully rolled the plastic into a tube and handed it up to her. "Drinking straw."

She brightened, and then hesitated. "What if I sip something creepy?"

"Start small."

She inserted the makeshift straw into the crevice and cautiously sucked, then smacked. "It's good, Nick. Clean. Climb up and share."

There wasn't much, maybe a cup of water each, but we were so thirsty that it was like a burst of adrenaline. "It's a start," I said.

We found another crack the birds flitted to and sucked that dry as well. Then, before we worked our way back down the boulders, I reached in the backpack for the spare T–shirt I'd brought.

"What are you doing?"

"Making a canteen. Don't worry, the shirt's clean."

I tied the cotton around one ankle and led the way downhill through dewy grass. Within minutes the fabric was soaked. "This won't work when the day heats up, but right now it helps." I took my empty water bottle and almost used my knife to cut the top off so it had a wider opening. Then I realized I'd be wrecking our only container that had a screw top. So I untied my T–shirt, held it over my head, and wrung the cloth. Enough water ran out to give me a swallow. I offered the wet rag to Ellie. She looked skeptical a moment, shrugged, wrung, and drank.

She wiped her face with the damp shirt. "Who are you, Daniel Boone?"

"Boy Scouts. And I read about this stuff for fun. You know about animals. I remember camping tricks."

"A team, like you said." It pleased me that she repeated that. We went on, venturing out from the rocks to the randomly placed acacia trees at the beginning of the savanna.

We passed some yellow fruit and I gave it the basic poison test. I rubbed some on my forearm to see if it stung. No. Then on my lips. Still okay. But when I bit it tasted suspiciously bitter, so I didn't swallow. "We can't risk getting sick," I said. "Pass on this one."

She looked disappointed and then summoned necessary cheer. "There have to be others that are okay. Cavemen eat something."

Next we found a shrub with some reasonably straight branches. I used my knife to whittle off two, each thicker than my thumb, trimming away stems and leaves until we had crude walking staffs. Spears! Holding something in our fists gave us a little confidence. We were Man, the Toolmaker.

Two teens with sticks.

When we left the shade of the last tree the sun was high, the dew gone, and the day had marched from chilly to hot. There was little to navigate by, so I took a bearing with my compass. My stomach was growling, my mouth dry. We should have a gallon of water on a day like this, not a few swallows. I hadn't gotten enough sleep and felt listless from the lack of food and drink. We hadn't been here twenty–four hours and already I was flagging.

I glanced at my partner. Ellie didn't look much better.

"I'm guessing ten or twelve miles," I said. "At two miles an hour through this grass, that's five or six hours. Then we tank up."

"Let's hurry. I feel exposed on the savanna."

But we couldn't hurry because we were low on fuel: Teenagers have to eat. I'd been hungry and thirsty in my life, but that was waiting for a McDonald's during a car trip with Grandma. This was serious. My mouth was chalk. My head pounded. My feet were lead weights. We trudged.

At first we watched the animals warily as they moved out of our way. After a couple miles, however, we took their courtesy for granted and plodded through, heads down like the wildebeest. Occasionally I looked backward at the rock pile to keep us aligned in the right direction. I also looked warily around for cats but didn't see any, so mostly we just slogged.

Slowly, however, nature intruded on my consciousness.

First, there were more kinds of animals than I'd originally realized, all of them flowing around each other without fighting, like kids negotiating a high school hallway. Small graceful antelope with beautiful striped hides skipped away. Big brown ones with beautifully curved horns loped like majestic deer.

There were ugly bristle–haired pigs with tusks that I thought might be boars, but Ellie called them warthogs. Gross, but Porky Pig might be tasty.

I saw what looked like small dogs skulking around the bigger animals, and she identified them as jackals. Then a bigger kind of dog, all head and shoulder like a bad atomic experiment. She said those were hyenas, and dangerously mean. We came close to a group of them chewing on something in the grass. They gave us the eye, ugly and tough, and we lifted our crude spears in response. It was like flashing gang signs.

We resisted the urge to run, and they left us alone.

But their sharing of meat gave me a thought.

Most interesting were the ostriches. Some were black and white and some brown, but they were taller than a basketball star, with sturdy white legs that reminded me of a male ballet dancer in tights.

Ostriches might have eggs. And an ostrich egg would make quite the Denver omelet.

I wondered where they nested.

White clouds sailed overhead like zeppelins, casting the savanna in light and shadow. Birds flew regularly over the migrating herds. Some orbited, and I guessed they were hawks or eagles looking for a snack.

Others flew more purposefully.

"Look, most of the birds are flying the same direction that we're walking," I said to Ellie. "I'm betting they're going for water, too. I wish they'd give us a lift."

"Yes. Too bad we're not waterbears." She was fanning herself.

"There are bears here, too?" Who knew what prehistoric Africa held? I glanced around, looking for a raging cave bear or sour–mood grizzly.

"Tardigrades. The oldest and most successful animal ever. They can go ten years without a drink while in deep hibernation. Then you drop water on them, and they come back to life."

"That's insane."

"It's true. They're tinier than a pinhead, and look like these weird, bloated caterpillars under the microscope. They've been found in boiling hot springs, ice, at the bottom of the ocean, atop the Himalayas, and even survived in space when astronauts put them outside. They can endure a thousand times the radiation we can, and have survived on earth a thousand times longer. Far older than dinosaurs. Five mass extinctions, and they sailed through every one."

"Never heard of them."

"We're tourists, Nick. We die if we don't get a drink. The waterbears – which have this weird face and shambling walk like a microscopic bear – will muddle right along. Maybe the Xu think *they* should inherit the earth."

"Well, if the Xu drop water on me, I'll come back to life."

The rocky outcrop where we'd spent the night eventually sank beneath the horizon. Now our environment was as featureless as the felt of a billiard table, and I spent the last three hours of our trek checking my compass every five minutes to make sure we were still walking east. Just to be sure, I also kept our backs to a sun that had crested at noon and was now sinking west.

Ellie didn't say much more. She'd long since taken off the raingear in the heat, letting me stuff it back in my pack. She seemed pretty glum. Or was she just habitually serious, like she said? Maybe the aliens had been careful not to snatch an airhead, but Madame Curie. Yet so far she didn't seem to have much of a plan beyond time jumping with boy loser.

Which was crazy.

You can't figure women out, Carl had informed me, giving me the gift of beer wisdom. *Easier if you don't try.*

The savanna wasn't quite as featureless as it first appeared. Termite mounds poked up everywhere, looking like tiny volcanoes pocked with vents. There were bones enough to stock a catacomb, testifying that life in the wild was nasty, brutish, and short. There were also chunks of loose white rock that I guessed was quartz. I pocketed small chunks for throwing and noticed one piece had an edge to it.

Maybe we could make real spears, with Stone Age spearheads. There were stringy–strong twisted vines in the grass that I could use to lash them.

The grass itself varied, high here and low there, a little greener this way and browner that way. Mostly it was tawny, the color of lions. Or, more accurately, the lions were the color of the grass. But as the clouds skidded and light played, the savanna also glowed tan, wheat, gold, straw, honey, sawdust, and sometimes a silver–green, rippling like a wavy ocean. I hadn't paid much attention to grass before, but this palette made me realize what a complex system it made. Not grass, but grasses, duking it out with each other, being eaten, watered, fertilized with animal dung, trampled, seeded, burnt, and regrown. A day ago, I would have said the most important being out here was *me*, torso upright above all these amber waves of grain. Now? Not so sure.

There were tracks everywhere, a billion of them, and I began to try linking print to animal. Isn't that what hunters do? Mostly hooves, but also paw prints. And some that looked like saucers.

"Elephants," Ellie guessed.

I tried creeping up on antelope but they edged easily away. How was I ever going to get close enough to kill anything, unless they attacked to kill *me?*

Then the grass became a deeper green, and the

ground dropped into a broad swale. There was a line of trees ahead that I guessed marked a river.

"Palm trees," Ellie said, her step quickening. "Paradise."

"Or at least Florida. Maybe people live *here.*"

"Maybe we can finally get a decent drink of water."

We waded into grass that heightened to our chests and stopped at the most magnificent sight yet.

A group of gigantic elephants, iron gray and ponderous, was stripping branches from trees. They were massive as dump trucks, their ears flapping sails and their eyes regarding us under great feminine lashes. The oldest were wrinkled, the youngest cute, and the smallest one tucked into the shadow of its mother's belly.

"Trying to suckle," Ellie said.

The tusks gleamed where not spotted with mud. Their hides were corrugated like fir bark, and their gazes were wiser than an owl's. An old bull turned and flapped his ears in warning, curling his trunk. Message received. Don't come close.

Beyond the elephants, rotating and dipping like golden construction cranes, were the necks of giraffes. They had a model's grace, majestically swaying as if they were strutting on the fashion runway. Other animals were bunching at what even we could smell was water, with zebra and antelope crowding each other as if at a shopping sale. There were big black buffalo with horns broader than anything I remembered seeing in a zoo or picture, and I wondered if we were seeing prehistoric critters that had since gone extinct. There were pigs with gray bristle like old man hair, weasel–looking slinky things that Ellie said were mongoose, and even a snout–nosed aardvark, which looked like a plush toy from outer space.

There was a reassuring peace to it all, these species mingling without killing in a way I hadn't thought possible.

"Eden," Ellie murmured. "Like the pictures in a children's Bible."

"Nobody eating each other, at least. But I'm starving. Do palm trees have anything to eat?"

"Dates, maybe. Coconuts. First I need something to drink; my head aches and my tongue is swollen. If only we had lemonade."

"With ice."

"Or a Frappuccino."

"No plastic. Frosted mugs."

"A frosted *bucket* to drink dry."

We began to trot, toward disaster.

CHAPTER 13

THE TERRIBLE POOL

THE SLUGGISH STREAM meandered through a series of marshy ponds, the water brown but alluringly *wet*. We were badly dehydrated. An animal trail as broad and beaten as a sidewalk led to a likely spot on the riverbank and I idly wondered what massive creatures used it. Fortunately, none seemed to be occupying this particular mud beach, and I didn't pause to wonder why. I gave Ellie the pack and took out my empty plastic water bottle.

"Wait on firm ground. I'll fill, we'll drink, and then look for a better camping place. This one is boggy and buggy."

"The water looks awful," she croaked. "But I'm dying of thirst."

The trail led to a pool dotted with big boulders and logs. A lone dead tree rose from a shore of goo. Not the choicest watering hole, but maybe we could filter the worst grit with my spare T–shirt. The water stank, and I wondered if we should have looked for something better. No, too thirsty. I sank a few inches in the sticky footing as I crept to the water's edge. Long–legged birds strutted, pecking at the shallows, but otherwise the scene was quiet. I squatted to dip the bottle, reaching to unscrew the cap.

The pool exploded with animal fury.

A "log" came alive, erupting out of the water with gaping mouth bigger than a bear trap, lined with reptilian teeth. Crocodile! Its tail oscillated like a whip, catapulting the predator with unbelievable speed and force. One moment the beast was imitating dead timber, and the next it was all moist throat and yellow, pitiless eyes. Its gullet was a black hole. Its breath was wet rot.

"Nick!" Ellie screamed.

I jerked in terror and dropped the bottle, and maybe that saved me. The croc deviated to bite at the bright plastic, letting me vault backward faster than I thought possible. I was electric with fear. Warm water arced as the monster swung its jaws back toward me and snapped. They closed on nothing as I darted behind the dead tree. The crocodile kept coming, its lunge throwing it against the wood. It grunted as its belly splatted down on the mud.

Maybe I could outrun it.

Then I heard the most gawd–awful bellow I'd ever heard in my life, far angrier than the lion calls or the grunt of the crocodile before me. The noise came from behind. The mud quaked like Jell–O. The rumble was like an avalanche.

Ellie hadn't been screaming about the crocodile.

I whirled. Charging with the weight of a runaway locomotive was a lumbering hippopotamus. Those blimps could run? Its gaping mouth was even wider than the crocodile's. Two saber–like lower teeth jutted upward toward crushing molars on the upper jaw, the dentistry so huge that it could use my bones for floss. The hippo seemed swollen bigger than a movie screen, heavier than an Abrams tank, and angrier than a disturbed hornet's nest. Its muscles rippled in positive rage. And it was aimed at *me*.

I didn't think, I jumped. I grabbed an overhead branch, levered myself with strength I'd never mustered for gym class, and scrambled into the dead tree's upper branches. Just as I did, the hippo struck the trunk like a careening garbage truck, its collision almost knocking me loose from my perch. The tree leaned precariously, wood squealing. But the hippopotamus charge brought it nose–to–nose with the crocodile on the other side, and so next came a crazy blur of scale and skin as the two confused animals went for each other. All I saw was an explosion of mud and water as the hippo's insane momentum carried them both into the river pool, and then the crocodile thought better of tangling with an animal several times its weight and thrashed frantically away. The hippo sank, bellowing, as it beat the water into crazy brown surf.

The tree leaned more, groaning.

I was in shock. The "logs" and "boulders" I'd casually noted became frantic animals, crocodiles skimming away while sympathetic hippos roared, moaned, and farted in a pool as agitated as a washing machine. The charging behemoth that had rammed my tree submerged amid its fellows, slowly calming as water closed over and gave it a sense of safety. It nuzzled friends before turning to trumpet angrily at me.

The tree went the rest of the way over. I bounced off it into the mud, rolled upright, and ran for my life.

Ellie had already disappeared into the high grass. I did the same, tensed for snapping jaws or goliath legs. Once out of the hippo's sight, however, I seemed to be out of mind. I thrashed a hundred yards through the reeds.

Finally I stopped, panting and shaking. I'd never been so frightened in my life. An angry animal is like a crazy person who can't be reasoned with. An angry *wild* animal seems as impossible to appease as an earthquake. I couldn't stop shuddering. It was like I'd been electrocuted and reprieved. Every nerve jangled.

"Nick!" Ellie's call was high and hopeless, and I knew she thought I was dead and she was alone.

I had to catch my breath before I could answer. "Here!" My voice broke as I shouted.

"Where?" She was wild with anxiety.

I stood tall and waved, still wheezing. "Stand up on something!"

Grass moved and I saw her head as she balanced on a rock. I slowly beat my way over to her, spent and staggering.

She fell into my arms and we hugged in horror, realizing how narrowly I'd escaped. The contact helped. After a minute I could finally stop shaking.

Ellie was sobbing, taking great gulps of air. "This is such a horrible place."

"I was stupid. I thought the backs of the hippos were rocks, and the crocodiles were logs. We're idiots, but we're alive."

"I dropped the pack when I ran," she confessed.

"I dropped the water bottle, but we'll get them back. We have to get them back." I held her away by the shoulders, forced to sound confident lest we both get hysteric. "We learned from this. We're near water."

"We can't even get a drink," she mourned. "We're going to die." She snuffled, was embarrassed by her emotion, and then steadied. Her voice shook. "I'm sorry I panicked. I was afraid you'd been trampled and I was going to be all alone."

"I was too terrified to even panic. Everything happened so fast."

"Look at you." Her eyes roamed up and down. "Mud man." She stepped back. "Ugh."

Indeed, I was covered with sticky grime. "All mud, no water."

She shook her head. "You've made me filthy too." I'd smeared her with muck from our hug, her cheeks streaked, hair smudged. But suddenly she began to smile. "You look like a Hershey bar." Now she began to laugh. "Nick, I've never seen anyone so dirty in my life!" And now she was chortling, releasing tension as the absurdity of our plight hit home. Laughing was the only way to cope. "You're an ink blot!"

So I laughed too, my tension bursting in crazy hilarity, and pointed. "You look like a graduate of Mud Wrestling U."

We roared, shaking, and fell together again, until finally the tense merriment left us drained but released. Ellie looked at me more soberly.

"I'm so sorry I brought you here. I just felt we didn't have a choice."

"That's what Gabe told us, remember? He is one cold angel."

"What are we going to do now?"

Did she mean our mission? Jumping through time? Dueling space aliens? I took a shaky breath. *One thing at a time.* "We're still going to get water, because we don't have a choice on that, either. That hippo seemed pretty enraged at having me between him and his pool, so we find a hippo–free zone. No crocs, no lions, and not even squirrels if I can help it. I just want a quiet drink."

"I thought I lost you. I thought you were dead."

"Just about."

"I thought you were smashed or chewed."

"Just scared. Still scared." I stood straighter, trying to reassure her. "Permanently scared, but that's good if it makes me smarter. We need that pack or we're dead. Where is it?"

"Back in the grass," she said miserably.

"Okay, that's easy enough. Step one, right? I'll see if I spot the water bottle, too. You keep watch. See a hippo, call out. They use that freeway of a trail."

It wasn't hard to follow Ellie's thrash through the reeds back to the pack, and from there I could see the river pool again and my toppled tree. The "logs" and "boulders" of dozing animals had settled and the water was once more placid. There was no sign of the water bottle. I scooped our makeshift spears up with the pack and brought them back.

"Either the bottle sank or it floated downstream," I reported. "It still had the lid on. Let's search."

We paralleled the water, looking for a likelier drinking spot. Ellie pointed to a narrow stretch where the river showed some movement. A small herd of drinking zebra spied us and trotted off, one of them braying like a donkey.

"Maybe the zebras mean no predators," she said.

"Smart thinking. If you're right."

"Scared smart."

Cautiously, we broke through brush and reeds until we reached water.

No boulders. No logs. Maybe man–eating fish, but I was too thirsty to care.

We sprawled on our bellies to drink, slurping and rejoicing. The water was gritty but wet. Then I slid in, washing off my mud. "It feels good," I reported. "No wonder the hippos like it."

Ellie sensibly waited to see if anything ate me and then crept in too, both of us submerged in our clothes in water no deeper than a bathtub. It was almost as warm as a tub, too. "Now I'm worried about snakes," she said.

"I'm so worried about so many things that I'm not worried anymore. I mean, it's exhausting to worry so much, you know? So after the hippo, after almost being killed, I think I'm gaining perspective. I'm alive for a reason. You're alive for a reason. Somehow we're going to make it through this, Ellie. We're supposed to, you said."

Her smile was wry. "I wish I could believe me. So why are we starving?"

"At least we're not dying of thirst. Step One."

"You said getting the pack back was Step One."

"Right. Step Two. Progress!"

She stood, water pouring off her wet clothes. If she noticed my appraising glance she didn't let on. "I see your bottle."

I stood too. The floating plastic was caught in some reeds twenty yards downstream.

"See? A sign. Step Three."

She nodded. "But it's going to be dark soon."

"And we don't have Stonehenge to hide in this time."

"No, but there are lots of trees." She offered a tremulous smile. "Let's build a tree house, Nick. And then I've got ideas for food."

CHAPTER 14

HUNGER

MAYBE OUR ANCESTORS lived in trees. Maybe Swiss Family Robinson lived in a tree. But yours truly, Nick Brynner, found arboreal habitation to be even less relaxing than roaring lions.

Ellie and I were as clever as time allowed. I cut more staves and we gingerly built a crude nest in the crook of one of those thorny, yellow–bark beauties. We wedged our spear poles, too, and used pack straps as temporary rope. The wire cutter on my handyman multipurpose tool snipped some tough creepers to serve as additional lashings. Not bad for an hour's work.

When we hoisted ourselves aboard, our "bed" of woven sticks sagged slightly, but that just jammed it more thoroughly into the tree. We both slid into the middle of this stiff hammock, and for the first time in my life I found myself sleeping with a girl, sharing my raincoat as blanket. We were hip to hip with her hair drifting against my mouth if she turned my way. So this new intimacy was wonderful, right?

Not.

First, our perch creaked and groaned enough to make me fear it might collapse, so lying there was like trying to sleep on eggshells. Second, the night wind blew chilly and hard, and the tree rocked and groaned. Worst motel ever. Third, she fell immediately into exhausted slumber and I needed to do the same, so there wasn't even a chance at romance. Way too tired. Fourth, we had an animal chorus once more, this time grunts and thuds and a weird *whoop* that sounded like giant birds but which we later figured out were hyenas. If we tumbled, we might be gobbled.

And finally, her proximity kept me uncomfortably alert in more ways than one. Ellie didn't say anything about the instinctual reaction of my body but could hardly fail to notice, given how jammed we were. She'd scoot a few inches away but inevitably we'd slide together again, and shifting too much threatened to bring down the platform. I was balancing to give her space and trying not to embarrass myself, but when I dozed off we'd roll back. Then I'd wake, shift away, and stew.

What should have been funny was mostly just miserable.

Eventually I gave up trying for propriety and zoned out, as heavily asleep as if I were on an operating table. But when morning came I felt tired, cranky, stiff, and self–conscious. I was more than happy to stop playing birdman.

Ellie pretended it was just one more night at Holiday Inn Express and chose not to comment, but I could tell she was flustered too. What kind of friends were we?

I had to let her decide.

Meanwhile, we both were going to slide into depression if we didn't get nourishment. The day started without much talk. We drank muddy water and washed as best we could. Out of constant fear of animals we didn't move too far from each other even to pee, so we turned our backs to provide privacy.

"Did you bring toilet paper?" she asked.

"No." I felt I had to explain. "I'm a guy, going on a quick kayak paddle."

She was silent.

"Use leaves."

We were getting to know each other in a hurry.

Ellie coped by going brisk and practical. "Okay, we got water but we need food." She had unfastened her hair to wash and now she finger–combed it and wrapped it in a ponytail. "We're going shopping."

"Agreed." I felt as if my belly button had shrunk against my backbone.

"There're some lilies in the river. Roots can be edible."

"Water lilies?"

"People eat them, I read. We need to learn what

humans can eat." She led me back to the river, checked for crocodiles, hippos, and snakes, waded, and pulled. "They're rubbery and slippery. Bring a spear."

I did so. With trial and error, we managed to lever a few lilies out of the silt bottom, cut off the bulbs, and wash them clean. I took a cautious bite.

"Yuck."

Ellie tried them too. "Pretty bitter."

"How do you know these aren't poisonous?" "I don't."

"Maybe they need to be cooked."

"We need a kettle." She sighed, wiping her hair away from her forehead but refusing to cry. "Okay, we're experimenting. We've got these; let's try other stuff." She pointed uphill. "That's the rock where we'll meet. You take a spear and go hunting. I'll look for fruits and vegetables. We either succeed or we starve, and if we die our entire species dies with us."

"Not that there's any pressure or anything."

"We'll meet at noon," she said, pointing to the sun. "Don't take any risks." Which was pointless advice, since everything in prehistoric Africa was risky. I gave her the pack to use as a bag to gather plants. We separated.

I paralleled the stream again, keeping out of the thickest brush where I could be surprised by a predator. Meanwhile, I tried to play predator myself. It's surprisingly hard. I had a sharpened stick, absolutely no hunting experience, and gnawing hunger. Animals avoided me like I carried an invisible force field. Birds shouted warning. Mosquitoes made me slap.

But with the dawn stupor wearing off, I also found myself unexpectedly enjoying my roaming. Hunting forced attention, and I was astounded at the menagerie of animals. Planet Earth was capable of lots of life, and this place made civilized home seem like a biological desert. The animals fit so naturally that they had a presence, a cool, I envied. They belonged.

Palms, acacias, and eucalyptus cast dappled shade, and further upland were tree titans as fat as a sequoia. Their enormous trunks ended in stubby upright branches that resembled roots, so the tree looked upside down. I'd seen pictures of these and scoured my memory for a name. Baobab.

There were also low shrubby trees with glossy leaves and firm red fruits. I cautiously tried one, and at least it was better than the lily. Not very sweet, but not bitter.

Poisonous? I ate another, greedy from my hunger, and then prudently put more in my pocket to wait and see what my stomach would do.

Now, what could I kill?

I saw monkeys in the trees, but they swung away long before I got close. A troop of baboons allowed me to draw nearer, but big males moved to block me before I crept within spear range. They snarled, displaying enormous pointed teeth, and their surprisingly big bodies were barrels of coiled muscle. I sure as heck didn't want to pick a fight. I wondered what *they* were eating, but moved on.

Something flicked up high and I jerked from surprise. A big cat was resting in a tree above me. It stared at me with cold boredom, its tail rocking lazily as it read me like a menu. The feline was spotted, so I supposed it was a leopard. Or could it be a cheetah? Again, a mass of muscle, as if every creature but me was on steroids. I felt embarrassingly weak.

The cat didn't seem inclined to come down, and the reason was jammed in the crook of the tree. He had a dead antelope up there and was snacking. I could see blood on its muzzle.

I hurried on.

To eat, or be eaten? That was my Hamlet question. Likely prey for me was a rabbit, but when I spotted one it swiftly disappeared in the brush. How could I run down something that swift? Think!

Find a burrow.

I looked, and couldn't.

Some hunter, Brynner.

No poison cramps yet, so I ate more fruit, the sugary juice flowing through me like a rush. Food! I picked more for Ellie, too.

Then I had an idea and crept down to water's edge, stalking.

Yes, *that* prey was possible. I struck.

We reunited at the rock, both of us relieved the other was alive and unhurt. Even a minor injury could be catastrophic. Ellie set down the pack with a smile of triumph.

"I got something, Nick." She pulled out what looked like a velvet–covered coconut. "It's from the baobab tree and I heard it's good. Remember *The Lion King?*"

"I think I passed in favor of *Fast and Furious.*"

"Parts of the tree are edible. We need to crack this open."

I found a quartz rock with an edge and gave the fruit a whack. Tough as a lunch box. So I attacked frantically – when in doubt, whale away – and finally the nut shattered, revealing curious spaghetti inside. There were white chunks of pulp wound with dark red fibers. Ellie pulled out a piece and sampled.

"Seed inside." She spat out a dark seed concealed in the pulp, cracked it with her teeth, chewed experimentally, and swallowed. "Pretty tasteless, except tart. But the pulp is nourishment." She held up some dates. "These fell from a palm tree."

I shared the fruit I'd found. "Maybe these are a wild plum?"

"I'd say some kind of fig. What else you got, great hunter?"

I was a little sheepish, but proud, too. I pulled from my pocket what I'd already cleaned and then hid for surprise. "I speared a frog."

"Nick, that's wonderful!"

"It was sunning, but it's not as easy as that sounds.

They jump. I got this one, and I'm thinking we could try the legs." The emptied body seemed about as appetizing as a plastic bag, but the legs, I'd heard, were like chicken.

"Excellent, *mi amigo*. I think the French call them *cuisses de grenouille*."

"You know French?"

"My Dad knows French cooking."

"You're not a girl who squeals about frog dissection."

"Biology nerd, remember? I'm different. You're different. I think that's why we're here."

"Gabe said we were ordinary. Unremarkable."

"He just meant normal, not superheroes. But he thought we could play their game. We're going to prove him right."

"You're cockier than yesterday."

"Food will do that. Let's build a fire and put a flat rock in it to make a pan. We can fry the frog legs and the water–lily roots."

We spent the rest of the day cooking, experimenting, and eating, our smoke a signal for any cavemen or space aliens who cared to look. Our staple was the baobab fruit pulp, and while hardly tasty it was edible enough to finally give us a full stomach. Energy tingled back. I used my knife to cut off the frog's webbed feet and skin the legs. Then we fried them on the hot rock. A little like chicken. They needed salt, but the smidgen of protein was exquisite.

Ellie had another idea. There was a termite mound

nearby, so she probed it with a stick and pulled out insects, each with a body about the size of a shelled peanut. She shook them onto our hot rock and they jumped and sizzled. I plucked them clear with the needle–nose pliers on my multipurpose tool and accumulated them on a broad leaf.

Ghastly.

"More protein," she said. "Bon appétit." She popped one in her mouth, chewed quickly, and swallowed.

I looked at her with wonder. "So?"

"Nutty. Not terrible. For strength, Nick."

I tried to get up the nerve. "You should have left me to the gort."

"Come on, a hologram said termites are a delicacy in Africa."

"Maybe the Xu were putting you on." But I tried some, biting and gulping. Crunchy, bland, endurable. I managed not to lose the rest of my stomach. "A little like raw carrots," I said optimistically, trying to convince myself. I chewed and smacked experimentally. "But more like the worst meal I've ever had."

"Motive to get some real meat," Ellie said.

"Today a frog, tomorrow an elephant."

"So what about tomorrow? We can't just stay here."

"Why not? We've got food and water."

"There's no Adam and Eve, and the Xu are going to beat us to them."

"Ellie, we're eating bugs. We can't fight the Xu."

"We don't have to fight them. We just have to warn

our ancestors. They'll figure out the rest. They'll have food, too."

"So where *are* Grandma and Grandpa?"

"I don't know, but we can't see anything down here in this marshy valley. We didn't see any sign of them from those first rocks. I think we should keep going east, toward the mountains, and look for high places to spy from."

"Would they really live in mountains?"

"Water would be cleaner up higher. Fewer mosquitoes. " She looked evasive. Did she know more than she was telling me?

"Those hills looked days away. What do we do for food and water?"

"Carry, forage, hope. We take as much food as we can and make as much distance as we can."

I hadn't told her about the leopard yet. Sooner or later we'd be lunch here in the Garden of Eden, once we ran across a predator that wasn't already stuffed. We'd survived this long on dumb luck. So she was right. What little chance we had was with humans who already knew how to survive on this continent, and who could fight off its beasts. We had to find the cavemen not just for them, but for us.

"Okay, tomorrow we head east again. I hope you're right, Ellie."

"We don't know I'm wrong until we try." She picked up a stick. "I'm going to fry up more termites for trail food. We'll snack on them like gorp."

"Yummy."

"And Nick?" She turned on her way to the termite mound.

"Yes?"

"It's okay to sleep close tonight. It keeps me warmer. But just sleep, okay?"

I swallowed. "You bet."

"Girls understand, you know."

I turned so she wouldn't see my blush, feeling a thrill of possibility and the embarrassment of confusion. Understand *what?*

CHAPTER 15

PARTNERSHIP

L EAVING THE RIVER felt like letting go of a dock to strike out swimming for the other side. Having found food and water, we gave up fleeting sustenance to keep exploring eastward. Within a mile we felt swallowed by the vast savanna again, the wildlife once more mostly indifferent to our passage. When I looked back, the grass we'd disturbed had rebounded as if we were never there.

Or, we were a part of everything, with no walls or windows separating us from the planet we shared. It was like that first day of grade school when you leave Mom's car to join the world, no longer the special only kid and yet a part of something bigger. Frightening, but exhilarating, too.

Like a ship appearing over the horizon, a castle of erupting boulders again rose from a knoll in the plain ahead. These rocky outcrops were apparently a routine part of the savanna. Ellie and I altered course slightly to make for high ground that would serve as camping spot, observation post, and a place to light a signal fire in hopes of finding Adam and Eve.

Two new discoveries gave us a little more confidence.

First, Ellie pointed out that animals seemed to be congregating at a particular point on the prairie, their crowd marked by a pillar of dust. When we drew near we saw they were drinking from a water hole, with any lions or leopards apparently sleeping it off during the intense noontime sun. I expected a stampede when we strode to the muddy pool, but instead zebra and wildebeest simply shifted to make companionable room. They took a fast drink and moved off, wary, alert, and refreshed. We would copy them.

"The water still looks more like chocolate milk than Perrier," Ellie observed.

"We'll use my T–shirt to filter again."

The baobab fruit rinds made crude cups, and Ellie scooped up water with my bottle. I held the T–shirt over our make–do glasses. It filtered out the worst of the dirt, though not any bacteria. We didn't have a choice. We drank until we were bloated, filled my water bottle one more time, and went on.

I kept waiting for some dire intestinal parasite, but so far, so good. Maybe the germs of fifty thousand years ago hadn't evolved to torment us yet.

The second survival realization was that we could thieve like jackals. We spotted a pack of the dogs devouring lion leftovers and decided to test the territory. Leveling our walking sticks like spears, we took a breath for courage and marched toward the feeding dogs like gunslingers, pretending we owned the place. The jackals reminded me of coyotes. They looked up suspiciously, tensed, and gave high–pitched barks of warning. In any real fight they'd tear us apart, and it was all we could do to keep from running. But instead we started shouting, shaking spears and stamping feet, emphasizing our height. The animals sullenly slunk off. We ran forward, I used my knife to cut off some strips of fresh meat, and we backed away.

Vultures flapped down after us. Each animal took its turn.

Ellie pulled some grass to wrap today's steak and I put our scavenged meal in an outer pocket of my pack, which was already filthy. We were the dumpster divers of prehistoric Africa. We wiped our bloody hands on the grass.

"Not exactly mouth–watering," she said.

"Except we're starving."

The new cluster of boulders didn't appear to house any lions when we arrived in late afternoon, and we had time to gather firewood. I wasn't optimistic about water since we were on a small hill, but we actually found a shadowy puddle beneath an overhanging monolith. It was so clean compared to the savanna waterhole that we poured that liquid out, drank ourselves silly again, and refilled the plastic bottle. The puddle's depth had already lowered, but it should suffice for a couple days. We were far from relaxed, but survival had reduced our panic. It was our fourth night and we were adjusting, as people do. Both of us limped from blisters, so I dug out my supply of Band–Aids and applied them to our feet. I had half a dozen left.

"You don't talk about a dad," Ellie remarked as I bandaged her heel.

"That's because I don't have one. He died when I was ten."

"Accident?"

"Cancer. And please don't say you're sorry. You had nothing to do with it."

She was quiet, and I knew she didn't deserve the cutoff. I'd just heard the sorry business a thousand times, and it was one of those polite but empty sentiments with no adequate answer. It gives everyone else something automatic to say, except me. It's obvious losing a dad sucks. They're sorry, I'm sorry, he's dead.

"It's been a while," I added, trying not to be too brusque. "I'm used to it."

"I knew to ask because I sensed it. I lost my mom." She wasn't sad, just matter of fact like me. "Mine was an accident. This drunk crossed the center line."

I caught myself about to say, "I'm sorry." Instead I said, "Do you drink?"

"No." She rubbed her feet, which were beat up like mine. "Not after that. Do you have brothers or sisters?"

"No. Only child. Just me, my mom, and her moronic boyfriend."

"He's dumb?"

"Not really, but he's annoying. He doesn't do enough for her."

Ellie nodded. "I'm an only too. And my dad doesn't date."

"Both of us?"

"Weird, huh? I'm thinking about the Xu. Maybe they pick kids to play the game with as few family connections as possible. Fewer to grieve."

"I'll gladly give up my place to an orphan."

She laughed. "I guess no orphans went into that old fort."

So we had stuff in common. I stockpiled enough wood to last the night, we spitted and roasted the stolen meat – eight matches left – and reveled in the nourishment, trying to ignore the lack of spicing. When the sun went down night came on fast in Africa, so we spent a couple hours watching the light of stars turn drifting clouds into silvery gobs of gas.

No great cats came near this time, and the habitual animal calls faded in our consciousness the way city people get used to traffic noise. We huddled and fell asleep together, so wearily and so naturally this time that it wasn't a big deal. Ellie or I would wake to feed the fire, and then drift off again.

"Water and no lions," I said the next morning. "I like this place. Maybe we should rest here a day or two."

Ellie shook her head. "We're in a race with the Xu."

"We won't win it by collapsing."

"We'll win it by finding the right humans. Then they'll help us."

"How about them finding us, like we said? We light fires and keep watch. If nobody shows up after a few days we strike out for the mountains again."

She considered, slowly nodded, and actually looked relieved. "That's a good compromise, Nick. I could sleep for a thousand years. And I'm always hungry. Let's find more food."

Nature forces you to pay attention. Those furry hyrax animals were here again, and after futilely hurling a spear at two and missing entirely, I decided to watch, think, and plan. I moved from boulder to boulder, following them like a private eye. Ellie, meanwhile, inspected every plant. Pluck, dig, cautiously sample, cook if necessary, eat. There was no baobab here, but there were figs, plums, and roots.

I also spied rabbits hopping in and out of grass and brush, and studied them with the intensity of a scientist.

Surprise! Animals can be predictable, just like people.

I tried two experiments. I tied loops with a slipknot at the end of three lengths of fishing line. If I slipped my finger in a loop and pulled, it cinched tight. At dusk, just before the bunnies bedded down, I used sticks to suspend these snares over the paths the animals used to their burrows.

By morning one snare was knocked over, catching nothing. A second wasn't disturbed at all. But in a third, a rabbit had caught its foot. The more frantically it kicked, the tighter my loop held.

I snapped its neck, slit its throat, drained the blood, and experimented gutting and skinning. I found that by gripping the legs with one hand, and tugging the skin with the other, I could peel the animal like a peach, the fat ripping as I pulled.

It was him or me.

For the hyraxes I tried a different tactic. First, I improved my weaponry. I kept my eye out for loose quartz, found a shard pointed vaguely like a spearhead, notched my stick with my knife, and managed to tie the rock in place with vines. Poor work by caveman standards, but it should suffice for overgrown hamsters.

In studying hyrax routes, I found a point near their trail where they often hesitated and where I could hide. I waited, spear poised, until one came by.

It was maddeningly hard to be that patient. If there's one thing kids expect in the twenty–first century, it's instant gratification, instant messaging, instant popcorn, and instant soup. Time definitely ticked differently here. I waited three hours without moving. That's enough time for two movies, six sitcoms, a page–turner of a book, a football game, or a party. It was half the class time of a school day. All I did was watch, and wait. And watch. And wait. That hyrax trail was my paycheck, my lottery number, my holy grail. I stayed, or we would starve.

Four hyraxes darted by too quickly for me to aim and thrust. But each one that went by let me anticipate a little better how they moved, how they dodged, when they sniffed, and which way their heads turned. I observed, and I plotted. I studied as if this was my SAT exam. Hunger will do that.

My heart was pounding when I finally thrust successfully, impaling the little critter as cruelly as a vampire hunter. It thrashed like a landed fish.

So I bent, opened the knife, and slit its throat, too.

We stayed two days, killing, gathering, and eating. Ellie began raiding bird nests she found on rocky crannies, and searched the savanna for more eggs. She even stole an ostrich egg, which indeed made a hearty meal for two. We cut a small hole to get the goodies out, and then used the shell to hold water.

The more I ate the more famished I felt, and realized we were making up for lost calories. As we did, however, strength and ambition returned.

Butchery became routine. The insides of the creatures seemed as unremarkable as machine parts. Mechanical, stripped out by Man the Predator like shucking corn. Get hungry enough, and all hesitation vanishes. You eat your fill and the only feeling is satisfaction. I don't know if I could ever be a cannibal, but for the first time I suspected how cannibals think.

Me Tarzan. You food.

The beckoning mountains began to seem less distant as we gained confidence from our experiments. The idea of finding Adam and Eve, even though still crazy, seemed less impossible. Ellie discovered a dozen fruits, nuts, and seeds we sampled, including seeds from the acacia trees, and we started to catalog what was edible and what was not. I roamed for wood, both for small fires to cook and for a larger bonfire we planned to try as a signal.

We also swapped jobs, and Ellie was at least as successful a hunter as I was. She had a science nerd's gift of stealthy movement and patient observation. As we experimented with snares and trails, we traded tips. Our friendship deepened.

She treated me like a brother. I could never forget she was a girl.

On our third night in Boulder City, we set our signal fire. First a column of smoke rolled up, and then sprays of sparks worthy of a blast furnace. We had to guard to keep the blaze from spreading in the dry grass. I stamped out wayward embers.

Surely our signal could be seen for miles.

But nobody came. Disappointed, we fell asleep at midnight when our signal was crumbling into a cone of coals.

By morning it was smoking ash, and nobody had walked up to say howdy.

"I guess it's not going to be that easy," I said.

"We have to try the mountains," Ellie agreed.

"Do these cavemen exist at all? Are the Xu playing us?"

"They exist. We know that from the fossil record. And I think the Judgment is real. But we need to take as much food as possible. I'm going to try to make a bag by sewing some skins together with the rest of the fishing line."

"What if we want to fish someday?"

"Then I'll unsew them."

"Okay. I'll spend the morning hunting, you forage, we'll check our snares, and set off at midday." I looked east across the haze. "We'll probably have to spend at least one night on the open savanna."

"We'll take turns to watch."

Yep, we had become a regular Lewis and Clark. Or Lewis and Sacagawea. So we thought with our new cocky confidence. We'd watch birds and animals for signs of water, stare down jackals, and share a lion's breakfast on the plains. Meanwhile, since the hyraxes had learned to avoid my happy hunting grounds, I decided to try a new spot between two boulders that ballooned over the grass like giant beach balls. I'd hide under one, wait, and pounce.

So I dropped onto hands and knees, the grass still dawn wet with dew, and backed into my ambush point like a sniper. *Hooah!*

And then my luck ran out. Maybe I was being punished for overconfidence.

Something bit my calf with fangs of fire.

The pain was like a splash of hot lead. I didn't know such agony was possible. I erupted out of my hiding place, yelling in terror and dancing like a madman.

"Snake! Snake! Snake! Ellie, it's got me!"

I rolled, the serpent ropy, thick, and leathery as a whip. It wouldn't let go. I grabbed the writhing tail and pulled. Futile. So I rammed my leg and the snake into a rock, grinding the reptile until its jaws finally released. Blind with rage and fear, I seized its tail, swung it in an arc through the air, and brought the viper's head down at a hundred miles an hour. There was a crack, and the snake shuddered. Had I killed it?

No matter. As venom overcame me, I collapsed.

One last conscious thought.

I'm dying.

CHAPTER 16

BOY

SOMETHING WAS BITING my calf again, and I writhed in protest as I slowly swam upward into painful consciousness. My body ached, my leg was on fire, and my head pounded. What happened to peaceful death? No, my only option seemed to be agony and discomfort – I realized rocks were digging into my back, as well – and so I gave up on my blackout and squinted against being alive. Then I shrieked, or would have, except that I was too weak to make any sound at all.

A dark, ugly imp out of a nightmare painting was crouched over me, studying me with curious and proprietary eyes.

That's what I thought in my initial confusion. Then I realized the face, while foreign, was actually quite human. The skin and eyes and hair were dark brown, the whites of his eyes yellowed. The mouth had bright teeth but was grimacing. His cheeks had parallel scars as if raked by claws.

It was a young caveman.

One of his hands clutched my neck and the other held a cup made from gourd. He grunted, as if giving a command.

There was also something incongruous on the guy's head, I woozily noticed. An American baseball cap turned backward.

My tormentor had my hat.

Before I could muster the will to try to snatch it back, the demon hauled me to a half–sitting position, forced the cup against my lips, and pressed.

"Drink!" Ellie cried from behind me.

I startled at her voice, my mouth opened wider, and hot, acrid brew sloshed down my throat. I swallowed and hacked before I could think. The vile potion burned all the way down. When I jerked my head away this witch doctor of a savior slapped me, hard, and pressed the cup once more. I coughed, sputtered, and spit, so he dropped me back to the ground where I could roll away and curl into a fetal ball. Then the poison hit like a punch to the stomach. My insides seized in agony, gorge rose like a geyser, and I projectile vomited like something out of an exorcism movie, spattering the ground up to six feet away. The cap–snatcher leaped back to avoid the mess.

"Eww," Ellie said. "It's working."

I vomited again, and then heaved and heaved some more, even though there was nothing left to come out. Still my stomach roiled, my entire body wracked with spasms. It was awful. Finally I lay limp, shivering in warm Africa. Ellie threw the raincoat over me.

"Wha… what?" I couldn't form a proper question.

"We had to get the venom out, Nick. He cut your leg with a flint and sucked and bled."

I managed another word. "Who?" My teeth chattered.

"I call him Boy."

And then I fell blessedly unconscious again.

I woke sometime that night, my leg throbbing. A campfire was burning, and I saw the boy who had poisoned me crouched with Ellie over its nimbus of warmth. Lions roared in the dark beyond. Hyenas answered back. Africa would never shut up. I was fiercely thirsty, but couldn't summon the energy to speak or stir. So I slept again, and when I woke once more it was daylight. My brain buzzed. How much time had gone by?

My mind was still mud, but with patience I slowly took stock of my sorry state. I was propped semi–upright against a boulder, the raincoat wrapped around my legs. My boots and socks were off, my Band–Aids dirty and fraying. A fire still burned low, and the carcasses of small animals had been spitted to roast over the coals. Baobab fruit husks, gourds, and ostrich shells were lined up in a neat row, and grass had been gathered and laid into two crude mattresses. No, three – I was resting on one too. In short, I was still breathing in a campsite with a degree of primitive order. The only thing disturbing was the presence of the caveman.

He was a chocolate–colored boy entirely naked except for a loincloth and my baseball cap. He looked about ten or twelve, and tough as a leather shoelace.

I was looking at one of our ancestors.

Boy was wiry, with a slightly protruding belly taut as a drum, and no body fat that I could see. He was dusty up to his thighs. The youth's skin was dark but not as black as the blackest I'd seen pictured in *National Geographic,* and he wasn't particularly Negro in his features. He didn't look Caucasian or Asian or American Indian, either. His hair was long, black, shaggy to his shoulders, and wavy, but not kinked. His head was large and his face broad, but he didn't have the flat nose and thick lips of some modern–day blacks, or the thin beak and thin lips of some modern–day whites. It was as if no racial characteristic had quite yet set. If you crossed an Australian aborigine with an Amazon Indian and a South African Zulu, you might get something close to what Boy looked like, but he preceded all these. The perceptive might detect a yellowish or even reddish cast in his skin.

Boy wasn't ugly, I saw now, but his face and arms had ritual scars. His chest was painted ochre, the ceremonial color eroding like paint on an old barn. It probably hadn't been touched up for some time.

Even while squatting to work on a hide, Boy had the same springy strength I'd seen in the animals. He lived outdoors in constant movement, and his poise came from being perfectly adapted. We lost that when we moved indoors.

Was this Adam? And had we found him, or him us?

"Finally, you're awake!" It was Ellie, coming up from the grass with my pack filled with fruit. My genuine relief and joy at the sound of her voice was a jolt of strong medicine. She cared about me. Or at least cared that I cared about her. We were fellow conscripts, trapped in the past. I'd almost died, and she and our new companion had saved me.

"Thirsty," I managed.

"I'll bet you are. You threw up all your insides. We drank that pool dry, so Boy has been helping find water." She picked up a hollow gourd, which made a natural bottle. "Here, drink this."

Ambrosia. My throat was too constricted to glug, but I sipped and felt a glow inside me. *I once was lost but now am found,* the old hymn went.

Ellie knelt. "Do you remember anything?"

I shook my head.

"You were bitten by a snake and even though you killed it, you went into shock. I was certain you were dying. I was crying, completely freaked out, and then Boy came out of the bushes and scared the wits out of me. I suspect he was watching us for some time; maybe after that first bonfire we built. We scared him, too. Pale, weak, and covered with a new kind of fur – our clothing. But I gave him your hat as a gesture of peace and showed him the dead snake, since I didn't know what else to do. He ran like the wind and came back with plants to brew for you. Then he sliced where you'd been bitten, forcing puss out and sucking and spitting more, and got you to throw up. You were so sick I was certain you might die anyway, but after a while you stopped shivering and just slept. We've been waiting a night and a day."

I blearily looked past her. The sun was low to the west. "My batteries are dead, Ellie. I can hardly move."

"You need food. Fruit first, and then some meat." She stroked my cheek, which startled me, both because of the intimacy and because I realized how much stubble I'd produced. Bearded! Okay – fuzzed.

"We've been saved, Nick. Boy knows how to survive here, and I think he'll take us to his people."

"Boy?"

"I didn't know what else to call him. He made you a sleeping potion, too. He's learning our names. He's quick." She beckoned.

The caveman shuttled over to us with a peculiar crab–like walk and squatted on his haunches. He seemed light as a heron, springy as a kangaroo, as curious as a chipmunk. Ellie pointed to herself.

"Aie–ee," the caveman said. He touched her blond hair in wonder.

She pointed to me.

"Nig." There was an odd guttural clog to his voice as he said it.

I drank more water. "So is this Adam? We found him?"

She shook her head. "I tried the instrument and the result was close, but no jackpot. I think he's related, and that we're near. I think the couple we're looking for might be in his band."

"What's he doing here alone then? He's just a kid."

"I don't know. He's painted and scarred, so maybe this is a rite of passage. Hunting. Spirit quest. Vacation."

"Some vacation." I included us in that assessment.

"That's my old sourpuss!" She leaned forward and lightly kissed my forehead. Being the awesomely cool dude that I am, I jerked like an idiot in response, but she took no offense. *Very smooth, Brynner.* Every time I think I might be clambering out of the embarrassments of junior high, I act like I'm still in junior high, maturity receding like a rainbow. Is social clumsiness a life sentence?

"Which means you're not going to die," she went on. "Have some wild plums."

The sugar was an electric shock. I could feel the old batteries stir. I also began to cheer up. I'd survived a poisonous snakebite. We had a new ally. A girl had just sort of kissed me. Maybe we could find what we came for. And then? I pushed too much of the future out of my mind. My spirits continued to rise through the evening as I sipped, chewed, and stretched. My leg throbbed, my body was rubber, my headache lingered, but the Tin

Woodman had definitely been oiled. Not long after sunset, however, I was ready for more sleep.

"Ellie, you saved my life."

"Boy saved your life."

"Maybe we can really get through this thing."

"He knows a lot of tricks."

"I didn't think there was any other water here. That's a great trick to find some."

She smiled. "He collects dew, and finds little seeps. But his real cleverness is the water we shared with you."

"Why's that?"

"He squeezed it out of elephant dung."

CHAPTER 17

SWIMMING

BOY REGARDED MY baseball cap as fair payment for saving my life, so I cut a piece of my spare T–shirt that we'd used to filter water and tied it on my head like a pirate. Our new companion also seemed impatient to leave, which was good because we hoped he'd lead us back to his people. Using simple signs such as pointing to my bitten leg, we persuaded Boy to wait a day to let me recover my strength and accumulate more food. I limped. It hurt like hell, but I could travel.

Boy seemed proud to have adopted us, and was adept at spearing small game. He proudly displayed hyrax, rabbit, and porcupine, and we smiled and nodded to encourage him. We became student butchers, watching his far more skillful evisceration of our dinner. He could do more with sharp flint and quartz than I could with my stainless steel multi–tool. Cut, drain, slice open, scoop out, start the skinning like prying up the edge of tape, and pull. No plastic wrap, no bar code, no expiration date. Eat, or throw it away.

Oh, yes: And no seasoning. No salt. No sugar. No fork, no napkin, no dishes to wash. No manners, no tux, no flowers, and no dessert. No assurance where the next meal would come from, except we always seemed to find it. Boy gave no guarantees, and seemed to have no worries.

"I'm picking the last of the fruit that I can find," Ellie reported. "We need to move on."

I learned to use a sharp stone to scrape fat off the hides and dry them in the sun, flies buzzing. Ellie carefully plucked and bundled porcupine quills. "Maybe these could serve as needles," she said. "Or safety pins. I sewed a bag to take with us, but there's not much fishing line left. I'm trying to figure out how to use vines or strips of leather to make laces."

"Katniss, Rachel Carson, Betty Crocker," I teased. "The perfect woman."

She smiled. "Try to keep up, Nick."

Having Boy as a companion restored our spirits, and when I went from hobble to stiff walk, we slowly set off east across the savanna. I was sore, but survival more than made up for the ache in my calf. I was finally getting enough nourishment to equal the energy burned. I'd lost weight the first few days, but now I suspected I was adding muscle.

Certainly I benefitted from the resiliency of being a teen. Work hard, play hard, sleep hard, repeat. I was walking out the venom. I did miss my hat brim, but feared that if I tried to take it back our guide might desert us in resentment. Ellie and I shared the last of my sunblock and hoped our deepening tans would prove sufficient. The equatorial sun was fierce.

Boy roamed ahead to scout and dropped back to urge us on. My cap's red color helped us keep track of him. Sometimes he'd just silently amble beside, no doubt impatient at our turtle pace.

I'd learned to be careful in Africa, because vines in the grass could easily trip a hiker. The young caveman, however, positively ate ground as he strode, and we marveled at the efficiency with which he traveled. He was so scrawny that if you put him in modern clothes and stuck him on a playground, he'd be picked last for any team. But every ounce was dedicated to muscle and movement, and he had an endurance that left Ellie and me wheezing. His head only came up to my chest, but he could lope like an antelope when chasing something, and slither like a snake when sneaking. He climbed the occasional tree like a monkey to peer ahead, and then dropped down to rest as still as a lizard.

Boy carried a bundle of three spears tipped with stone, just as you'd expect from a caveman, and had a short club of wood tucked in his loincloth. He'd also slung gourds of water over his shoulder and ours. These vegetables could be hollowed out to make a thermos. I took the pack with our store of fruit, while Ellie shouldered her new bag stuffed with smoked meat. Flies orbited us like a planetary system.

I checked my compass and confirmed we were still heading due east. Boy was mildly curious at the instrument, but didn't understand its utility. However, his eyes feasted on my multi–tool the way I might admire a sports car or a mountain bike, so I kept that one close.

When Boy abruptly stopped to rest, he squatted like a garden gnome while insects buzzed. His eyes would half–close as he dozed, but I don't think he ever stopped watching either the landscape or us. Ellie and I would collapse in the grass, groaning about his endurance and our lack of it, and after a few minutes of recovery we'd begin our twenty–first century habit of chatting. We'd been raised that it was rude to be in company and not talk, and to abhor silence. Boy would listen, mute, his head slightly cocked. Then he'd suddenly rise and set off, us leaping to follow.

The caveman seemed to know exactly where he was going, but I could never decide if he was in a hurry to get there or on no schedule at all.

He was much less obsessed with time. From habit we tracked the arc of the sun and guessed what hour it might be. Boy seemed not to care, except to seek shade in the hottest part of the day. Then he'd march on until the shadows truly lengthened, when he'd unerringly find a camping place near water just before sunset. Our course meandered with no discernible pattern. There were no clear goals, rest stops, landmarks, or maps. Yet he navigated as confidently across the grasslands as a ship across the sea.

"I hope he knows what he's doing," I panted once.

"We're in no position to argue."

"He zigzags all over the place."

"But always ends up where he wants to be."

Boy was so quiet that I got the sense his band barely talked. Sometimes he'd swing his head to watch in consternation as we babbled on about temperature, bugs, hunger, water, the Xu, or our destination. He wondered why we needed to make so much noise.

He did mimic us in other ways. The caveman had no words for objects he'd never seen, such as shoes, pack, clothing, or dead flashlight, and no words for concepts that hadn't occurred, such as mile, degrees of heat, altitude, or the subtleties of weather. But I taught him hat, which he pronounced as "hT," with an emphasis on the T. When he said hat, it was almost like spitting. Boot became "oot." He fingered Ellie's hair, rubbed his hand on our arms to make sure our paleness didn't come off, and lifted and closed the flap of my pack like a toddler with a toy.

The thing he liked best was my dead cell phone, using its dark glass as a mirror. Boy would find an angle at which he could see himself, cackle with glee, dance a few steps, and then solemnly give the phone back. Maybe he believed it magic.

Our guide hiked barefoot, the soles of his feet hard as leather. A good part of his attention went to where he stepped. Despite his swift stride, he quite precisely avoided stones, thorns, animal droppings, ant colonies, and snakes. Three times he spotted serpents I might have stumbled on, swerving to give the reptile time to slither away in the other direction. "Vok," he called them, a name which apparently applied to all snake species. He also moved silently, never tripping and never snapping a stick.

Accordingly, we became more conscious of where we were stepping, of the easiest route through grass and brush, of our own noise, and of the position of nearby animals. We developed wilderness radar.

He still saw things we didn't. We followed him on a swerve around a grove of trees, and it wasn't until I looked back that I saw the silhouette of a lion standing up to yawn in the shade, looking at us with sleepy disinterest.

I stayed edgy about the predators. How many were giving us the eye as we passed, judging whether it was dinnertime?

Once Boy pointed to a ripple in the grass and we got a view of a male lion mounting a female from behind, much to my embarrassment and fascination. The girl lion nuzzled and licked to signal her readiness, and then they went at it with astonishing endurance.

"Aana," Boy said with a grin, showing the kind of local pride we'd have in pointing out a statue or cathedral. He made an obscene pantomime with his hands.

"I guess so," I replied.

Ellie and I glanced at each other but didn't say anything. We'd already gotten a barnyard education in a hurry watching other animals mate on the savanna. What nature seemed to be about was either making life, or taking it.

Boy lost interest in the spectacle before we did. He gave a grunt to get our attention and briskly led off again. It pleased him to point out other attractions, such as a flock of buzzards clustered on a corpse, or a massive black rhino as still as statue in the brush, its horn a poised missile. He led us wide clear of that one, too.

"I feel like I had gauze over my eyes and muffs over my ears," Ellie said when we rested briefly in the shade of a thorn bush. Boy was picking out fruits with green rinds, splitting them, and sharing them with us. The sugar was ambrosia. "He hears what I don't hear, and sees what I don't see. But then you start trying and Africa snaps into focus. How much have we been missing all our lives, Nick?"

"We just have other things to pay attention to. Less lion sex. More news, music, textbooks, and commercials. Texting. Spam. Google."

She laughed. "Progress."

"He eats ground so efficiently. He never stumbles and never pants. It's like he's floating. He walks easy."

"He walks like he belongs here, and we walk like we've forgotten how."

I changed Band–Aids on our blisters. Only two left.

Fortunately, our feet were toughening. "We're remembering the hard way."

And then I had a glimpse of paradise.

Foothills rose from the plain. At their base, shimmering like a mirage, was a broad, blue–tinted lake, the first we'd seen. Reeds grew on the shore. The water was the cleanest yet encountered. It wasn't alpine clear, but it wasn't Mississippi muddy, either. A cool breeze rippled the water. Hundreds of pink flamingos stepped as daintily as dancers, tiptoeing in the shallows as they poked their beaks into the water.

First we slaked our thirst. It was the best tasting we'd had, and I was becoming a connoisseur of H2O as if it were fine wine. This liquid seemed to balance all the dreck I'd swallowed. Elephant dung! I'd have been indignant if I hadn't been so grateful for the swallow. Apparently squeezing the poop was a last–resort source of the local Perrier.

Now Boy stood, clapped to enlist us, shucked his loincloth without embarrassment, and waded into the water to bathe and swim. I glanced at Ellie. She exaggerated a wide–eyed look of surprise at the nudity and shrugged. At thigh depth our companion plunged, the water exploding silver around his dark body. He disappeared briefly before surfacing farther out. Cavemen, apparently, knew how to swim.

"Oh my gosh I'm filthy," Ellie said. "I'm going in too. Turn your back, Nick."

"What about *his* back?"

"He's a caveman. That's different."

"You didn't turn your back when *he* decided to strip."

"I'm a girl, you're a boy."

I dubiously turned as she pulled off her clothes, and heard cries of delight as Ellie waded. Then a splash as she dove. "Your turn!"

She'd left all her clothes on shore but was submerged to her neck. How coy. And what the hell, don't we guys fantasize about this kind of thing? The popular kids in high school went skinny dipping all the time, or so they claimed, guys boasting of this and that. I hadn't had the invite.

So I turned, kicked off my own dusty clothing, and rather awkwardly backed in, coy myself. The water temperature seemed perfect, not too cool and not too warm, and once it was up to my waist I fell backward and let it close over my head. I tingled all over, the water stinging my snakebite scars and thorny scratches. The lake sloshed into dusty ears and nose. Heaven!

Then I surfaced with a shout. "Hooah!" This was the best I'd felt since setting out for Goat Island. I was still likely to die in prehistoric Africa, but at least we'd earned a recess. The water buoyed my spirits and washed away worry. Boy swam over, grinning at my delight, and then Ellie came too.

"It feels wonderful!" she cried. "I never want to get out!"

It felt like Eden, to tell you the truth. All of us

buck naked, splashing in water as perfectly temperate as a swimming pool, and not a test or deadline or alarm clock on the horizon. We were primly submerged, all right, but we could see enough of each other that inhibitions were increasingly obsolete. Ellie and I had slept together, cried together, eaten together, sweated together, been sick together, and now swam together. I was stunned not just at the peril of our situation, but its easy, natural, intimacy. I'd never had this kind of partnership with a girl.

At the same time, I wasn't bold enough to try to take advantage, suave enough to pretend this was normal, or experienced enough to do what half of America's teens claimed they had done. So I struck out swimming, and then paddled back. Ellie and I splashed each other, whooping and shrieking, without daring to touch. She was cautious, too.

"Nick, I need you to bring us our clothes. I'm going to rinse them out."

"I'm your servant now?"

"I'm too shy to get out of the water."

I didn't tell her I'd already seen quite a bit, thank you very much, and was working furiously to keep my mind from wandering too far in embarrassing directions. I just nodded with tight lips, as if this was the grimmest mission I'd ever been assigned, waded ashore, scooped up the clothes on the beach, and ran back into the water.

Ellie, politely and primly, had turned to face the beckoning foothills.

We moved apart to wash and wring our things, and put on underwear before coming out again. How Victorian. And yet to presume too much would spoil too much. Risk too much. Strain too much.

Boy, meanwhile, had gaped at both of us to satisfy his curiosity about our pasty bodies and that peculiar second skin, our clothing. He blithely came out stark naked and didn't immediately bother with his loincloth, so I don't think shame was much of a human concept yet. However, he had satisfied a question in his mind.

He pointed. "Aie–ee." At her body.

And then mine. "Ng."

He wasn't reciting our names, but rather what we were. Girl. Boy.

Did cavemen even have names? Maybe there were so few they didn't bother. So he thought we'd given him names for female and male.

Whatever.

Our guide led us away from the water for the evening. A lake would draw drinking animals, and drinking animals would draw predators. Lingering was an invitation to be eaten.

This time an isolated savanna tree was the anchor for our evening camp. Boy shared out the last of our meat and fruit with no concern about where breakfast was coming from.

I wondered if the lake had fish. I hadn't seen any jumping.

Since I had just a few matches left, I told Ellie we should hoard them for an emergency. I hoped Boy would kindle a fire on his own, but he made no effort to do so. He threw himself down and quickly went to sleep in the grass. We soon exhaustedly followed. My dreams were turbulent, which was the norm in Africa. Too much anxiety.

Once, however, I felt a stir and realized Boy had risen in the night and was peering out into the savanna, spear in hand. He was listening to the roars and grunts, his nose sniffing, gauging their direction and intentions in silver moonlight. After a while he sank down again, apparently satisfied with our safety, and quickly fell asleep once more.

It only took me two hours to relax enough to copy him.

CHAPTER 18

HUNTING

THE NEXT MORNING we rose with the sun and started climbing into the first low hills of the mountains. Boy moved more methodically than the day before, watching and listening. He had a new agenda. It was odd that our leader was a child, but then he was the one who knew what the heck we were doing. I was glad to not be the navigator. *Responsibility requires faith,* the Xu had posted. To which I would amend, responsibility sucks.

So as he crept, we crept. As he stalked, we stalked. We were the hunters this morning, not the huntees. Boy stiffened like a bird dog when we finally heard an odd whistle, and crouched. We copied, looking for what made the sound. He gestured with his head. In a shallow draw ahead was brown movement. Morning sun had broken clear of the misty heights and light was rolling down the ridge like a rising curtain. The illumination lit a tiny deer, no taller than a medium–sized dog.

Its horns were little points, and it moved by alternately mincing with ballerina grace and springing like a rubber ball. The critter also whistled.

Animals can surprise.

Boy took from his loincloth a piece of carefully carved wood the size of a popsicle stick, and blew. I jerked at the accuracy of the mimicry. The little antelope poked its head up at the whistle. So did a couple more I hadn't seen, stirring in grass the same color as their fur.

Boy turned to look sternly at us, a pint–sized sergeant in charge of his squad. He pointed to himself, and then to a point where the draw widened into a grassy swale. The mouth of this gully was half–dammed by boulders that eons ago had rolled down from the heights above, the rocks giving him a place to hide and wait. He pointed at Ellie and swung his arm, indicating the high point of the draw above the tiny antelope. With his other arm he pointed at me and swung it in an arc the other way. He indicated a fold in the savanna I could use as cover while circling. Ellie up, me sideways, Boy below. He put his hands together twice without making a sound, but the urgency was unmistakable. *Chop chop, go fast.* Breakfast was grazing.

I was excited. This wasn't scavenging lion kills or stabbing over–sized hamsters. It was a real hunt for a swift and wary antelope, even if the deer was the miniature poodle of its kind. Ellie nodded. We split up and she bent as she climbed, showing the athletic vigor with which she'd led me back to Fort Whitman. In minutes she was high above the antelope, creeping over to the top of the draw to drive the game down toward Boy.

I went the other way, dropping downslope to circle. Once I was certain the animal couldn't see me, I ran. I did my best to make no sound, and even had the bush craft to notice that the breeze carried my scent downhill, away from the animal above. My brain, freed of YouTube and instant messaging, was noticing things.

Boy was creeping to the boulders, spear ready.

Ellie slowly worked downhill, pushing the antelope without spooking it. The animal looked up in consternation and angled to get out of the draw. I rose to push it back toward the boulders, where Boy crouched in wait. The animal hopped that way and hesitated, probably thinking the rocks might hide it. Warily, it peeked back at us.

Boy's spear was a swift dart, plunging into the antelope's shoulder. The poor animal jerked and sprawled, kicking as it tried to get up to run. The caveman sprinted to seize the shaft of his weapon. I came charging too, my breath hot. As the quarry frantically pivoted under Boy's spear, still very much alive, I jammed my point into its chest. The antelope whistled and squealed, and I saw several of its fellows erupt from the grass and scatter before a descending Ellie, like a flushed covey of quail. Then Boy and I leaned to press our weapons and the antelope died, blood spurting.

I didn't feel guilty. I felt triumphant.

Boy picked up a sharp shard of quartz. Every yard

of ground was a potential hardware store to him. He worked with his usual astonishing efficiency, slicing the antelope's throat to bleed it, then gutting and skinning. The carcass was pink with a marbling of outer fat. Boy reached into the chest cavity and hoisted up the heart as an offering. When we both recoiled, he shrugged, bit, and swallowed. He popped out the antelope's round eyeballs and ate them like candy. Then came another organ that I guessed was the liver, or maybe the kidney. Blood surrounded the caveman's mouth like a clown's smile. Happy with these appetizers, he bent and hacked off steaks of raw meat and gave one to each of us. Clearly we weren't going to take time for a fire.

"Sushi for breakfast," I said.

"Steak tartare," Ellie replied.

We got it down because hunger will do that. I'd have preferred an ostrich egg omelet with a rasher of warthog bacon, but we'd neglected to bring a kitchen. So we chewed and chewed, the meat still warm from the animal's heat.

"That was intense," she said, pulling a tendril of fat from her teeth.

"Exciting. Basic. Savage."

"Are we becoming savages, Nick?"

"No. But surviving shows where savage intensity comes from. Where animals are coming from. Dog eat dog."

"Maybe where civilization's aggressiveness comes from."

"You hear that, Xu?" I looked at the sky, working out a piece of gristle. "Boy doesn't seem to worry a lot about where the next meal is coming from."

"It's whatever walks by. And something always walks by."

"I bet they go hungry sometimes."

"And I bet we'll find that out, too, sooner or later."

Boy cut more steaks that we wrapped in grass, working until we heard low growling. A pack of hyenas had paused twenty yards from the slaughter site and were eyeing our modest kill and us. I knew what they were thinking: "Our turn." They looked like drug cartel hit men, all jaws and shoulders. Boy stood, stuffed the meat he'd butchered into my pack, and left the ribs and innards for the hyenas. We quickly climbed away, spears ready if attacked.

The hyenas fell on the carcass, snarling and snapping at each other.

We were already filthy again, our bath of the day before now old news. Clothes made it worse. We sweated more than our companion, and the fabric trapped dirt. But we weren't ready to go au naturel. We'd grime like a proper lady and gentleman, until either our fabrics or our modesty gave out.

So we lived from moment to moment. By the end of the day we were once more out of water and no lake or spring offered itself. Boy led us down into a dry riverbed in the hills, its dusty sand cobbled with animal prints. There were huge disks left by lumbering

elephants, sharp hoofmarks from wildebeest and antelope, pans of dust where zebra had rolled, and cat and
hyena prints. Every creature seemed to use this silt bottom as a highway. I kept nervous watch behind.

Our guide stopped at a spot where the riverbed
made an outward bend, knelt at its lowest spot, and
began digging with a stick. Even I could smell the damp-
ness as he burrowed down one foot, then two. The river
wasn't gone; it had simply sunk into the soil. Finally the
hole began to fill with water, and a half hour's patience
allowed the worst of the silt to settle so we could dip
from our tiny well.

I fished out my water bottle. If the caveman was
impressed by plastic, he gave no sign. I suppose everything about us was strange to Boy, and plastic held no
more wonder to him than nylon, cotton, denim, cell
phone glass, or billed cap.

We slowly drank our fill, capped bottle and gourds,
and climbed out of the wadi and through some trees
to a cluster of boulders where we sheltered under an
overhang. This time Boy impatiently motioned to me
to light a fire, since he'd seen Ellie do so when I was
sick. He watched with fascination as the match flared
into flame. I worried that he thought such magic was
inexhaustible.

As the daylight died and our fire burned, we saw
the gantry necks of giraffes pivoting in the trees. A con-
voy of elephants passed by below, the young ones like
docking spacecraft beneath the blimp of their mothers,

the trunks of the tender animals as delicate as stroking fingers. Monkeys swung through the branches, yelling abuse, and birds were silhouetted against blue dusk as they flapped down toward their roosts. There was a sweet smell of dust, wood, and manure in the world, of a planet impossibly old before people ever showed up to explore it. And thinking of the world, I wondered if our dusty guide could give some idea of where we were and where we were going.

So I made a map.

I sketched the empty riverbed in the sand. A couple feet away I piled some pebbles to represent the boulders we'd come from. I inserted three sticks to represent us in a new stack of rocks, and then swept clean the area beyond and offered Boy a stick to draw on it.

He looked at me blankly.

"I think maps are too abstract," Ellie said. "They haven't been invented yet."

"How does he know where he is?"

"Maybe this is his home territory. Or maybe he doesn't care where we are."

"How can he not care?"

"We have homes and farms and factories and roads. We have places to go. These people follow the sky. They wander with the game and the weather. When it rains they get wet. There is no this way and that way. Everyplace is here. Every time is now."

"But how do they know if they're getting anywhere?"

"There's nowhere to get to because they're already there. There's no destination, only the journey. Maybe this overhang is as much of a home as Boy has ever known."

"That's just weird."

"Is it, Nick?" She fingered her hair to retie her ponytail. "I've been thinking. I know animals have territories, but they don't need to map them. They can see them. Sense them. Smell them. They do whatever they need to survive and make a den, but no more. Maybe we're the ones who are weird, dividing everything up, digging mines, plowing fields, and pouring foundations. Maybe that was our wrong turn, and the Xu think the way to properly live is to live like animals."

"The Xu don't live that way. They have spaceships and time wormholes."

"But they shepherd the creatures who *do* live that way. Maybe that's what they are, shepherds of the universe."

"To kill us, the wolves of progress. Who might discover what they have."

"Kill Adam and Eve to get a *new* Adam and Eve, in an unspoiled Eden. What if our ancestors cast themselves out of Paradise not by eating forbidden fruit but by building cities and waging wars? Is that what the Bible means? What if an alternate future was Boy drifting with the herds? The Indians following the buffalo? No borders. No countries. Nothing to own, because nothing ever gets made."

"So they'd live for nothing. Boy is really just an animal, you know. He's got a human brain but he's more like the wildlife than he is like us."

"So we're not animals? And if not, when did it change?"

"When we started thinking about where we are, who we are, where we're going, and what time it is. When we invented hot showers."

"And what a hassle that is!" She was enjoying our discussion.

"Hot showers?"

"All our worry to invent them, and pay for them. Think how many people go crazy or commit suicide or live with depression in our world. I think Boy lives like nature intended. You have to admit it's beautiful here."

"Beautiful and precarious. Stark. Uncomfortable. Scary. No Pentagon, but no hospital, either. No veterinary clinic. No tree huggers, no gardeners, no Old MacDonald, no Muppets."

"Just earth, unspoiled and untrammeled, spinning around the sun."

"Untrammeled? My, you do use big words, girl."

"It's how Congress defined wilderness."

"You *are* an egghead." We teased each other as friends. "Well, keeping the world a wilderness apparently means wiping out Adam and Eve and every person, building, and achievement we know. I'm not going there, thank you very much. I like iTunes and Dairy Queen blizzards and the Eiffel Tower."

"The Xu would wipe out a lot of glory," she said judiciously. "But a lot of sorrow, too."

"Ellie, come on. We're on Team Human. Aren't we?"

"Of course we are. But maybe we don't just save our ancestors, we instruct them. Maybe there's more than one reason we were put into this game. Maybe we don't just judge, we teach." She nodded at Boy. "And save the world in more ways than one."

CHAPTER 19

THE CAVEMEN

O N THE THIRD day of our journey with Boy,
everything changed. We came to the People, and
life got way more complicated.

In retrospect, weather was an omen. The land rose
in earnest after our camp by the wadi, and then began to
fold into real mountains. The herds of animals became
sparser as we climbed, and the air became cooler. The
sky's blue deepened, the freshness initially reminding
me of home.

Before long, however, the atmosphere turned ominously hazy. Boy kept looking back toward the savanna
we were climbing from. The cooling breeze died, and
humidity cloyed like a damp blanket. A flock of yellow
birds erupted from the grass ahead and winged away
to find better shelter in the trees. Insects went quiet.
The western sky darkened, and clouds mounded so
thick they seemed made of stone. They chased us like a

rushing mountain range. Lightning lit their edges with silver, stabbing the distant plain.

Boy said, "Giz," and began trotting uphill. We anxiously followed.

Thunder rumbled and the wind gusted, grass bowing before it.

A thought occurred. Was something alien disturbing the sky?

"Aka," Boy said. Water. But whether in this case it meant rain, storm, or flood, I didn't know. "Giz."

"Nick, I'm afraid of lightning."

"And I'm afraid he's leading us up to that ridge crest to get hit."

But our companion had actually spied a fold in the ground. There was a hollow beneath the lip of an eroded gully. "Aka, aka." We crawled in just before the storm hit, all of us squeezed and panting.

First the lightning came, terrifyingly close. A nearby tree was struck, sparks arcing like a broken transformer and dry branches flaming like a torch. Ozone filled the air, and our hair bristled with static electricity. The tree ignited a grass fire. Thunder boomed as if we were trapped in a metal drum. Then this violent, violet edge of the storm moved on, it got even darker, and rain sluiced down like an overturned bucket. The rain beat the grass flat, steamed away the grass and tree fire, and dribbled miserably into our niche.

I'd learned to seize opportunity. "I'm going to fill my bottle."

I caught some and shared a swallow with Ellie. Boy looked at us as if we were crazy. Didn't he want a sip? And then there was a new rumble, an ominous rush reminiscent of that chamber in the spaceship, and water began pouring down the little ravine in a torrent of foamy water. Flash flood!

"Aka!" Boy pulled us into the open again before we washed away. We were instantly drenched but we'd successfully sheltered until the lightning moved on.

Now we lurched vaguely uphill, soaked and disoriented. The wind slowly calmed, the lashing rain fell more vertical, and suddenly stopped as if someone had turned off a tap. Light grew as clouds began to rend and gleam.

Beside us, the gully chattered with water. Boy took my bottle, hopped down, and filled it in an instant.

"Well, that was interesting," I ventured.

"Refreshing," Ellie tried. Our hair was plastered, our jeans smeared with mud. We laughed at ourselves. Boy held up the bottle and grinned. "Aka."

We camped in a grove of trees, falling asleep while sitting up in order to keep off the chilly, wet ground. Ellie and I sandwiched Boy between us.

Long before I wanted it, birds and monkeys erupted in concert to herald the next dawn. Our companion had disappeared, but soon returned with breakfast fruit to go with gamey antelope. I wolfed it down, trying not to think of French toast and cinnamon rolls. How long could we keep this up?

A lifetime, in theory. That's assuming I had a lifetime to look forward to.

"Aka," Boy offered. He shared a gourd with water.

"We're going to need a dictionary," Ellie said.

"It will be a short one."

Now our companion's leadership seemed eager, and we guessed we were nearing his home. We climbed steadily for three hours and came to a gap in the ever–rising mountains. The ravine was like a gate in a rampart. A stream flowed from the draw and plunged down a series of rapids and falls. Peaks high above were hidden by clouds. A trampled game trail followed one bank into the gap.

The trail angled up to a grassy bench that gave a view ahead. We gasped.

"Eureka," Ellie assessed. "Archimedes said that."

"Bitchin'," I contributed. "The *Breaking Bad* guy said that."

Ahead was the enormous crater of an extinct volcano, its plain about ten miles wide. Ringing this platter was an enclosing wall of corrugated slopes and cliffs. Dense green jungle spilled down the far side of this vast stadium. Thin waterfalls chalked lines, their streams feeding small lakes in the amphitheater. These in turn fed the stream we were following through the entrance. Herds of animals dotted the arena floor, and a smudge of smoke drifted from a stand of trees near a lakeshore.

"Gann–tekla," Boy said. Eventually we translated this as 'the People.'

Meaning, Us.

This clan title wasn't a tribal name because so far as the cavemen were concerned, there were no other tribes worth listing. Enemies, maybe, but no allies. Just the People, camping in this extraordinarily sheltered animal park like their very own private lost world.

Boy pulled his wooden whistle from the belt of his loincloth and called like a bird. Answering birdcall came from concealing brush ahead. Our scout trotted forward and a muscular adult rose out of perfect concealment. He and Boy hugged, which seemed reassuring since I was betting that cannibals and slavers didn't embrace much. Then Boy proudly led the newcomer to his prize, Ellie and me.

Even as a grown man, this new fellow stood half a head shorter than I am. He too was dark, scarred, and shaggy, and carried a stone–tipped spear. He wore a bone necklace for decoration.

"Jewelry has been invented," Ellie murmured.

"Beauty before the wheel."

This new caveman looked at us ghost–colored beings with amazement and trepidation, more wary of us than we were of him. Boy pointed proudly and the two conversed in their odd, guttural tongue. Clearly we were trophies. Failing to learn how or whether these cavemen named themselves, we would eventually dub this guy Hercules, because he was the strongest of the clan. His muscles glistened in the sun.

"We found them, Nick."

"I think Boy is saying he found us."

The pair led us home.

Their village, if you could call it that, was little more than a dusty campground in a grove of trees next to a small lake. The hamlet had only the crudest of shelters, since the climate was benign and these nomads moved frequently in search of food. Blink and you'd miss it. The cavemen had no need of caves, and neither were there log cabins or African mud huts. Just beds of bundled grass and animal skins under lean–tos of hides and brush. The most ambitious structure was a fence of thorns to keep out predators. The People tended just one communal fire since the crater floor had limited trees and firewood. Hollow gourds, leather satchels, reed baskets, and wooden and bone implements made up the furniture and dishes.

The fire left a smoky pall over the encampment. When the People surged out to greet us, the air was filled with dust, the fluff of floating seed, and the pungent smell of unwashed humanity and nearby latrines. We braced against the grit. These humans looked stringy but tough.

Our hosts were neither friendly nor hostile but instead cautious and curious, as well as smoky, sinewy, and surprisingly fashion–conscious. People like to look good. The caveman hair was sometimes cropped short, sometimes bound in back by a leather string, and in the case of women, more elaborately combed and braided. Both sexes wore primitive jewelry. They had flowers in their hair, amulets on their neck, leather thongs on their wrists and ankles, and bits of bone through their ears. Some had stripes of ochre paint like Boy.

There was also the type of nudity you get on a National Geographic special. A few prehistorics had capes of antelope hide, but the majority wore only Boy's loincloth or a microscopic skirt. Women's breasts were bare, and you could tell a female's age in part by the size or sag. The younger children, who ran wild and seemed to have both everyone and no one as parents, were entirely naked. I stared and Ellie looked uncomfortable, but whatever prudishness remained was discarded by necessity. After a few hours, the bare skin didn't seem remarkable.

I realized that what really makes people naked is clothing. You have to have something on to make taking it off significant. They gawked at our cotton as much as we did at their skin.

We eventually counted thirty-eight souls. There were nine boys ranging from infant to my age, eight men older than me, ten women, and eleven girls.

"More females survive because the men die hunting," Ellie guessed. "Or the guys eat too much meat and not enough vegetables."

"Not enough to get fat," I observed. "Everyone here could write a diet book." They were as fit as the animals they hunted. The couch and chair had yet to be invented and if they rested at all it was often on their haunches, since the dirty ground had bugs, pointy rocks, and splinters.

The eldest prehistorics were graying but barely wrinkled, which made me guess senior citizens were in their late forties. Beyond that an individual couldn't keep up, and became lion meat.

Now the tribe pressed close, surrounding us to exclaim and poke. The concept of personal space hadn't been invented.

"Now what?" I said to Ellie. "If this bunch are really our ancestors, how the heck do we protect them from marauding space aliens?" The People didn't seem much more organized than a baboon troop. Several, their curiosity satisfied, had already wandered off.

"We have to check the genetics first. And then somehow get them to move and hide until the Xu give up. Win the game and defer the Judgment."

Boy was explaining us to the cave people who still crowded around, some summoning the courage to sniff warily and others drawing back as if we might carry disease. We were, of course, aliens ourselves: sunburned pink, dressed in colors they thought reserved for birds and butterflies, and with our feet swollen from an odd rind called boots. Ellie's eyes were blue as the sky, while mine were a less remarkable hazel. Her long blond hair drew exclamations, while my mop of brown did not.

"Aie–ee," Boy said. "Ng."

The most formidable–looking man bulled to the front. Like Hercules he was half a head shorter than me, but built like a barrel and burly with muscle. His suspicious, scowling expression was worthy of a drill sergeant, and he examined us like trouble. This must be their chief.

He considered all three of us as if Boy had brought back unwanted pets.

Then, reaching with the lightning speed of a gunfighter, he snatched Boy's hat.

The youth gave a cry of protest. The leader ignored him. Comically, this older man puzzled a moment about how to wear his new prize, and finally jammed it on his head sideways, the fabric inside out.

"Mine," I complained, pointing at the hat. I don't like bullies.

The chief couldn't understand the word, but my meaning was clear enough. He smirked in reply.

The others howled at the headgear, but whether it was mockery or appreciation I couldn't tell.

The aggressive man had a club tied to his waist, and several men held stone–tipped spears. We dared not antagonize them, and yet I sensed we were establishing the tribal pecking order here. This dude wanted his dominance acknowledged. He sniffed, fingered my grimy T–shirt, and pulled the fabric to test its strength.

Then his gaze turned to Ellie.

Boy said, "Aie–ee." A girl.

The chief grasped her T–shirt, pulling it away from her right breast.

Without even thinking I slapped his arm away. A

hum of surprise and alarm went through the crowd. This was a guy you didn't mess with, apparently. He glared and reached for Ellie again.

"Nick!"

I slapped his arm away once more.

Now he growled questions at Boy. Our scout answered, but whatever he said wasn't satisfactory. The hulking bruiser pulled his club loose.

What happened next was pure instinct, which means that if I'd thought things through I might have chickened. I swung and punched him, hard, in the face.

He didn't duck. He didn't go down. His head snapped back and he reeled. More important, he looked astonished. He began to raise his club so I waded in, hitting him several times with both fists. Pow–pow–pow! I was fighting for Ellie. The chief was so shocked that the club never came up. Neither did his arms in defense. Surely these people knew how to fight? But real boxing hadn't yet occurred, so it was if I was a master of martial arts. I'm no fighter, but I was punching out of fear and frustration. The fourth or fifth time I hit him, the big man finally sat down hard.

The crowd gasped.

My opponent looked at me in confusion. His nose was bleeding and an eye was swelling. He literally looked like he didn't know what hit him.

Boy dragged me backward, frantically shouting. Several spears leveled. I knew I'd been a hothead, but his touching Ellie had set me off. There's a bully in my high school named Seth Rutledge who swaggers down the halls in dark frustration. He's a complete screw–up, most likely to matriculate to prison, we joke. He's shoved me once or twice in hopes I'd be foolish enough to challenge him after school. Needless to say, the fact that I have the good sense to ignore him did nothing for my manly reputation, or my own self–esteem. I'd have that dumb tightening of the bowels that I hated, and I always vowed to make a better stand. But I never did.

So this caveman bully was simply in the wrong place at the wrong time, with a girl between us.

Now I might have killed us both.

The chief jumped up, angrily snarling questions at Boy. But the guy didn't charge. He regarded me with wary truculence, and just a touch of respect. Their language had a weird glottal click to it, a throaty catch to the words. That evening, Ellie and I would name our headman Click.

Boy answered quickly, pointing at Ellie, me, and back at Ellie. His explanation was clear even across fifty thousand years. She was my girl. Hands off.

My knuckles ached and one was bleeding, but I puffed with pride and anger. Ellie was looking fearfully at both of us, understandably alarmed at how all this would shake out. I was feeling cocky that I'd won the fight so far, and worried I might be spitted on a stake for my machismo.

My opponent glowered, clearly debating whether

he should give it another go. He wouldn't think twice, I knew, about bashing my brains in.

So a frantic Boy dragged my backpack off my shoulders and onto the ground and dug out my lifeless cell phone. He hurriedly gave it to Click, pointing to the black glass screen and Click's face.

The puzzled caveman held the phone up and his eyes widened in amazement. He could see, barely, his own mirror image in the glass.

The assembly gasped.

If the phone hadn't flooded and I could still take pictures, they might have made me Merlin.

No matter. Click looked at me narrowly, the way one looks at a dangerous rival, but then threw out his arm in dismissal. "Aie–ee." It was a grunt, giving Ellie up. Then he walked away to examine his new toy, half the tribe following in his wake.

My hat was still on his head.

CHAPTER 20

PREHISTORIC HIGH SCHOOL

THE PEOPLE ROSE with the sun and nearly went to bed with it, but otherwise were *way* more laid back than your typical twenty–first century stressed– out, uptight, American teen. They hunted and gathered but couldn't hoard, since there was no freezer to hoard to. Their attitude reminded me of the school cafeteria rule, "Take what you want but want what you take." The planet was the only grocery store, and everyone shopped every day. Once food was obtained, the workday was pretty much over. Sweet.

The People had the kind of gender differences you'd expect, with the men the primary hunters and the women sticking closer to camp to gather plants and watch the kids. Two females were visibly pregnant. In other words, sexism was alive and well in 50,000 BP, and when Ellie first set out with her own spear, a woman slapped it out of her hand and gave her a reed basket instead. Ellie complied, since we had to fit in.

There were no child labor laws. As soon as they were able, kids gathered food and firewood, practiced with spears, explored, dug, swam, hunted small animals, wove baskets, and helped dry hides. But nobody worked particularly hard because there was nothing to work for. There was a lot of play and a lot of resting. Frankly, it was kind of boring. No screen time. No taxes.

Call them hippies. Call them lilies of the field, neither toiling nor spinning. Call them lazy. Or call them smart. Certainly you could call them mostly good-humored. By knowing how to punch, I was a tough guy.

I guess you could also call them communists or socialists, except the whole idea of "isms" had never occurred to them. They didn't have any government. Click was a leader only when they needed one, which was rarely. They were comfortable in their own skin. We civilized folk always reinvent ourselves, or try for self-improvement. The People just were. I yam what I yam, said Popeye.

That didn't mean there wasn't quarreling and flirting. Cavemen didn't club their women and drag them by the hair, as they do in old cartoons, but they did court them. The girls not yet paired off might get a pretty flower, bloody rabbit, or shiny stone. The young women made their own interest plain with offerings of fruits or berries, shy glances, sinuous walks, or coy over-the-shoulder come ons. They'd shove or snub rivals, and ignore men they had no interest in with cutting indifference. That game wasn't all that different from a school dance.

Click kept the baseball cap he'd seized, but gave the cell phone mirror to the woman I judged the prettiest and sauciest of the tribe. This temptress guarded the artifact zealously and preened in its reflection whenever possible, to the annoyance of the other females. What a prehistoric heartbreaker! Ellie named her Foxy.

Foxy deserved her sense of self–importance. Ellie's genetic testing machine still worked, since it was recharged by the sun and impervious to dirt and water. The sampler didn't require a finger prick of blood, but it did give a sting when it scooped a few cells to sample genetic code. I had to serve as guinea pig to persuade the cave people to try it. I smiled bravely as it pinched, pretending it was fun. Ellie read my results.

"You're a long ways from Adam and Eve, Nick. Fifty thousand years, I'd estimate."

"I wish," I said, looking at the circle of dark aborigines. "I've bet my life that I'm actually quite close to the happy couple."

Boy persuaded Click by pointing to his own skin. The caveman seemed to decide the DNA machine might confer some kind of power or immunity. And once Click consented to being tested the others followed, and afterwards walked tall.

We checked the digital readout. The Xu had indeed put us down near our quarry. Click and Foxy registered as the ultimate ancestors, so we could guess how their romance was going to progress.

"Should we rename them Adam and Eve?" I asked Ellie.

"That's just too weird."

I looked at the pair in wonder. Great–great–great–great–grandparents… as many greats as one could count. They were tough as nails and innocent as children. Once they followed a bird that Ellie called a honey guide. It led them to a bee's nest in a hollow tree that Click raided with a stick for a honeycomb, ignoring the stings to share honey with his honey. The two reveled in the treat, the sweet dripping on their chins as they licked each other's fingers. Kill those two and everything changes? Save them and they produce civilization? It was hard to believe.

Yet they were the game. We had to judge them and, assuming they passed muster – and how could they not, given that they were us – protect them, and presumably soon. How far behind could the Xu assassination team be? Had that storm really heralded the alien approach? How could we possibly shelter Adam and Eve?

"Job one is to get acquainted," Ellie said. "We have to get them to trust us so we can get them to hide."

"Hide from what? Even if we learn their language, they can't begin to imagine what we'd tell them."

"We just have to persuade them to move. Somehow."

Geezer and Nana were our names for the tribe's

two elders, who may have reached the ripe old age of forty–five. As near as we could tell no one kept track of how old they were, since the entire concept of years and seasons was sketchy in equatorial Africa. Nonetheless, tribal members treated the two like oracles and psychiatrists, bringing food in return for advice or instruction. This was given with a combination of words and sign language. We could often get the gist of what was said.

Typical problem: My child is eating too much fruit when we pick, instead of carrying it back to share with the community.

Typical solution: Don't give them any meat or plants that others have gathered, to show selfishness doesn't work.

Take that, Dr. Phil.

By the standards of the People, I was an adult at sixteen. Even Boy had that status, thanks to his recent quest. The scars marked coming of age. You grew up quick or didn't grow up at all. Boy had also moved up the pecking order by discovering us. The dude didn't need to shave but girls his age were already giving him the eye. He strutted around like a rooster.

Hercules was the most obvious tribal athlete, the go–to guy in a hunt or a fight. He had the chest of a lifeguard and the elastic thighs of a basketball player. His slim, rather elegant mate we dubbed Lady, to whom he'd given a lion's–skin cape. That impressed the heck out of me. How do you kill a lion with a stone–tipped spear?

Mother Hubbard was a busybody organizer, Scout

given to wandering, and Woody tapped logs in rhythm like a woodpecker. Sleeping Beauty was the laziest.

The biggest caveman we named Bunyan, after the legendary logger. The darkest was Iron Man. The tribal tinkerer was Megatron.

Meg, as we inevitably came to call him, was skilled at hurling a spear with a mechanical throwing device that I learned later is called an atlatl. A two–foot stick with a leather pouch for the butt of a spear is used to throw with greater leverage and power. The resulting speed could bury a flint or obsidian weapon into the trunk of a tree fifty feet away. The man would practice at least an hour a day.

That inspired me to try inventing the bow and arrow. Okay, reinvention, but I did start fantasizing about becoming the Thomas Edison of fifty thousand BP. I wondered if that would break some unwritten rule of time travel, and decided I didn't care. It's not like I asked to be dumped here.

Ellie and I knew that our nicknames for the People sounded as if we were naming dogs or horses, but we couldn't quite tell what the clan's own names were, or even if they had them. Was it just a word describing what people did? Or maybe both, like "Smith" in English?

Nor could we pronounce their weird language. We struggled with the odd, guttural clicking. It was like trying to talk and gargle at the same time.

What language they had was punchy. Gestures,

head nods, and foot stamps added sense and emphasis. And so much silent communication went on that the People seemed telepathic. I'd watch Click sit brooding, his gaze to the dirt. Suddenly two or three men would show up next to him, spears ready, and they'd all abruptly leave on a hunt. Eerie.

Maybe mind reading was a prehistoric talent we've since lost because of our incessant chatter. Maybe animals communicate that way. Certainly Ellie and I occasionally spooked each other with anticipation of each other's thoughts, probably the result of our isolation and mutual dependence.

"You like being a part of this, don't you?" she asked me once.

I'd been thinking I felt more accepted here, by these dark-skinned primitives, than in the frenetic world I'd come from. "You read my mind. And you like living in a game park."

"I see balance that I don't feel in our world."

"Brutal balance. Everywhere we walk there are bones."

"Yes, but the result is harmony. Or maybe I'd call it rhythm."

Caveman culture wasn't utopia, it was high school. There was a clear hierarchy of cool kids the others instinctively followed, like Click, Foxy, Hercules, and Lady. There were nimble nerds, like Megatron, Woody, and a homely stumblebum of a sweet girl we called Clumsy. There were teachers: Geezer, Nana and an awkward medicine man who walked with a limp and oddly splayed arms, dubbed Crow. There was plenty of jealousy, with Click and Hercules sometimes snapping at each other around Foxy, a rivalry she loved. There was resentment, with Lady sulking when Hercules gave Foxy the eye. There was preening pride, when Bunyan brought in a fresh kill and struck a red carpet pose. And there was resented sloth, when Sleeping Beauty's water went unfetched or her firewood unstacked.

There were mysterious rules, as when Crow angrily shooed us away from one of the trails leading out of camp. There was something weird out there and we'd not yet earned the trust to see it.

There were grudges, anger, affection, and charity. Gift giving was a way to gain status. The more you gave, the more popular you were.

There were no laws beside common sense. I wondered if murder had even been invented yet.

This was the simple society the Xu thought deserving of annihilation.

It was high school all right, which made me wonder if adult life ever escapes high school conventions, or alternately whether high school has been fiendishly designed to train teens for the cold cruel world. Does misery serve a purpose?

We were like a tree of monkeys or a troop of baboons, sharing a banana one moment, pelting someone with its skin the next, and slipping on the leftovers a third time. Ellie and I were inducted into the pack almost instantly because clan numbers were small and new recruits boosted survival. Welcome aboard! But it was like being adopted into a commune with a long, complex history we couldn't fully understand. They saw a million things in nature that we missed. Yet they had no science, no geography, no mathematics, and no history. They couldn't count, tell time, or plan. Everything was now. Everyplace was here.

How were we going to persuade Adam and Eve?

We pitched in to earn our keep. Ellie gathered edible plants, and discovered it was possible to find melons, tiny sour apples, and oranges, or something close to them. She experimented sewing hides, making porcupine quills into very unsafe safety pins, and weaving grass baskets. The cavewomen were already capable of crude bags and skirts, but Ellie won their appreciation by using my multi–tool to shape skins into patterns. She experimented with a cap, a mitten, and a crude moccasin. The other women gave us two hide blankets as a reward.

I hunted, or at least helped. My job was as a driver, since my height and youth made me a swift runner while my spear throwing needed practice. I'd circle around, creep up, and then push game to be intercepted by the others.

My brain was stuffed with possible inventions to improve my status, from the button to the wheel. But the People had no clothes requiring buttons, and no roads for wheels. They had little to carry, and nowhere they were inclined to go, at least until food became scarce. Every bright idea I brought from the future seemed to need a dozen other bright ideas to make it practical.

I did try the bow and arrow, and found it as complicated to make as a machine gun. First, I had no good bowstring, and my experiments with braiding some from grass or vines were unimpressive. I tried a strip of leather but it stretched too easily and broke too quickly, like a bad shoestring.

My bow was equally poor. Any wood I could find lacked the spring to provide much tension. My arrows weren't straight, and I had no idea how to fasten feather fletching to the shaft.

It was a science project in which everything goes wrong. When I finally demonstrated my brilliant invention to an assembly of men, the arrows flew only a few yards, veered unpredictably, and plopped harmlessly onto the ground. While I tried to fix broken bowstrings and hunt for wayward arrows, the cavemen became bored and wandered off.

So much for being the Edison of Africa.

We couldn't even get by on looks. I worried the cavemen would be all over Ellie as an exotic blond, and that I'd get a spear in the chest for trying to protect her. I also secretly anticipated that maybe I'd finally fulfill a fantasy as the only handsome guy in town, and have to beat off the native girls with a stick.

Negative. We palefaces looked about as alluring as

the belly of a dead fish. I realized that Click's initial paw-
ing of Ellie was cautious curiosity, not lust, and that the
women seemed to regard me as freakishly undercooked,
oddly restless, and weirdly ambitious in a world where
ambition hadn't been invented yet. Dashing time travel-
ers? Meh.

Yet they shared food without question and taught
their survival strategies for food, water, and shelter. The
lessons were as basic as deciding which side of a ridge to
follow in order to stay warm or cool, or to be conscious
of being upwind or downwind of animals. Often we felt
dumb. I tagged along on a hunt with Hercules once and
a rainstorm blew in. We sheltered in a grove of large acacia, but he pulled me away from the first trunk I picked
for protection, pointing out that it was occupied by a
line of ants. He suggested another tree, watched me
crouch, and then screwed up his face in mystification. As
thunder rolled and heavy raindrops began to patter, he
shifted my position until the trunk and branches actually helped intercept the deluge. To the People, I was the
mystifying maker of oddball artifacts who lacked sense
to get out of the rain.

CHAPTER 21

ELLIE'S SONG

ELLIE HAD HER own adventures, and came back
with shocking news.

We were as curious about Crow's forbidden path as I'd
been curious about forbidden Goat Island. The People
seemed so casual about everything else, so why would
Crow care if we followed one particular trail?

Crow wasn't crazy, but he was the tribe's philosopher
and brainiac, a man intense about the world in ways the
others were not. Click might be the biological father of
our future species, but Crow had the mental instincts
of modern man. He examined my bitten leg and gave
me leaves to chew, which made me vomit again. Was he
trying to restore me or poison me? I finally realized he
wanted me not to swallow the leaves, but to masticate
them into a paste to put on the wound.

The tribesman also showed me a red flower, a
poppy, that he harvested after it had dried into a pod.
He scraped the pod's insides for a powder that helped

me sleep when the leg throbbed: weak opium, I finally figured out. Boy must have used the same plant. That scared me, but I ground some any way for emergency use. I thought of it as a last–resort sleeping pill to get me through pain I couldn't ignore.

Crow walked with a limp and was definitely a tribal loner, with no mate. So Ellie piled on the charm. At first he ignored her but she was persistent, flattering him by asking about medicinal plants using sign language and the few words we'd picked up. She also kept pointing to the mystery trail. A water buffalo skull had been placed on a rock to serve as signpost and warning, and Ellie's curiosity clearly agitated the odd man. He groaned, he trembled, and he turned his face away, but she kept on in a soothing tone. And her attention, to a man starved for it, slowly won him over.

One morning Crow permitted her to follow him. The pair disappeared in high grass, dropped toward a gully, and was gone for at least two hours. I was beginning to worry when she reappeared, unharmed but perplexed.

"So what's the big secret?" I asked her.

"The People have religion, or at least the beginning of it," she said.

"Crow is a priest?" He'd come back a few minutes after she had and was sitting proud, as if he'd shared a great treasure. He knew we were talking about him, too, and he enjoyed it.

"I don't think they're organized enough to have

titles like that," Ellie said. "I'm guessing Crow is simply mystical, and is their one guy who wonders what it all means. He found a talisman for them. Instant prophet."

"Talisman?"

She was clearly troubled. "Brace yourself, Nick. The trail leads to a dry wadi. There's this sheltered spot where floods have eroded dirt away and left some big black volcanic boulders. The rocks make an open–air room. The roof is an old tree. Sunlight comes through all dappled and filtered, like a stained glass window. Very peaceful, but powerful too. Spooky. The place felt sacred, like a focal point. Like coal squeezed into a diamond."

"And they worship some kind of trinket god?"

She shook her head. "I don't think they're far enough along for gods or creation stories or bibles. Spirits, maybe. They respect the world. They appreciate good fortune. So Crow puts flowers, skulls and red paint around this thing he found, and it was so unexpected I'm still trying to process."

"What's unexpected?"

"A belt buckle."

She had me confused. "What belt buckle?"

"The talisman he reveres. It's an old brass buckle from maybe a hundred years before our time. Modern time, I mean. It has two crossed rifles engraved on it."

I was chilled. "You mean like an Army buckle? The square kind that holds a webbed belt?"

"Yes."

"Ellie, it's that guy Gabe told us about. The soldier."

"Yes. The one who stumbled into the wormhole when the fort was built."

"Private Ruben Dunbar. Disappeared, 1921. I read about him in old newspapers. The Sheriff said people went to Fort Whitman and didn't come back."

"And the army realized it had poked into the wrong place and left."

My mind whirled. "Gabe said Dunbar died here. Did the Xu kill him?"

"I don't think so. Maybe lions ate him and all that was left was the buckle. It's shiny. Crow found it."

"Or maybe these cavemen killed him."

"Crow doesn't act like that. The People haven't been hostile."

"True." I tried to imagine Dunbar's plight. "And who knows what time he landed here? Last week? A hundred years ago? Maybe he's become a tribal legend and the buckle is all they have left. I've heard of South Pacific tribes getting excited about stuff leftover from World War II, and waiting for flying visitors to return like gods."

"If Crow is paying attention to this belt buckle," Ellie said, "it means your soldier has already changed history in some slight way. Which means we could too."

"Maybe the Xu killed him because he changed too much."

"Or not enough." Then she was quiet. Dunbar had never gotten back home. Was that our fate, too?

"How crazy," I finally said. "Their saint is a belt buckle. Talk about old–time religion."

Ellie glanced at Crow, who had gotten bored with our conversation and was fixated on a bright blue lizard darting haltingly across a rock. "It was actually kind of touching," she said. "But sad, too. The birth of superstition. Ignorance. Fear."

I raised my eyebrows in mock shock. "You're not religious?"

"Science nerd, remember?"

"Fear of what? The People don't seem to be afraid of much to me. Or need to be afraid – at least until the Xu show up."

She screwed up her face and looked away. "I'm bugged by what Crow is doing with that talisman. His shrine is harmless now, but after thousands of years of development and worship? There will be gods, sin, and sacrifice. What if men invented religion to make other men afraid?"

"Afraid of what?"

"Existence. What if men started fearing the natural world once they started moving away from it? Suddenly, nature needs to be appeased. All that's natural becomes unnatural, so suddenly they need the supernatural."

"Whoa, what? Ellie, it's just a water buffalo skull and a belt buckle."

She was serious. "Isn't this what we've come to pass judgment on? Human progress, or human wrong turns? I'm trying to see how we got from this world – this quiet, sustainable, prehistoric world – to our noisy and polluted one."

"It's only harmonious until a volcano or a crocodile comes along. Our world is way more comfortable. Lounge chairs. Penicillin."

"Our world is way more anxious. The more people advance, the more natural disasters can knock down their advances. What cavemen can simply walk away from becomes a threat. So civilized people begin to pray. Spirits. Demons. Human sacrifice. Aztec pyramids. Why can't we just *be*, like animals?"

"We are animals, sort of, and we do just be." I grinned at my own sentence. "Most of us do–be, anyway. But we're also more than animals, girl. And what's wrong with faith? My Mom needs faith. Maybe Crow is just saying thanks to this wonderful nature of yours. Saying grace. Don't you believe in anything?" I wasn't religious either, but her hostility took me aback.

She looked stubborn. "I know this sounds extreme, but we've got to ask how we got from this Garden of Eden to thousands of nuclear weapons."

"Wow. Whoa. Not from poor weird Crow. And that savanna was no garden, no way. We got to nukes from your science, it seems to me."

"Belief gets in the way of rationality, Nick. It starts promising another world so we feel permission to destroy this one."

"Nobody wants to destroy our planet. Folks are just trying to get by."

"Not the greedy ones. And the more we get comfortable, the more we consume. The more we destroy, the more we fear. And when I saw the belt buckle, I thought, 'This is how it starts.'"

I laughed. "Poor Private Dunbar!" Ellie certainly could paint a dire picture when she wanted to. She had a lively mind, and was the most provocative girl I'd ever met. Good debater. Good lawyer. Yep, Eleanor Terrell will go far, once she figures out which way to go.

"We have to save these people from the Xu, Nick. But then we have to teach them not to make all the mistakes we've made through history. Let's sustain *this* heaven instead of counting on the next one."

I smiled at her earnestness. "And how do we do that?"

"I don't know. I just feel this terrible responsibility of trying to fix things, to save things, to reform." She looked at me, sad, beautiful, seeking my help. My stomach did flip flops. Guys want to fix things. She wanted them fixed. "We've got an awesome duty, Nick. Save them. Save the world. Save *us*."

"You *are* serious, girl."

She nodded, sad, pensive, and apologetic. "I'm a drudge, I know. You're not the first boy to say so."

But I hadn't said so. And I knew that for me, Eleanor Terrell was anything but a drudge. I didn't agree, but I knew what she was driving at. Somehow we went from coexisting with nature to exploiting it, and of course that's what brought the Xu calling. That, and the heat signature of Hiroshima. Of course they were the ones with the spaceships, and who knew what their environmental record was? But meanwhile, was Crow pious? Batty? Inspired? Misguided?

"This is too heavy for you and me," I finally said. "We're struggling to survive in a game we never asked for, and trying to shelter Click and Foxy from the bad guys. I'm not ready to judge science or religion. Frankly, I wouldn't mind a priest right now. Or a cop. Or an ice cream man."

"We just have to be very careful with what we leave here," she said. "Your cell phone, for example. And I don't want them worshipping your multi–tool."

"I think my red baseball cap is more likely."

"Yes." She was still serious. "We have to get that back."

So she was a very pretty worrier. There are worse things. Ellie had been trapped on that spaceship longer than I had, had talked with Gabe at length, and had been thinking about the dilemma we'd been hurled into much longer than me. So I needed to listen. We had to do the right thing – just as soon as we could figure out what the right thing was.

I did know not to fret over a belt buckle.

That evening I saw another side of Eleanor Terrell, and out of it came one of those moments that mark your life, making you jump from one chapter to the next. Sometimes teenagers wait for life to start happening to them. And sometimes it happens, big time.

Every night after the sun went down, some of
the People would finish eating whatever it was they'd
caught, killed, or plucked, and sit around the fire for a
spell, the sparks dancing upward as if they planned to
join the stars. No other animal made fire, I reminded
myself. Ellie was missing something. No wonder people
needed myths to explain who they were, and how they
came to be. Who else had fire? Who else *thought* like
Homo sapiens? Worried like Homo sapiens? It was a
blessing and a curse.

Anyway, I liked these evenings. Sometimes Geezer
and Nana would tell a story with a smattering of words
and a lot of gestures, an exercise similar to charades.
We didn't always follow the narrative, but we followed
the spirit of storytelling. Sometimes Click would mut-
ter and grunt what I supposed were marching orders for
the next day's hunt. Or Hercules would boast, or Foxy
and Flower would give a shimmying little dance while
Woody hammered out a rhythm on his logs. The beat.
The body. The beat. The body. Music made us different,
too, I told myself. Or did it? Were we just copying birds?

Then Ellie shocked everyone by breaking into song.

The People had never heard a melody before. They
sat back: alarmed, enchanted, perplexed, stunned. Oh,
they knew how to thump. A little chanting, maybe. A
puffed chest or a hip wiggle. But not words to classic
tunes. I don't know if it sounded like discordant yam-
mering or the most exquisite thing ever heard. I do
know they stared at her, dumbstruck.

Just like I did. Ellie had a lovely voice.

She sang *Silent Night.* Odd choice from a pretty atheist, if that's what she was, but it doesn't get more classic than that. Her voice was strong and clear, and the quiet lyrics and simple notes drifted upward with the sparks. I shivered. *All is calm, all is bright.* For just a moment, our world joined theirs.

"Come on Nick, join in!"

"I don't know that one." I'm bashful about singing, for good reason.

"You don't know *Silent Night?* Talk about no old–time religion!"

"I only sang in camp."

"Well, camp ones, then." So she coaxed until together we sang *Home on the Range,* and *Coming Round the Mountain,* and *I've Got Sixpence,* and *The Ants Go Marching.* It was ridiculous, but fun, too. Our audience looked at us open–mouthed. Nothing we'd done was more amazing than this.

"Maybe they'd like Pink," I said. "Or Macklemore."

"No, this is an oldies but goodies crowd." She got me to help sing *My Favorite Things* from *Sound of Music,* a movie my Mom and Grandma still loved. It has a nice patter to it. Our audience was utterly silent, looking at us as if we might vanish in a puff of smoke. I was kinda thrilled, to tell you the truth. I'm no performer, but finally had an enraptured audience. It was like singing to little kids. Guaranteed appreciation! *Raindrops on roses and whiskers on kittens.*

Ellie smiled at my willingness to join in, and when I pleaded that I was sung out she performed a quite credible version by herself of *Over the Rainbow,* the Oz notion of 'we're not in Kansas anymore' making the choice painfully appropriate. The sentiment drifted out across the crater. Birds fly over the rainbow. Why can't I?

Was she singing it *to* me?

Don't get ahead of yourself, Brynner. You always make a fool, remember?

But oh man, did I want to kiss her then, a full–bore smacker right in front of everybody. She was smart, she was contentious, she was lovely, she was brave, she was curious, and she could sing like a pop star, it seemed to smitten old me. Timidity kept me where I was, of course, timidity and dread. *Boy loser.*

Now our caveman audience started making an odd buzz, like the sound of a hive. I think they were trying to sing.

Score one for Oz.

And I realized, with that utter certainty that eventually sweeps over everyone who ever feels it, that I was falling in love with this strange, pretty, sweet, contradictory girl beside me. Hopelessly. Helplessly.

Is anything more dangerous, more painful, and more exquisite? I knew she didn't share my feelings – not yet. But for the first time I didn't care that we were marooned in prehistoric Africa. I had Ellie. We were partners, dependent on each other. My heart swelled with excited hope.

She smiled at me, so radiant in the firelight that I almost fell over. Man, did I love her! Never felt anything like it before. The sparks swirled, the stars swirled, and I was floating. I was as high as a rocket, as weightless as an astronaut.

She knew it, and flipped her hair, rocked her body, and wordlessly promised me companionship and completion. I grinned like a fool.

But I also felt very frightened.

Because even as I fell for her, head over heels gob–smacked smitten, I had a vast, tragic foreboding of doom.

CHAPTER 22

FIRE

THE NEXT MORNING I saw a boot print.

I'd left before dawn to go hunting with Boy, the caveman I felt closest to. Not only had he saved my life, he also seemed the most appreciative of my strange clothing, weird artifacts, and odd experiments. I suspect his tolerance came from youth. He was a friend, and while we were adults by caveman standards, I felt more kinship to someone still growing up, like me.

He literally looked up to me because I was tall. I relied on him.

We'd used our sparse vocabulary and sign language to settle on a hunting ground. As light slowly grew, we hiked west to the gap that led into our crater refuge, like the broad entrance to a vast stadium. It was a good place to stalk game because it served as a funnel for animals going to and from the savanna.

The two of us sidehilled up the north slope of the draw, using our spears as walking sticks as we climbed from one grassy bench to the next. We reached a crow's nest view.

In one direction was the circular amphitheater of our extinct volcano, ten to twelve miles across. The crater walls, I guessed, were about half a mile high, and the ones farthest from where we stood caught the most clouds. In the opposite direction were the dry broad hills Ellie and I had climbed with Boy. Beyond was the grassy savanna we'd first landed on, faint in the haze. A brisk breeze blew from a western horizon still dim in early morning.

The panorama pumped me with joy, which I suspected was a side effect of my crush on Ellie. The view was beautiful, serene, dramatic, stage–lit, and filled with animals. I felt connected. Our planet was magnificent and I was lord, surveyor, and steward. As the coming sun nicked the eastern crest, everything turned gold. King of the mountain!

Except I wasn't the only king. Just as we began looking for game, Boy took my elbow and pointed. There was a dusty wallow at one end of the grassy bench where we stood, a place where animals rolled to give themselves a dirt bath. It was a good place to look for tracks of what else might be lurking about, including lions.

And sure enough, there were enough cat paw prints to take the edge off my euphoria.

But Boy wasn't pointing at that.

He'd discovered a boot print. Or at least some kind of shoe, with a very peculiar waffle sole. The pattern left little pyramids in the dust. The footwear was also weirdly broad and splayed, different than any human boot I could imagine. In fact, it was just the kind of shoe you might design for a webbed foot, or a three–toed reptile, or a flipper. Unworldly. Alien.

The kind of boot a Xu hunter might wear. Or even a gort.

Game on.

My skin crawled.

Understand that I still had no idea what the Xu actually looked like, beyond the angelic Gabriel. All I knew was that they were supposed to come here too, that we were in a wicked race between slaying and saving Adam and Eve, and that warm–up time was apparently over. Some kind of Xu assassin had recently stood at this very spot, gazing into the crater we called home, maybe observing our evening fire and hearing Ellie sing. He – it – was probably calculating that our cozy little stadium was very much like a bag to trap us in.

I felt that tightening of gut and muscle you get before a fight, the electricity of nerves getting ready. Beside that boot print were the barefoot tracks of some very, very big human feet. Basketball player feet. Football linemen feet. Had a Xu assassin recruited cave-man help? And were they rival humans, or some kind of bruiser Neanderthal? Boy fell to his knees to examine the prints with alarm. He sucked in breath, said something like "Mordis," and made rapid signs. He pointed to himself, then the footprints, and then shot up his arm and stood on tiptoes to suggest great height.

Message received. The Xu had recruited thugs the size of club bouncers or Mafia enforcers. Terrific. Did our space assassins want to use earthlings to do their murdering handiwork? Maybe the rules allowed, or required, that our alien opponent not get their own hands dirty. Or talons. Or claws.

Or maybe the oh–so–superior Xu thought caveman versus caveman was entertaining. Gladitorial. We who are about to die salute you, blah blah blah.

I looked wildly about. I saw no gorts, angels, aliens, or prehistoric pack of Bigfoot. Africa still looked like a game park, unspoiled and nearly uninhabited. Only experience allowed me to pick out a tiny smudge of smoke that marked the People's encampment a few miles away. But somewhere out there, stalking us, was the Xu execution posse. And if they succeeded in murdering Click and Foxy – and presumably the rest of the clan as well – then history would be Reset. A possible Consequence, I'd seen, was a world with no people. No Mom. No friends. And perhaps no Nick and Ellie.

Would we be murdered too? Or if our genetic Adam and Eve were killed, would we suddenly vanish, never having existed on this time track? Or would we simply be marooned to rot in prehistoric Africa, spending the rest of our nasty, brutish and short lives chewing gamey meat, sleeping on animal skins, and picking off ants and lice?

I pointed urgently and shoved. "Run!" If Boy didn't understand the English, he understood my meaning. He had to dash to warn Click and the others. He especially had to warn Ellie. It was the first time I'd thought of anyone else in that way, except Mom. She – they – were more important to me than me.

That's what love said, anyway.

So I gripped my spear, crouched to be less visible, and thought furiously. Somehow I had to delay or stop any invaders until… what?

Until Adam, Eve, and Ellie had escaped.

The People were probably already out for the day, hunting, gathering, wandering, and perhaps being picked off one by one by creeping enemy cavemen.

So Boy took out his whistle and gave a shriek different than the timid whistle of the antelope or cheerful bird. This was brazen alarm. It pierced the African air, shrill and insistent.

Then he set off running.

I stayed as rear guard, horribly alone. Visions of every movie monster I'd ever seen flitted through my brain. Would the booted Xu have some kind of ray gun? Would his henchmen be cannibals?

You can always imagine something worse than reality. There are always monsters under the bed.

Movement uphill! The bad guys had heard our warning whistle. I looked up with dread. The side of the draw we'd climbed continued stepping toward the crater rim, and the Xu posse rose out of brush well above me. Several shaggy heads loomed above grass and leaves. They stared intently, and I stared back. I didn't see gargoyles, angels, or lizard men.

There was something peculiar, however. One of the menacing cavemen was wearing one of those flat, World War I army helmets that look like an upside–down soup bowl.

Private Dunbar had left more than a belt buckle behind.

Or perhaps that *was* private Dunbar. Anything becomes possible in a time–tossed world. My mind was galloping.

The grass moved. About twenty cavemen in all, two hundred yards upslope, began descending toward my dusty wallow. They were tall, burly, and dark, armed with spears and clubs. If I ran, I'd just lead them to the others.

Unless I ran the other way, out onto the savanna, to buy a few minutes of time.

Far from Ellie.

And then a lion saved me.

There was a blur in the grass, a rippling glimpse of tawny fur faster than a sports car, and one of the would–be attackers gave a guttural scream and tumbled under a male lion, the beast roaring like a gort. The kill was quick as a thunderclap. Gruesomely, I could hear snapping bones. One moment the tall caveman was striding arrogantly toward me like a naked Goliath, and the next he was dead. The man's arm thrashed upward a final time, straining, and then fell. The growling beast began dragging its kill, even as the other cavemen shouted and followed the cat.

The lion let his victim fall and roared warning. Other roars echoed. The enemy halted, wary and uncertain. Where was the lion pride?

At least they'd stopped looking at me. Reprieve! I fought down fear and thought what I might do. In my backpack I still had a couple of matches.

There it was, then.

Fire.

I snapped off a branch of a nearby bush, heedless of painful thorns, and ripped up grass to wind around its tip and make a quick torch, clumsy with panic. I looked up. The Xu posse was still facing down the stubborn lion. In my haste I lost one match in the grass, but fumbled out the last one and looked anxiously for a rock to strike it on. There! A flame, my torch lit, and I plunged the incendiary into the tinder–dry browse of the hillside.

Flames flared like charcoal with too much lighter fluid.

I began weaving along the draw, igniting the grass between the hostile cavemen and myself. The brush caught surprisingly easily. The flames crackled upward as high as my head, smoke boiling off and drifting into the crater. The intensity of the heat was scary. Already I couldn't see our foes. I began trotting back toward the crater and home, dipping into the gap and torching the grass every ten feet or so. I could hear the brutes shouting, lions roaring, and flames snapping. My torch scorched my hand. I hurled the last of it away and set off on a dead run.

Behind me, the grass fire blossomed like napalm. Smoke roiled up into a mushroom cloud. The rising sun lit the cloud to an ominous black, and animals in the refuge were beginning to lope this way and that in consternation, braying, bellowing, and grunting.

My arson had sealed off the crater's only natural exit.

It was a three–mile race back to where the People had their camp. I was gasping, side aching, when Ellie anxiously met me.

"Nick, what have you done?"

"A Xu is coming, or at least the cavemen he's recruited." I was panting for breath, and slick with sweat. "I saw their footprints, and a weird bootprint. An alien boot. An Army helmet."

She was bewildered. "A helmet?"

"From Private Dunbar, I'm guessing. Someone found it, or he's still here. I don't know. I think he died a long time ago and these souvenirs are still rattling around. All these huge guys rose out of the grass, a lion attacked, I started a fire. It's showdown time, Ellie."

She looked past me to the fire. "The wind is blowing this way. The fire is coming into the crater."

Indeed. I hadn't just created a temporary firebreak; I'd ignited the savanna in our amphitheater. Sparks were dancing ahead, bounding like pixies and igniting smaller fires everywhere they alighted. I'd set an inferno between the Xu and us, but I also might have trapped us in a fire pit of my own making.

"It was either start a fire or fight off an attack by more muscle than the Green Bay Packers," I said in my defense. "We have to get out of here." I pointed toward the jungle on the far crater wall, several miles away. "We retreat to the green and lead these people somewhere safe. Does this contest end at some point?"

"Who knows? Gabe wouldn't tell me the rules, or if the Xu even have rules. But you're right, that way is wetter, maybe too wet to catch fire." Now smoke was beginning to blow over us, pungent and perilous. A thought occurred and she excitedly grabbed my arms. "And this is an excuse to get them moving, Nick. Your fire might actually be a stroke of genius. They *have* to run now."

I brightened. Arson has its uses. "Boy was frightened by the jumbo footprints of the enemy cavemen, too. Maybe they're someone our clan has fought before."

"That will help, if it's true."

We trotted into camp. The People were frenzied, scooping up skins, baskets, spears, and implements. In less time than it takes to play a song, they were packed. That's one advantage of simple living.

"Gabriel kept calling this a game." Ellie was thinking hard. "Which suggests it can be won. Clan against clan. Maybe the Xu don't use weapons; they're too advanced. Or maybe they want humans killing humans.

Clear conscience. Being chased by cavemen makes it a fair fight, don't you think? How many?"

"Maybe twenty that I saw. One was killed by a lion."

Boy was exclaiming excitedly and using gestures while other tribe members snapped sharp questions, watching the lid of smoke. Click seemed hesitant to retreat, but Boy was insistent. He kept shouting, "Mordis, Mordis!" It seemed to have the same effect as yelling "snake" or "wolf." Yet they couldn't agree on going.

Maybe it was my new self–confidence. Maybe it was my love for Ellie. Maybe it was my annoyance at losing my hat. With impulsive drive that surprised myself, I strode over to Click, snatched off my red base-ball cap, and jammed it back on my own head like a royal crown. It was a coup, or at least an assertion of authority. I knew what we must do.

So I gestured urgently toward the far crater wall and arched and dipped my hand, mimicking the idea of climbing over the rim of the old volcano. "We have to go this way, this way!" The cavemen looked where I gestured.

Still they hesitated.

But the smoke was climbing higher. Embers were wafting over our heads. I grabbed Geezer's arm and pointed. "That way!"

Finally the elders nodded to the others. Run.

I got out in front, hoping like any leader that someone might follow.

Then I risked a look behind.

It was as if a dam broke. Everyone was trotting, children wailing in fear. Click was sulking, but jogging. Boy skipped anxiously as he prodded the others. Scout ran ahead. Mother Hubbard helped herd the young ones. Hercules dropped back to serve as rear guard.

Animals ran with us, the species intermingling in confusion.

Once they got going, the People sped with their customary endurance. Foxy scooped up a toddler. Woody hurried the normally shambling Crow, who'd taken the time to fetch his belt buckle. Ellie took Clumsy's hand. Our nation, no more populous than a school classroom, had begun to migrate.

This tiny band was the future of the human race.

We loped toward steep crater walls with only the unknown on the other side. It was like running for the edge of the universe, and hoping there was something beyond.

Behind us, fire was spreading across the crater floor. The blaze was spotty enough that some animals were running back through its gaps toward the open savanna, galloping over scorched spots and kicking up puffs of ash. I saw no sign of pursuit by the Xu gang. Had the lions scared them off? The flames? My bold vandalism gave me a secret thrill. Let it burn! I wasn't just playing the hero; I'd tapped my dark side.

But wasn't that precisely what the Xu were worried about?

Click caught up with me but didn't take back the baseball cap. I hadn't become chief, but I'd become emergency leader. By default, Ellie and I were the ones with a plan. So he went along.

And then stopped.

CHAPTER 23

STAMPEDE

THE CAVEMEN WERE never single minded. As animals paralleled our progress to get away from the fire, Click eyed them the way a modern guy covets a hot girl or a hot car. Here was meat in abundance, going our way and near at hand.

I shook my head, a gesture he'd come to understand. "Hurry!"

But that just made him stubborn. Click stopped and pointed. "Yagwa!" he shouted to the others, jerking his head. Between the crater wall and us was a milling, confused herd of wildebeest. The men bunched, hefting their spears. I was alarmed. A fire and enemy behind, and we were going to stop and shop for dinner?

"We have to run," I protested. I kept gesturing toward the crater rim. "Hurry, hurry!"

Even Boy shook his head. "Lachka. Lachka." Meat.

This was crazy. Our genetic Adam wanted to stop and hunt?

"Nick, we might go hungry if they don't," Ellie said. "We haven't stockpiled food to travel, and who knows what we'll find in the forest or the other side of the mountain. It's not escape if we starve. Click knows that."

I saw the point. Wildebeest were a rare target because they were swift, ornery, and hard to bring down. But now the fire was cornering them.

"Yagwa," Click repeated with relish. Our chief began giving commands again. The pause, I realized, was a way for him to reassert authority.

And if I tried a power struggle, I might lose completely.

The men shouted and signed, fanning out to envelop the herd. This would take forever! The women and children, expecting exactly that, sat or squatted. Click's enterprise had brought our flight to a complete halt, even as the grass fire ran this way and that. It was burning thousands of acres, but leaving large stretches untouched. Sooner or later, the Xu goon squad would march through.

"We're losing our head start," I groaned to Ellie.

"They won't move without meat."

I stewed, studying the lay of the land.

Then I called. "Boy!"

He'd learned our name for him. The youth trotted over and I beckoned him to follow. By now the older men had flanked the wildebeest but were still a hundred yards from striking. The animals were getting nervous, and might bolt back towards the fire.

I had a better idea. Stampede.

I'm no physicist but I do understand gravity. Even mountain goats, which escape bears and cougars by hanging out on sheer cliffs, sometimes fall.

Life is tough all over.

I'd spied a shallow canyon ahead, creating a thirty–foot drop in front of the herd. At the bottom was flood–washed rubble. It was why the animals were milling in confusion. So instead of waiting for Click's signal to stealthily converge, I charged the wildebeest like a wild man.

To our prehistoric forebears, this was a new idea.

Click and Hercules shouted in protest, thinking I'd spook the quarry. I ignored them. Boy ran with me, the day recklessly exhilarating. Flames flying, Mordis on our tail, and meat on the hoof!

"Yee–hah!"

Boy hollered too, waving his arms and spear.

The wildebeest bolted. Horns tossed, tails bounced, the ground shuddered, and dust roiled to join the smoke.

The herd leaders saw the danger and swerved. Those behind were blinded and panicked by pursuit. Some galloped straight over the cliff.

I slowed. The remaining wildebeest slackened their panic enough to see the danger and charge off in all directions, horns lowered to gore. We dodged out of their way as they squirted from the hunters' cordon and loped toward the center of the crater. Click was shaking his spear furiously.

But the other cavemen followed me to the lip of the ravine.

A dozen wildebeest had gone over and been killed or crippled. Those still alive were bellowing. Some shook their great necks in dazed stupor, and others hobbled on broken legs. Instead of spearing a single animal, I'd used good ol' modern brainpower to quickly doom a dozen – far more than we needed or could use. The excited hunters skidded down the canyon wall and darted in to finish them off. It was slaughter. Blood flew. Hearts were yanked out and devoured. Men hollered and capered.

"Nick, why?" It was Ellie, who'd run up to watch with me from the gully rim.

"Quick. Efficient. We have to get going." I was brusque because I felt guilty.

"It's a waste."

"Yagwa are dangerous to bring down. We can't risk injuries."

That's what I told her, but I flinched from her disapproval. Nick Brynner was not just a firebug, I was a one–man extinction machine. Impatiently, I'd given humans a new lesson in overkill.

I had seen the future, and it was me.

We butchered two wildebeest for the best haunches and abandoned the rest. As we moved away under a ceiling of sparks and smoke, other predators moved in. Hyenas were laughing, and vultures orbited. I told myself I'd fed the entire ecosystem, and that the vast wildebeest herds would quickly recover from my morning of carnage.

But I also remembered that over–hunting had nearly wiped out the American buffalo. Mr. Faunus said the first American Indians might have done the same to Ice Age species such as the woolly mammoth.

My new comrades – my followers – were rejoicing at the easy kill, replaying with their hands the swerve of the animals and their fatal fall. Megatron acted out the spectacle by falling on his back and kicking his arm and legs in the air, like broken limbs. The others hooted with laughter.

Click was scowling, because once more I'd usurped his authority.

Was I defying the Xu or proving their point?

I was doing what I had to.

We climbed into the forest. Behind us, the crater floor burned like an apocalypse.

CHAPTER 24

FLIGHT

I T WAS A steep, desperate climb in which no one was left behind. Geezer and Nana were pulled, toddlers rode shoulders, children scrambled, and every skin and basket of bloody meat and mangled fruit was determinedly manhandled up the slope. Boy had an instinct for the terrain and led the way up a forest ravine laddered with muddy roots and logs. This was real jungle, with dinosaur–scale trees. Some figs and banyans had buttressed trunks that sprawled as wide as a house, their twisted wood as complex as a wire bundle in a supercomputer, and their spilling vines as thick as climbing ropes. Branches above were broad as sidewalks, under a canopy that cast eternal shadow. Brilliantly colored birds scolded us as we puffed upward, and monkeys shrieked and pelted us with nuts.

The rim of the ancient volcano was a circular for-ested ridge a hundred yards in width and thirty miles in circumference. It plunged almost as precipitously on the outer side as it did into the crater. We pushed along this jungle catwalk in fog, since we'd climbed into the clouds. And then shivered when we rested, even while still smelling the smoke. I gave Ellie my raingear again, reasoning that my own chill gave me the same incentive as our near–naked cavemen to get off the top and down into warmer regions. Interestingly, after Click conferred with the other men – ignoring Ellie and me and scowling at my reclaimed hat – he ran his own proposed route past Geezer and Nana. The old woman was the tribe's loudest critic, skeptical and sharp, but once persuaded she gestured with her arms. Go, go!

So we slogged north and came to a break in the foliage that showed a precipitous but feasible route down a ridge on the outer cone. Ahead was land I hadn't seen before. Maybe Click had.

From our high viewpoint, volcanoes and deep valleys marched north toward a horizon that looked a hundred miles away. Lakes shone silver, and a platinum river snaked across a hazy plain. We stood so high that we were above the birds. I saw a formation flying below us.

The tribe sat to rest.

"The way to the future," Ellie said.

"Which implies we have a future." I grinned as I said it.

"We're looking at this big rift in Earth's geology." Ellie could unconsciously take on a schoolmarm tone. "They mentioned it in school, and Gabe reminded me. There's a crustal crack that runs north from Africa, through the Red Sea to what will someday be Israel and the Sea of Galilee. The Dead Sea is part of it. The rift makes a valley and ridge that runs all the way to the strait that has Arabia on the other side. And from Arabia, people could spread to Asia, Europe, Australia, and eventually the Americas. That's the way Adam and Eve need to go."

"Can Click and Foxy walk all that way?"

"They won't have to, because their children and grandchildren can finish the trip. Adam and Eve might die before ever leaving Africa, but their descendants inherit the earth."

"Awesome. We win."

"If we escape our pursuit."

Click and Foxy were huddled together, her head against his shoulder. "Mr. Faunus talked about them in class," I said. "It seemed so irrelevant, but now it's… now." I shook my head. "If Faunus was really ever a teacher." I looked out at the vast landscape, unreeling for many lifetimes to come. "It's like a dream. A bad one."

Ellie plucked at grass. "Some people think life is a dream. Or dreams are reality. Maybe reality is something we don't really encounter until we're dead. Or reality is made up of things we can't detect. Maybe the Xu figured out how to jump around in dreams."

"Murder isn't a dream. You're either alive or you're dead. To hunt down and kill two harmless cavemen? That's psycho."

"Gabe said it was mercy, by not having to kill the rest of us."

"Thanks a lot, Mr. Angel. Just make the future vanish instead. I didn't hear him volunteering for that kind of charity."

She stretched. "We just have to outrace them, Nick. At some point the game ends, right?"

"How do we know? A gong? An angelic choir?"

"I suspect it's like everything else in life. You just know. You keep going, doing your best, not knowing how or when it ends. And then it does."

Which made me think of falling in love with her. But what she meant was death.

We started downhill, picking our way down the steep ridge until the mountain flank broadened and our pace quickened. Foggy jungle gave way to open forest and then, thousands of feet below the volcano's summit, rolling savanna. The People visibly relaxed. This was the environment they were accustomed to.

The sun set behind the shoulder of the extinct volcano. The fugitives stopped wearily in a grove of acacia trees and sagged onto the grass. Woody started to make fire, using friction, but Click wisely stopped him. No fire, no smoke. We were still being pursued, or at least might be. We munched on scraps of smoked meat and fruit, saving the fresh wildebeest for a fire.

Before dark I walked clear of the trees to look back the way we'd come. An orange moon was rising like a fat balloon in the east, and a couple of the brightest planets glittered in the twilight sky. The mountain was tinted amber. I didn't detect any movement. Maybe we lost the Mordis raiders in the smoke and confusion.

But I doubted it.

The night chorus of animals started up. I listened to the tick of insects, the hoots of hyenas, and the distant whuff of lions. Jackals called. What were they saying? I went back and curled up with Ellie in the grass, pulling the baseball hat brim low over my eyes and wondering if we could really win or if the entire insanity was rigged. My mind churned. I felt emotionally ragged. Africa always had me looking over my shoulder.

My solace was the girl. It was remarkable how little she complained, and how quick–witted she was. Had I ever seen her really cry? She'd been hurled into the same nightmare as me, boy loser was the only person she could rely on or relate to, and there were no red ruby slippers to get us home. Just Click and Foxy, Adam and Eve, and the need to save the whole bleepin' world.

Meaning us? Or save it *from* us? I was proud of getting us out of that crater and any Xu trap, and yet still felt inwardly embarrassed by the fire and the wildebeest slaughter. I felt I'd staged a sorry preview of so–called civilization. I hadn't invented the bow and arrow, but I'd demonstrated mayhem.

The bad news was our dire peril. The good news is that I cared deeply about this girl, even if she didn't seem to care quite the same about me. And yet caring only heightened my fear. Now I had something to lose besides my life. I wanted to protect her, and felt inadequate to the task. I needed help.

Which jump–started my exhausted thinking. I *had* help, sleeping all around me. The People! Our tribe, clan, family, fraternity, and congress. But I also needed a gang. An army. And maybe it was up to me to make one.

Would that be sin or salvation?

Thoughts swirled. I didn't have the outdoor skills of these rugged cavemen, but I did have fifty thousand years of historical knowledge. So even though I was just a teenager I was also the old man of this group, which is probably why Click was willing to leave me the dirty old baseball cap. I *knew*. Yep, Nick Brynner was the grizzled coach of a hundred sports movies. The slacker student of Caesar, Napoleon, Crazy Horse, Rocky Balboa, and Wolverine. What would James Bond do? Michael Corleone? Frodo? Harry Potter? Katniss Everdeen? I was out of my element in prehistoric Africa, but Ellie and I were the only ones who knew how many other elements were possible. We were being hunted, but what if we became the hunters?

What if we got the ball?

And then I fell into weary sleep.

CHAPTER 25

ARGUMENT

A CLAN OF CAVEMEN doesn't move as efficiently as a high school tour group checking off thirteen countries in Europe. Fear fades. Hunger doesn't. The People's inclination was to settle down and look for opportunity wherever they happened to be, since hiking made it difficult to hunt and gather. When the whole world is a grocery store, and expedience has forced you from aisle three to aisle four, why move on to aisle five?

So there was debate about the day's plans. Ellie and I kept pointing north, Boy chimed in to remind them of my heroic cleverness, and hey, I had the baseball cap! Finally they decided to follow the chain of volcanoes along the rift valley, but not because of Ellie and me. We were still perched high and most game roamed below. Pickings would be easier if we drifted downslope.

So we set off again, following grassy ridges north and kicking up puffs of volcanic ash. We circuited around a younger cone that had burnt chocolate slopes and streaks of white ash worthy of Mordor. Steam hissed from its forbidding summit, and occasionally we could see dust plumes as the mountain shook itself like a sleeping bear, rocks rattling down its sides.

"Now we have to make sure Adam and Eve don't get entombed in lava," Ellie said, only half–jokingly.

"Leopards, lightning, crocodiles, brush fires, snakes, and scorpions," I listed. "We're not getting paid enough for this kind of babysitting."

She looked back at the pair, trudging steadily. "I bet they don't kill easily."

"I want to guarantee they don't, if the Xu posse picks up our trail. I've been thinking, Ellie."

"Uh–oh." It was encouraging she still had energy to tease me.

"I'm guessing any kind of fight in this world is pretty much a free–for–all. No strategy, since these guys don't even know how to box. But what if we get our team organized?"

"How?"

"By making an army, and throwing in artillery."

She stopped, pulling me out of line as the dust–covered People filed by. "Nick, isn't that exactly what the Xu are criticizing us for?"

"Criticizing, or exterminating?"

"I know you were desperate yesterday. But we burned half the crater and killed animals we didn't need. Now you're talking war. Which means corrupting a gentle tribe that was doing just fine until we came along."

Her blue eyes had that intense glow that made her so beautiful, but I was annoyed at her challenge. "You mean until the *Xu* came along. I'm talking about defending ourselves in a game I never wanted. We don't have a choice, Ellie. The People aren't gentle, they're hunters. Haven't you ever met a bully on the playground?"

"I just fear screwing up the natural order. Fighting a little battle that sets us on a path toward World War III."

"Come on. Your 'natural order' fights all the time. Nature red in tooth and claw, remember? We're supposed to let Click and Foxy be stood up against the wall and executed by space aliens? If this is really a game, it's a game we need to win. Me. You. All the People in this clan."

"I don't mean don't try to save them. Run."

"And if we don't run far enough, fast enough?"

She shook her head in frustration, uncertain what she believed. "I'm just worried that the real game is to see how aggressive we are in this prehistoric petri dish. Maybe it's a set up, you know? They watch the modern teens foul everything up. Checkmate."

"So the contest is rigged? That's not what I gathered from the gloriously feathered Gabe."

"What if they're testing whether we can come up with something better than an army? I don't think the Xu like armies."

"I don't give a crap what the Xu like. Your space aliens are bullies. They're chasing us with Bigfoot thugs and trying to assassinate our forebears. Maybe girls don't get sand kicked in their face, but sometimes you have to fight back."

"That is *so* sexist. Girls *do* know, and we *do* get bullied and hurt – by men, especially. But we also know that sometimes fighting backfires. It makes things worse, not better. So we talk, and try, and forgive, and make up. Men have fought wars from the beginning of time and all it's produced is sorrow."

I shook my head, certain her hesitation came from not thinking the situation through. "No. We're being hunted down, and I for one am going down swinging."

She closed her eyes. "Can't we just hide them?"

Her plea tore at me. I wanted to satisfy her, but didn't see how. I flung my arm. "Where? For how long? Ellie, I don't want a battle, and maybe they're already off our trail. Maybe we've won, for all I know. I'm just saying what happens if we haven't? If we can't hide long enough? So sure, let's keep running, and hide when we can. But if push comes to shove, let's be ready to fight. Otherwise, all this is pointless."

She moaned. "It's like there are no good choices."

"I thought *that* was clear from Day One of this absurdity."

She looked at me sadly. "I'm so sorry you got dragged into this."

My heart lurched, as it will in response to any kindness from girls. And I knew the right aw shucks response from old movies. Tough and gruff. "Thanks, but I got myself into it, remember? Curiosity killed the cat."

"Don't say 'killed.' It's bad luck."

I could feel her shivery seriousness. "We're not going to die, Ellie. I feel it. There's an end to this somehow. I'm going to get us home."

I wished I believed that.

She wearily leaned and kissed me, softly, sadly, on the lips. "You're a very sweet warmonger." Then she sighed and swung around to follow the rest of our little nation of hominids. "Let's go find the end."

It's funny how little things can boost your spirits. Ellie's kiss was hardly a serious mash–up of romantic passion, but the affection injected helium into my hiking boots. I floated.

It helped that our course was a gradual descent along a high, grassy ridge that gave a glorious view in all directions. Africa was all 3–D, High–Def, Imax magnificence, an unpolluted, untrammeled, undepleted paradise yet to be tamed. Nobody had given us dominion over the earth. Not yet, anyway.

So we hiked through a primeval park of animal abundance unimaginable in the used–up twenty–first century. Maybe the first mountain men who saw the vast Great Plains bison herds felt this, or ancient Egyptian pharaohs who could go lion hunting in what is now metropolitan Cairo. All I know is that I counted more elephants that day than there were people in our little band. We spied two rhinos, a sprinting cheetah, more types of antelope than I could sort, loping zebra, towering giraffes, rooting warthogs, brawny buffalo, and lizards that glowed pink, blue, and green. There were birds without number, and snails the size of a football.

No nature documentary I'd ever seen suggested this many animals were even possible. And yet we *belonged*. We didn't kill anything that day. As the sky glowed late, the acacia trunks bright as ribbons of neon, Click and Foxy picked a new camp and allowed a fire. We roasted the wildebeest we'd slaughtered in the crater, and then they snuggled contentedly in a partnership that, according to the Xu, would someday produce the future human race. Did they sense their destiny?

Nearby was a broad lake, riffled by wind and fringed by trees, and at dawn our group rose to explore it. A huge flight of flamingos lifted off the far end before settling uneasily down again, and Ellie pointed out herons, ibis, egrets, and storks. The early sun struck sparks off the wavelets, and a herd of zebra drifted up a slope on the far shore. In the opposite direction elephants were moving like a column of tanks. Despite myself, I was falling in love with Africa.

I hadn't guessed the People were watery, since they'd done nothing with the lakes in the crater but wash and drink. Here, however, they built a raft.

The difference was that they'd spotted fish jumping.

Part of their meager luggage was a basket I'd never seen raided for food. From it came crude nets. The men dragged small logs down to the lakeshore while women cut vines for ropes. Timber was lashed together into a float just big enough to precariously support one person. Three more logs were tied perpendicular, to make a crude outrigger.

Woody balanced on the contraption and they pushed him off, bon voyage. The light was still growing, insects orbited over the water. He poled and drifted, and then cast the net like a cape. His hips rotated with easy, practiced grace. The sardine–sized silvery fish he scooped up looked like coins cascading into a basket that balanced on the logs. It was like watching ballet.

Other men posed in the shallows as still as herons, spears upraised. Then they thrust to strike more fish and frogs. Ellie and I sat in the grass, watching. There was a peculiar peace to the harvest, if you didn't think about the fish.

"Ellie, I think I know how this ends. We're going to float these guys out of Africa."

She was humming softly as she watched the group gather and laugh, letting tension release like air from a balloon. "A navy, Skipper?"

"You said this valley rift eventually leads to the Red Sea. The cavemen know how to boat and swim. We guide them to the narrow part at the bottom and point them across."

She nodded. "The ocean is shallower now because the Ice Age has locked up so much water in ice sheets. Which probably means there's less water in that strait and more islands. Hop, skip, and jump."

"Maybe *that's* the game." If so it could take years to play. A lifetime.

"For history to produce us, everything has to fall into place. They have to migrate more than a thousand miles, get across the straits, and have their descendants spread across the globe. It's such a long shot. And yet scientists theorize that's exactly what happened."

A new hope occurred to me. "If they're being chased, they have motive to travel. Maybe in trying to murder Adam and Eve, the Xu are going to accidentally cause their success. Maybe it's a time–travel paradox, and the more the aliens try to exterminate us, the more we prevail."

She shook her head. "You saw the Consequence of that emptied town. There are different time tracks. The Xu want a Reset so that in the new time track Earth has a different history. No strip mines, no clear–cuts, no Dust Bowl. Just wilderness and Eden."

"Red in tooth and claw."

She laughed. "You're always going to use Lord Tennyson on me, aren't you? Life can be cruel and hard for individual animals that are preyed upon, yes. But most live full lives. The result is pretty stunning."

"You sound like you're on the Xu side again, Ellie."

"I simply see their side. Or rather, I see Africa."

"Well, I'm on Team Homo sapiens, and I say we encourage the People to float their boat. I say we don't change history, we guarantee it."

She nodded doubtfully. "With all that's to come."

"Michelangelo."

"Hitler."

"Isaac Newton."

"9–11."

Why had she turned so contrary? "It's beautiful here, Ellie, but it's boring. Nothing ever *happens*. Progresses. People aren't just animals; we're supposed to accomplish things. I don't know why. But the Xu can't just squish us like a bug and shuck human history. We do a lot of bad, but we do a lot of good, too. That's what they should want in their galactic fellowship. And it's our planet, dammit."

"Is it, Nick?" She looked across the lake. "That's what the Xu are questioning. What they want us to judge." She shook her head. "It's like every outcome is bad."

"No. We win, they lose."

We ate our fish and trekked on, the People still pushed by fear. Clearly they'd tangled with the Bigfoot gang – Mordis – before.

We wound up and down ridges that led north, following that great rift, staying above a vast valley floor. Dotting our route were volcanoes, some smoking and some quiet. The highest were capped by snow.

The prevailing wind was out of the west, bringing a steady scud of puffy clouds. Occasionally they'd gather themselves into brief, serious rain. We could see squalls twenty miles away, brushing ridge tops and flickering with lightning. The thud of thunder was a distant drum.

The epic emptiness was awesome, yes, but it also gave me a feeling of planetary ownership. Our brains made us top dog. Was that the will of God? Evolution? Or was my conceit just satanic pride? I was quite the slogging thinker, but Africa made you ponder.

All I could 'judge' is that I couldn't abandon these cavemen. Odd though they looked and sounded, they were capable of excitement, worry, jealousy, sacrifice, caution, bravery, and love, just like us. They watched over their children with fondness and impatience. They paired with each other to support and squabble.

High school, I said. Or humanity.

We camped that night in a gully with a trickle of spring water, stopping early so men could hunt and women could gather.

Ellie and I climbed a nearby knoll to once more look back the way we'd come. Our course wound like a snake toward the now–distant high forest of the extinct volcano, blue in the haze. Possibilities overwhelmed me. Once we saved the Xu, we could walk anywhere. Live anywhere. We had freedom no modern human would ever know. It was frightening. Empowering. Like growing up.

"It gets to you, doesn't it?" I said.

"Africa?"

"The prehistoric."

She brushed a tendril of hair from her eyes. "The planet certainly didn't need humans to complete it."

"Maybe it needed us to appreciate it."

"That's pretty deep, Nick. Does something need human applause to be valuable?"

I laughed. "That's like the old question of whether a tree makes a sound when it falls in the forest and no one is around to hear."

"The Xu say we're an invader. A parasite. A microbe."

"And I say they're the ones butting in where they don't belong."

As the day's sun sank, holes in the overcast allowed last rays of light to poke through, lighting the earth with spots of drifting golden fire. We watched with quiet appreciation until the illumination shifted onto a dusty ridge many miles from where we were. The sunshine seemed to spin, and I realized it was playing on a plume of dust. Animals? I looked hard. No, dots moved beneath in orderly single–file.

My heart sank. "They're coming."

Ellie looked where I pointed. "You think it's them?'

"Who else but hominids walk like that? And who else have we seen?" There was a brief glint, like reflection off an old polished army helmet. "It's the enemy, Ellie, and our tribe can't outrun them with our kids and elders."

"What are you going to do?" Her question was glum.

Soon the sun would set and our pursuers would camp for the night. It was dangerous to push through lion country in the dark. I looked back at our camp.

"Invent victory."

CHAPTER 26

WAR

AND SO I played general in what was probably the first organized battle in human history. My job was to put coordination into a caveman clan that ordinarily had the discipline of a preschool at recess. They had mankind's hunter instincts, but they were the cautious, impulsive instincts of the natural world.

I remembered a school DVD of primitive New Guinea tribes. War to those guys meant paint, dancing, bluffing, and tagging. Sure, some of their warriors were grisly headhunters, but when it came to battle they shrewdly fought as briefly and at long range as possible. Injury in a primitive place could mean a long painful death. Glorious last stands threatened extinction. There were no medals, no flags, and no home front demanding unconditional surrender. There were no antibiotics and no doctors. The basic idea was to scare the enemy away.

So my guess was that the People might holler, jump, throw rocks and, if absolutely necessary, jab a bad guy with a spear. They'd hope one good wound was enough to settle a war.

That wouldn't cut it with the would-be assassins of Adam and Eve. I had a grimmer idea, imported from my own time.

My belief was that we needed to give the Xu posse such a thrashing that they left us permanently alone to migrate, meaning we won the game for good, and sealed our Judgment.

I used to groan about all the trivia that school stuffed into our heads. But now I was Mr. Know-It-All by a margin of fifty thousand years. Remembering a world map let me guess, very roughly, where we were. I knew that the world is round, and that the stars are really distant suns, and that invisible critters called germs can make us sick. I knew about the lever, the wheel, gravity, the fact hot air rises, oxygen, and weird stuff like the fact metal will float if you shape it into a ship. I wasn't a trained warrior, no way, but I'd watched a billion battles in movies and computer games, meaning a billion more than anyone here.

The Xu had rounded up cavemen mercenaries to do their dirty work. Maybe this meant space aliens were squeamish about war. Maybe using cavemen made the game fair. Maybe it was sadistic, pitting prehistorics against each other like roosters in a cockfight. Didn't matter. What if our pursuers fought like barbarians, and we fought like Romans?

That was our only chance.

If our pursuers won, Adam and Eve were dead and the future altered. Which meant that if Ellie and I didn't vanish immediately, we'd likely be either killed in the attack or marooned in Africa. I was fighting for them, fighting for us, and fighting for everyone who will ever live.

I was also scared. I hate playground fistfights, let alone kill–or–be–killed combat. What courage I mustered came from being cornered.

First I made a shield, which was far easier than inventing the bow and arrow. I lashed branches in a rectangle and fastened another branch across the middle to serve as handle. Then I used leather strips to sew two layers of antelope hide to the frame. It wouldn't stop a longbow or sword, but it might ward off rocks, clubs, and stone spears. It also looked novel and empowering.

"I don't think anyone has ever seen a shield," I told Ellie.

"Nick, we're escalating things."

"Balancing things."

I went to Click, shield in hand, and provoked a mock fight. After I shoved him backwards a couple times the chief came at me as expected, his eye once more on my baseball cap. I planted my feet, crouched behind my invention, and let him pummel it. Then the other men tried. They had great fun in pushing matches.

We set up a shield–frame factory, using every scrap of hide we had.

I sketched a battle plan in the sand. Boy, who'd

first puzzled over my maps, got them now and helped explain. I'd point to pebbles and then point to the people they represented, slowly assembling our defense. I pantomimed, shouted, crouched, and thrust. I led them a short distance up the gully where we'd camped and showed a place where the ravine made a convenient choke point. This would be our ambush.

They got excited. The People hated Mordis.

Then I drew a line in the dirt and put the men shoulder–to–shoulder along it, completely counter to habit. Their macho code rewarded the bravado who dashed out in front. He'd boast, preen, and flirt.

"There's no 'I' in team," I told them. They looked at me blankly.

So I gave spears and the shields we'd completed to the smallest and weakest half of the men and let the others, including Bunyan, Hercules, and Click, attack. Normally those shielded would fall back from the brawniest hunters, but I mimicked raising a spear while shouting "Up!" It was a simple English word they could remember.

A hedge of spearheads, including mine, rose to point, and Hercules stopped in confusion. Bunyan backed up. Click scowled. He sidled to the right and the spears tracked him like radar. He drifted to the left and we swiveled with him. Then I shouted, "March!" Even though the cavemen had no idea what the word meant they came with me, keeping rank. The 'enemy' fell back.

Once exposed to an idea, the People were quicker

to understand than some moderns. They had fewer preconceived ideas. Fear began to turn to confidence. They even helped dig a shallow trench I ordered. Man the builder!

I knew things would quickly become confused in a real fight, but at least I'd planted the seed of organized combat. Click would anchor our center. I'd be at one end to command. I suggested Ellie lead one of the female wings, but she declined.

"I'm a conscientious objector."

"We came to save Click and Foxy. How else are you going to do it?"

"I don't know." She looked around as if seeking an escape hatch.

I swept my arm. "You said yourself this is all untouched, pristine. Where are they going to hide? How fast can they run? Surrender doesn't work. Appeasement doesn't work. Begging doesn't work. The only thing that works is fighting back, and if that's what makes us human, so be it."

"Aggression."

"Guts."

"You're so stubborn!"

"I'm tired of being pushed around." I didn't add that she pushed too, but I didn't have to – she knew what I meant. We were both tense from the approaching danger. "Ellie, I need support here."

She looked heartsick. "We're going to lose this game by winning it."

"Then it's not a game. It's a trap." Our quarreling frustrated me. What was wrong with her?

"I don't care. I'm going to take care of the little kids."

I looked away, hurt by her desertion.

"But I'll stand with you until it starts." She touched my arm. "I know you're doing what you think best."

I deployed the other women and the older children into ambush on both flanks. They'd be my artillery. Mother Hubbard commanded one wing and Foxy led the other. I hated to risk our ultimate ancestress in battle, but we men were outnumbered.

Nine guys, including me, formed our battle line. Megatron laid down half a dozen spears he'd throw. Iron Man showed off a big, new, white–quartz spearhead. Woody tapped his shield like a drum.

"Mordis," Hercules would growl. Then he'd pound the earth with a club. The other men would grunt and hoot.

We crouched in the grass to wait. Time seemed to stop, the air hot and still in anticipation. Finally we heard the tramp and grunt of approaching men, or approaching hominids, anyway.

I don't know quite what I expected. Some kind of Xu ringleader in a silver space suit, maybe, the bug–eyed alien urging his assassins on. Or an angel with demonic intent. Some kind of outsider, like Ellie and me.

But all we saw trudging toward us were hulking male cavemen with rocking spears and pug–ugly faces. They were dark, dusty, naked, and tall. Their eyes seemed sunken because they had a curious ridge of bone and flesh on their foreheads, like a bony brim. This was topped with shaggy hair. Their bodies were hairier than those of the People, and their muscles bigger. They looked like a particularly dark and foul–tempered mob of pro wrestlers, or a criminal motorcycle gang.

One of them, however, wore the World War I helmet. Was he their boss? It was buffed clean of paint, glinting like an old hubcap.

"Look at the size of them," I whispered to Ellie, who knelt beside me. "Are those Neanderthals?"

"I don't know if Neanderthals got to Africa. Besides, they weren't that tall. I'm guessing Homo erectus."

"Meaning?"

"Big. Tough. Ancestral. But ultimately extinct." She grasped my forearm. "I'm off to guard the children. But… good luck." She gave a light peck on my cheek.

Some of our opponents carried two or three throwing spears. Others had clubs. Helmet–head was the biggest and his gaze pivoted like a periscope, taking in the landscape and keeping track of his fellows. Yep, he must be their chief. I crawled to Click and pointed at him, then mimicked a thrust to the chest. Take that dude out and the battle was half–won.

Our chief nodded grimly. I crawled back to my place.

A hundred yards. On Mordis came, a cloud of dust moving with them, insects darting in the harsh afternoon light, sweat a sheen on their hairy bodies. We could already smell them. No wonder Boy had urged our clan to flee. Bigger, stronger, meaner.

Fifty yards. I rose and my companions rose with me, presenting shields and a row of leveled spears. This was surprise number one. The opposing cavemen gave an astonished shout and bunched, dumbfounded by our shields.

So helmet–head shouted at them. They hesitated, muttered, and finally charged at his urging.

With a crash, the legs of their front rank disappeared.

The bad guys howled. At my direction we'd dug as deep a trench as we had time for, three feet down, bridged it with brush, and covered the brush with sand. At the bottom were stakes and thorns.

That was surprise number two. My own side whooped.

The enemy leader snapped at his men, urging on the rearward ones and shouting at the forward rank to extricate itself.

So we attacked.

Our enemies desperately threw spears to stop us but they bounced, clattered, or got stuck on the antelope hides. We hurled the missiles back. Several bit flesh and Homo erectus howled even more.

Then we were stabbing the ones who'd fallen into the trench.

It wasn't a disciplined thing by Roman standards,

but even a ragged line of warriors attacking behind rectangular shields was novel. Three of the enemy managed to scramble out from the booby trap in hasty retreat, hopping on wounded feet. But three more were caught and killed, dropping into a ready grave.

They were the first dead humans – if Homo erectus was human – that I'd ever seen, except for my Dad.

We leaped across with battle lust, encouraged by the success of surprise. Somewhere along the way I'd lost my own fear. This was prehistoric shock and awe, and I'd engineered it. As we advanced the enemy cavemen fell back in confusion, colliding with each other. Our spear points jabbed several without suffering a counter–blow. Blood spurted, hot and red, and the sight set our hearts pounding. A couple more enemies fell and Hercules and Crow swung clubs to finish them. I heard grunts of exertion and an awful cracking of bone. There was no kinship between these rival hominids.

"Keep in formation!" We were losing cohesion, and risking an enraged counter–attack.

My soldiers couldn't understand a word.

Fortunately, it didn't matter. With a shrill scream and warble, the women and older children rose from both lips of the gully and hurled down a storm of rocks and spears. This was surprise number three. Sleeping Beauty actually showed fiery energy, and Clumsy an effective aim. Desperation will do that.

The enemy flinched, staggered, and cried out in confusion and pain. The People all learned to throw in

WILLIAM DIETRICH

order to bring down small game, and they were vicious in a rock fight. The Mordis were battered. I saw an eye put out, teeth flying, and a javelin sticking in a meaty shoulder. Their gang began to panic. The few fierce enough to push forward fell under our shield wall. The guy in the helmet was roaring at the others, urging them to attack, but they were wavering.

It didn't help that their leader hung back. He wanted the others to do all his fighting for him.

But finally he waded in, eyes tight with fury and frustration, and his World War I helmet almost comical except that he was a head higher than any of us. The bruiser swung his war club in a great arc and bashed Click's shield, hurling our chief aside. Another swing forced Hercules to jump back, the club's wicked slice making an audible whoosh in the air. Then he turned on me. The helmeted brute had black eyes, a hateful expression, and the bulk of a gorilla. I crouched behind my own shield, tensing for a hammer blow.

He raised his club to crush me, and that could have been it. But then he astonished by raising a rusting automatic pistol with his other hand and taking aim. If it would really shoot, he'd start a massacre.

So I didn't think, I reacted. I powered off my haunches and thrust my spear to beat him to the draw, my weapon ramming their leader's midsection. His torso was solid muscle but the flint was sharp. The point lanced into his stomach with surprising ease, like a knife stabbed into hot bread.

The pistol arm jerked and the gun went off, a bullet sizzling past my ear.

My spear impaled him.

My opponent's eyes bulged in surprise. He opened his mouth to cry out. The fury in his eyes turned to wonder. He looked at me in horror, as I looked back.

Then he exploded.

In stars.

What I mean is that a brute the size of a football lineman, and as solid as a stone statue, suddenly vanished in a bang of sizzling golden sparks. I had just a shadowy glimpse of something reptilian and strange in the fireworks, a slick hide like leather or plastic, and then it and its corona of light snuffed away.

The metal helmet hit the ground and rocked back and forth like a dropped pot lid.

The pistol fell to the sand.

I was stunned.

The enemy was even more shocked. With a cry of despair, those attackers still fighting broke and ran. There had been perhaps twenty in the original posse. Half escaped, some wounded. The others were dead or about to be. The People finished them off with no more sentimentality than they'd expended on the wildebeest. Clubs and spears chopped down like pumping pistons. Men and women shouted in triumph. Heads caved in. Chests sprayed blood. Hands and feet were hacked off as grisly trophies.

This was not the first clash between these groups, I

sensed, but a long–simmering enmity between similar but warring species. Only one was going to inherit the Earth.

We had no choice. There must not be any Xu Reset.

So my soldiers killed in a great swale of blood and dust, driven by fear and vengeance. And by doing so they preserved, perhaps, the future of my own kind.

Ellie led the children back at the end of the slaughter, the little ones wide–eyed but not shocked. They'd seen animals butchered their entire lives.

I was shaking and tried to hide it. Every nerve tingled. Every breath seemed a miracle.

"I heard a shot," Ellie said.

"One of them blew up into little stars," I told her. I held up the rusty gun. "Army issue, I bet. One minute he was going to shoot me or bash my brains in, and the next I speared him and he vanished like dandelion fluff."

"Was he their leader?"

"Yes. But he hung back until the last minute."

"I think you killed their Xu."

"So he recruited the Mordis by looking like them?"

"What else? He couldn't look like a space alien without freaking them out. I think you got the key guy, Nick."

"He didn't die, exactly. He flared like a sparkler. Was he really alive in the first place? Was he just a hologram?"

She shivered. "I don't know. I think Gabriel would say that we saw for a moment what life really is, or isn't.

That what we think of as solid is frozen energy. That everything, twisted the right way, is a package of sparks."

I nudged the old Army helmet with my foot. "So did that ugly dude kill poor Private Dunbar?"

"I don't think so. The pistol looks too old. Maybe the Xu guy found it himself, or more likely took it from a caveman. We'll never know."

"Why was he wearing an alien boot before?"

"Maybe to announce himself. A challenge."

I stooped, picked up the metal rim, and hurled the helmet like a Frisbee into the trench we'd dug. I considered saving the pistol but was afraid it would go off accidentally. Nor did it belong to this time. "Rest in peace, Private Dunbar." I threw it into the trench, too.

"How lonely Ruben must have been," Ellie murmured.

"So we've won?" I persisted.

She looked at the bodies strewn in the dirt. "That's the question, isn't it?"

CHAPTER 27

A NEW ADAM AND EVE

AFTER OUR VICTORY I was afraid the People might retrace our journey back to the extinct volcanic crater, their temporary home. But they seemed uneasy instead of reassured, and were nomadic in nature. With the help of Boy I got the sense that they feared the erectus tribe would seek revenge. The crater had already burned. Best to move on.

So we used the trench as a shallow grave for our enemies. Crow muttered something over the piled dirt and we set off north again. The farther we traveled, the easier it might be to keep Adam and Eve alive. And when did this gladiatorial contest end? I looked up at the sky as if a God–like voice would make a pronouncement, and waited uneasily to be plucked back to that nightmare spaceship. But nothing happened. It was just us, Africa, and yours truly as killer, or at least the vanquisher of a disguised space alien.

Despite our win, I couldn't enjoy it. The game rules

were hidden. The end point was a mystery. Ellie had turned aloof. I was so tired, confused, and guilty that I scarcely cared anymore.

I just wanted everything to be over.

My emotions tumbled. If blood left a bitter after-taste, there's also nothing like danger to make you feel alive. Then guilt would come and I'd muse I was Cain, the first murderer, and we were somehow reenacting the Bible's story of our fallen beginnings. Wouldn't that be a twist? I get back home, take out the Good Book, turn to Genesis, and say, "Guess what, Mom, that's me."

We made a quick march to get away from the bat-tlefield, camped in exhaustion, and pushed hard the next day. It helped that we were still slowly descending, the land broadening and the air getting thicker. We came to a muddy river and forded upstream from a flotilla of lurking crocodiles, long as torpedoes. We waded to our waists, shook ourselves like dogs, and went on.

Dogs! I assumed they hadn't been domesticated yet. A troop of jackals skittered ahead of us and I eyed them with speculative interest. I still wanted to be the Stone Age Einstein.

The Xu wouldn't approve.

Ellie kept glancing back for pursuit. Nothing.

Hercules stayed behind a few hours to watch too, and then jogged to catch up, looking relieved.

I hoped my girlfriend, if that's what she was, would in time accept our victory and even be a little appreciative of my prowess. But she was subdued and gloomy, so all I could do was wait out her mood.

Meanwhile, Africa continued to unfold. Zebras were not just herds, but hoards. Wildebeest seemed to create their own weather when moving, churning up vast thunderheads of dust. Lions and leopards rose to peer as we trooped by, stretching lean muscles as they sized up our spears.

Grassland alternated with park–like groves of trees. The sun was warm, the sky bright, and butterflies darted. Women veered off the main path to collect any number of foods, including more bird eggs. Men trotted ahead and returned with an antelope for dinner, a subtraction balanced each day by a thousand savanna births.

After we ate saltless meat for the millionth time – how I missed sugar and spices! – I called the adults to a council. I built a dirt map of the world I'd explored so far, and this time they got it. I made a crater to show where we'd escaped from, and other mounds to represent the volcanoes we'd skirted. I dug a small trench and crossed sticks at my best guess of the battle site, and was rewarded with excited recognition. Several shouted and pranced.

Then I took a deliberately big stride, surprising them, and sketched in, as best I could guess from vague memory of classroom maps, the horn of Africa, the Red Sea, and Arabia. The result was as crude as a medieval chart, but I hoped to give them their goal. "Aka," I said, pointing to where the Indian Ocean would be in my dirt atlas. And then jabbed again and again. "Aka, aka, aka."

Water.

They squinted with bewilderment. I knew they were picturing lakes. They'd never seen an ocean, and a sea that stretched to the horizon was beyond their imagination. But I pointed to the narrow strait at the bottom of the Red Sea, repeated "Aka," and then sketched a log and fisherman. I hopped. Then I thumped Arabia. "Safe," I said, using the English word since I didn't know if they had a prehistoric equivalent. Thump, thump, thump. Go there. It was if I were trying to give a command to dogs. "No Mordis." I shook my head violently and thrust my palms down. "No Mordis." I had no idea if that was true, but they'd picked up the English words 'no' and 'ok,' as well as 'up.'

They studied my scratching with narrow eyes. I was proposing a journey of a thousand miles, a migration that could take a generation or more. They couldn't know that. But I was the person who had set the fire and beaten the bad guys and driven the wildebeest off the cliff, so maybe I was right about this journey, too. Would any of them remember my directions years and generations ahead? Would any of them care? There was a gulf not just of language, but of thought. And yet I was confident they grasped the central conviction: that mankind would be safer if the People got out of Africa.

"Safe," I repeated. I left them to brood on my scratchy chart.

As the fire burned down, Ellie finally came over to sit beside me. The light from the coals gave her a ruddy beauty. The moon overhead turned her blond hair silver, like an Elven queen. I was relieved she'd relented enough to join me. But her skepticism hadn't changed.

"Nick, you shouldn't have shown them that map," she said.

Was she just going to nag now? I tried to answer evenly, but felt defensive. "Says who? I don't know the rules of this crazy game. Our job is to protect Click and Foxy. The farther they run, the safer they'll be. Maybe we've already saved them, but if not, they should keep going."

"I worry about directing history too much. Trading one Reset for another."

"Why are you so critical all of a sudden? What choice do we have? Aren't we on the same side?"

"Yes." She looked away into the night. When she first started to speak, her voice caught, so she took a breath and tried again. "I just fear we're making a terrible mistake."

"How?"

Her voice went to a whisper. "By saving Adam and Eve."

"Ellie, good God! That's the whole reason we came here, isn't it? Survived those crazy rooms on the spaceship? Crossed the savanna? Fought a battle?"

She gave a low moan, rocking back and forth. "It's so beautiful here."

"What's that got to do with anything?"

"Nick, don't you see? If saving them is our Judgment, and the Xu are right, that couple is going to produce our civilization and all its destruction. They're going to give birth to Adolf Hitler and Genghis Kahn and acid rain and the extinction of the passenger pigeon."

"Plus the Empire State Building, Leonardo da Vinci, Abraham Lincoln, and the national parks. The Bill of Rights. Mozart. The Taj Mahal. We've had this argument already. Don't go all space alien on me."

"But what if we're *wrong?*" She leaned into me, and even in the dimness I could see her eyes were wet. "What if the population explosion, the atom bomb, and global warming trashes Earth? Extinguishes this for all time?" She thrust out her arm. "What good is the Taj Mahal if we take down the whole planet? All these magnificent animals and this magnificent ecosystem paved over, polluted, poached. Isn't that what's at stake here?"

"Plus everyone we know and every good thing they stand for."

"No, Nick, listen. What if this isn't a threat but a chance?"

"What   is?"
"The game. The Xu. Our being dumped here. All of it. What if we're being given a choice of not just saving Adam and Eve but doing a genuine Reset that makes things *better?* Which saves everyone but sets civilization on a whole new course. Which doesn't start with spears

and battles and escaping across the Red Sea, but starts here, now, with a better world?"

Had she gone crazy from all the stress? "What are you babbling about?"

"What if *we* became Adam and Eve?"

That shut me up. I was stunned.

"We," she repeated. "You and me. Get Click and Foxy out of the way and we become the ultimate ancestors. Maybe cross the straits to Arabia, maybe not. But we use all the lessons our species has learned in fifty thousand years to start mankind on a better path. We teach the People to be stewards of the earth. We reinforce the good instincts they already have. We lead by example. We teach our children. Their children. We stay here and make things right. We pass on a kind of Ten Commandments on how to sustain the Earth."

My mind was whirling. "Our children."

"We pair up, Nick. Marry. We're old enough by their standards. I know it's a hard life, but it's also a lovely one. We escape all that modern stress. And we lay the groundwork for a peaceful, productive, artistic society that doesn't triumph with war and cruelty. Instead of Adam and Eve being shoved out of Paradise, we stay here and make paradise *better.* Nick, do you love me?"

Girls are always six steps ahead. "Yes." My confession was glum, as if I were embarrassed to be found out.

"There you go, then."

"There I go *what?* Do you love *me?"*

She smiled sweetly. "You know how fond I am of

you. And we'll care even more after we're together. After children. After we've done our best to start our species in a utopia that protects nature instead of exploits it."

"Wow." Some of this, of course, was appealing. Flattering. Daunting. Scary. Commitment. Children. And yes, that meant sex, and yes, that meant Ellie was choosing me for all time, and yes, we could probably do a better job at getting things going than our caveman ancestors. And yet...

"What happens to Click and Foxy?"

"We have to murder them." She said this so matter–of–factly that I almost fell over.

"Ellie, no."

"I'm sorry to use that word, but this adventure has made me blunt. We've escaped wild animals, chewed on raw meat, killed rivals in battle, and made new friends. We're learning a little of their language, and teaching them ours. But at some point we have to get rid of the ultimate ancestors if we're going to do a Reset and save the earth. I know I sound ruthless. I didn't even want to be in the battle. I even hate the animal butchering. So maybe we just don't heal them when they get hurt, or give them the wrong directions, or they choke on a bone. I don't know. But we take their place, you as king and me as queen, and it's our children who become everyone else in the future. We build a better society."

I tried to twist my brain around this. "We give birth to the ancestors who are going to give birth to us? Does that work?"

"It must."

"You've gone nuts. Loco. Crazy."

"Have I? Or have I found the only way out? Click and Foxy will die in a few years anyway, of natural causes if nothing else. They've been dead five hundred centuries from our point in time. Taking their place is the only way to save the planet from humans, and our species from the Xu. Don't you think this is what Gabe really put us here to figure out? Why else pluck us out of the twenty–first century and drop us into this crazy marathon? Why pick teenagers, a boy and a girl? Because we're young, and have our whole life to teach these cavemen, and because we can have children."

I was shaking my head, a mass of longing and confusion. "No, no."

"You want me, Nick. I know you do. And you can have me – tonight, even – if we're honest enough to admit this is the way out. We're supposed to become Adam and Eve. It's the only thing that makes sense."

She leaned close, her hair a halo around her beautiful face, and all I had to do was reach out and touch her and change all human history, maybe for the better. I ached to kiss her, and do much more! She was offering herself! But she was also suggesting a wilderness marriage, a trip of no return, and kids. Whoa, whoa, whoa. Was I ready for any of that?

But I hadn't been ready for surviving outdoors or hunting animals with a spear, either. Or fighting and killing burly cavemen. But if I was inventing battle, wasn't I a worse Adam instead of a better one?

My mind churned. I wanted her. I was afraid of her.

And murder? That was different than war. My stomach turned.

Not to mention staying here for the rest of our lives. Give up on ever going home? Betray the mission we were given?

Or fulfill the mission in a different way?

"No." It was the hardest word I ever had to choke. "Not yet, Ellie, I'm not ready. For you, for this, for deciding the future." I was in a panic. "Please wait. Let's think about this. Talk it through. Give me a little time."

She had that same steely intensity I'd first seen in the speedboat, the determination I'd fallen in love with. "The game is still on Nick. We may not *have* any time. We're not going to let this beautiful world, and all these amazing animals, be doomed by our doubts. We need to save them. We were put here to save them."

I stalled. "So we save them tomorrow. Or the next day. I can't decide this now. Children? Destiny? It's too big. Ellie, I need to breathe."

She was disappointed, frustrated, even rejected – but she reluctantly nodded. "Okay, think it through. You'll see I'm right. We can do better, Nick, because you and I know the consequences of *not* doing better. We can reset everything and try to avoid world wars, global warming, and extinctions. We can retain Eden. With the two of us, there is no apple in the garden, and no fall from grace."

"It seems presumptuous."

She looked at me sadly, fondly, patiently. "It seems logical. Sleep on it."

I was relieved to have a stay of execution, not to be asked to reform the world this night. What was that old book? *Atlas Shrugged*? I had just shrugged. "You've got my brain on fire." I looked at the skin pot the cavemen used as a kettle, debating. "Let's have that grass tea before we sleep. Let me think."

"Yes, think. You'll see I'm right."

So we drank. Because I *had* decided what I must do.

Chapter 28

BETRAYAL

ELLIE SLEPT THROUGH the entire next day. I'd drugged her with Crow's potent poppy husks that I'd picked along the way. It was highhanded, but I figured I was saving her from herself, and humanity from us.

I pantomimed to the People that Ellie was sick, that I would look after her, that they must hurry on for their own safety, and that we would catch up. They looked doubtful, but finally went. Boy tried to linger on a hill until I threw rocks to drive him away. Maybe he sensed that I was doing something private, and important, that still had to play out.

The departure gave our cavemen a good head start from whatever threat Ellie might pose. I didn't believe she'd really have the ruthlessness to kill Click and Foxy, even if I went along. But just to make sure I bound her to a tree with vines and scraps of my old nylon fishing line. I tied her ankles for good measure. If we were going to play Adam and Eve it was going to be well away from the People.

They could pick their own destiny now; we were going to set off in a different direction. The Judgment was over, at least for me. The universe could go hang.

She was groggy and thirsty when she finally awoke. "Nick?" she croaked.

I was quiet, still debating what to say.

"Nick!"

"I'm here," I said from behind the tree. "I won't leave you, Ellie."

She struggled against the bindings. "What's going on?"

I came around with a baobab cup. "Have some water." I put it to her lips.

She jerked her head back, looking at me with suspicion. "What's in it?"

"Nothing this time."

Ellie hesitated, and finally drank. Then she shook her head to clear it. "What did you do to me?"

"I had to knock you out with Crow's flowers. You were talking crazy. We need to be by ourselves for awhile and sort things out."

She wrestled against her bonds, increasingly annoyed. "You can't tie me up!"

"Just until Click and Foxy get far enough away. Then we'll take the next step."

"What next step? Nick, untie me!"

"Go off on our own."

She thrashed, but I'd roped her good. The deed made me feel like a creep from a horror movie, but once again I had no choice. Finally she stopped and gave me a glare. "Tying people up is against the law, Nick."

"There are no laws, remember? Look, I didn't want to do this but you planned to murder Adam and Eve to save the animals. That's just nuts." "I wanted to save millions and millions and millions of *people* from ghastly deaths from the wars and genocides our species is going to produce. I wanted to *reset* things, Nick. To make Earth better. Us better. The Xu are right. You know it, I know it. And you've ruined it."

"Ellie, our Judgment was to save Adam and Eve. I saved them. From the Xu, from Homo erectus, from you. Checkmate, future assured, my Mom and my high school and even Carl the dopey boyfriend all saved. We live happily ever after." I looked away. The happy part, I figured, would take a while.

"Live as what?" She regarded me as if I were the crazy one.

I blushed and looked down. "I don't know." But I was secretly thinking we *would* live as a second Adam and Eve, only off by ourselves. We would let the genetic Adam and Eve make their own wilderness trek, for better or worse. Meanwhile, we still had each other.

But I didn't say that, or say that I was still in love with her, or ask for help in figuring things out. I just said, "Whatever."

"Nick! Oh my God." She rolled her eyes. "I'm

willing to give my life to save the planet, but to just wander off by ourselves and wait for a lion attack? You're the one who's crazy."

"Ellie, I had no choice."

"Yes you did." She was furious, and as truculent as a child denied candy. Did she really think we could become partners in murder? When we didn't even know what the Consequence would really be? Maybe she had some fantasy of becoming the ultimate green warrior, or the mother of the new master race. But we were just two high school kids with sticks, put here to keep things the way they were.

That's what I figured, anyway.

"I don't know if we ever get back," I said, "but if we don't maybe we can find another band of humans to live with. We can still make a life here if you'll let us." I tried a weak smile. "Just give it a chance. Give me a chance."

"Then untie me, Nick."

"No. Not yet."

"Nick!"

"It's best to wait for tomorrow morning. I know you're uncomfortable, but I'll make it up to you somehow." I held out my palm. "Do you want some figs or nuts?" I'd been gathering while she was conked out.

Ellie looked at me in disbelief. "I'm not a monkey."

"But you still get hungry."

She closed her eyes, leaning back against the tree. "Leave me alone."

So she sulked. I walked around as if tiptoeing on

glass. Hours dragged by. The sun finally went down, it was chilly, and I realized I'd have to eventually make fire from friction. I'd watched Woody spin sticks and catch tinder, but hadn't mastered it yet. It was lonely without the help of the others. It was *really* lonely with Ellie staying mad.

Eventually we both fell asleep to the usual night noises.

My dreams were turbulent, full of anxious chases and angry words and unspoken dread at murder. Then I was jostled awake.

"Nick." It was an urgent whisper. Ellie nudged me with her bound feet. "Nick!"

"What?" I sat up, grabbing my spear. The sky was just beginning to gray in the east. No animals were prowling near, however.

"I'm sorry."

"What?"

"I'm sorry. I don't know what I was thinking. You're right, I went crazy." Ellie was crying. "I'm so cold and stiff tied up like this. Nick, I can't lose you, I'm still too afraid. Please hug me. I *am* in love with you."

The words made me soar. Was she honest? I was wary, but I also felt guilty for drugging her and tying her up. I crawled over and put my arms around her. She buried her tear-streamed face in my shoulder.

"This has been such a nightmare." She shuddered. "I'm so tired and confused."

What to do, what to say, how to fix things? "Ellie, it's okay. Please don't cry."

"Nick, I need you."

"It's okay, baby." I'd never called a girl that before, and it felt thrilling and strange.

"Hold me. I'm so cold."

But I couldn't hug her very easily when she was trussed to the tree trunk. I knew the People were long gone. So I hesitated just a moment and then used my multi–tool to saw and clip her free, while keeping her ankles bound. She rolled against me and we lay together in the grass as the light grew, our bodies sharing warmth. Bird and monkey chatter rose in volume. Then we were kissing. Ellie pushed against me and before I knew it I'd cut her ankle ties as well, so we could wrap into each other even more. I'd never made out so passionately with a girl, and I was on fire with desire. Caution vanished. I felt greedy, kissing her lips, her ears, her neck. She moaned.

Ellie arched her body, pressing against mine, and I responded. We panted as our hands roamed.

And then she suddenly shoved me away, gasping. "No! Not yet. I'm not really ready. Not for a baby."

"Ellie…" I groaned.

She rolled and sat up. "I'm finally thinking, Nick. You were right; we have to wait. We're in the middle of a wilderness, and we've lost our tribe. There's no one to help."

Oh man, talk about whiplash. I was glum. "I know."

She smiled, her look one of pity and promise. "I *want* to, but we have to wait until we figure out what we're doing, you know?"

"I know."

"Do you understand?"

"Yes. No. I don't know."

"Girls have to think things through. It's a Consequence."

"I get it, Ellie." My fire was ash.

"Let's have some breakfast and talk about what comes next. Really talk. About us. Are you ready for that?" She had recovered some of her business–like briskness. She even rubbed her hands together. "Gather some more food, inventory our belongings, take our bearings."

"Got it."

"What do we have to eat?"

I rolled away, grunted, and sat up. "Some fruit, some smoked meat. We'll have to hunt by ourselves again." Dawn had turned the east pink. A glow kindled where the sun would crest the skyline. "Let me check this basket they left behind." I was on all fours to rummage. "I'm hungry too."

"Nick, you're a darling." She was right behind me.

And then she swung a heavy rock against my temple, the world exploded, and all went black.

CHAPTER 29

THE FINAL KILL

A SNORT WOKE ME.
Something rank and bristly butted my side. I
blinked, head pounding, and realized I was face down
in the grass. Flies buzzed. I turned my sticky cheek and
recoiled, despite the pain. One of the planet's ugliest
mammals, a warthog, huffed in indignation and stepped
back to hoof and snort. He'd probed me with his snout
to see if I was dead and dinner.

I was lucky he hadn't just taken a first bite.

Struggling to my feet, dizzy and wretched, I yelled
and waved. The pig backed reluctantly, snuffling and
grunting in disappointment. Several vultures hopped,
squawking. Jackals circled, yipping. Half of Africa had
turned up to chew on my remains, it seemed. Now I'd
spoiled the party.

There's nothing like being surrounded by wild animals in a cafeteria line to persuade you of your own
mortality and vulnerability. Where was my spear?

Ellie had left that, at least. I scooped, shook it, and hollered again. The animals backed some more. Ellie had also, surprisingly, left my pack, although the pig had rooted in it. The food was gone and the water bottle gnawed. I put the ragged knapsack on anyway.

It was hard to think. The sun was high and pounding, flies were feasting on the blood of my scalp, and my vision was blurry. She'd really hammered me, in more ways than one.

The baseball cap had fallen off. I jammed it back on.

A shaky meander downhill took me to a seep with water, where I drank and washed my face and hair. It hurt! So my tempting Eve had clobbered me like a devilish Delilah and set off on her own… for what?

To hunt down Click and Foxy, of course. To reset all of human history with Ellie as Eve.

And since she hadn't killed me, with me as Adam. That's what the crazy girl would figure, anyway. She'd calculate that I'd catch up with her sooner or later, find the dirty deed done, she'd say 'come hither,' and that would be that. What alternative would I have? She was the only thing I wanted in this wilderness, and the only human I had anything in common with.

Oh, she knew I'd be furious. First I'd blow off steam. Then I'd tolerate her. Then forgive her. Still be secretly in love with her. And the Xu would be proved right. We're a beastly, murderous species. But after homicide we'd pretend to take a gentler, kinder path, teaching our children well and abandoning violence like a prehistoric John and Yoko. The wildebeest herds would live happily ever after.

Yeah, right. We'd lead our Reset children across the Red Sea and into the vast continents beyond, peopling earth with our superior offspring.

Unless we failed to reform humankind and history, and the Xu came back to Reset us, too. Or unless Ellie had misjudged how time travel works and we'd simply vanish when Click and Foxy did, never having existed at all. So long, Homo sapiens.

That would make the wildebeest *really* happy.

Did I even care anymore?

I slowly turned and considered my surroundings. Africa *was* beautiful, as Ellie had observed countless times, with a divine magnificence equal to whatever we put in its place, be it Notre Dame or the Hubble Telescope. Was this the Garden of Eden? Wasn't the point of the Bible story not just that we'd disobeyed and been expelled from Paradise, but that by seeking the Tree of Knowledge we'd ruined everything? Why *not* do a Reset? What good were people anyway?

Well, art and architecture, I supposed. Poetry. Literature. Music. I remembered Ellie's singing. Would we bring melody into her remodeled world, and compose as we migrated? Would we develop the technology to make a piano and guitar, but not catapults or tanks?

My head was spinning with grief, and I was so woozy that I vomited, staggering away from my mess.

Then I began to feel hungry. Angry. Vengeful.

How could she clobber me so coldly? Did she feel nothing?

I'd never been so depressed. Or betrayed. Or alone.

Boy loser.

I leaned on my spear, stewing, and tried to summon strength and understanding. What was I really doing here? Why couldn't the Xu just zap me and put me out of my misery? Or were the Xu handing me the girl of my dreams on an African platter, and I just needed to accept it? What, really, was wrong with starting over, given the sorry record of human history?

Well, no castles, no cathedrals, no concerts, no Christmas. No us. And there was something more about this devil's bargain that was thudding in my pounding brain, something that nagged me from the night we first arrived here. Why me? Why humans?

Then I remembered. The stars.

Every animal roved under those stars, but very few looked up. I'd watched our animal companions quite closely, and they were pretty much preoccupied with the next tuft of grass or the next haunch of meat. Wolves might howl at the moon, but they didn't get spooked by infinity. It's not that they accepted or rejected the immensity of time and space. Not only did they not know about it, they didn't care that they didn't know, and didn't know that they didn't care. They never thought about infinity, or thought about much of anything.

They were animals.

Ellie wanted to turn us back to that animalistic kind of contentment and boredom. Exist with existence. Just be.

Yet why were we humans so different from every creature around us? What were we doing here? It was baffling when you thought about it. Evolution had resulted in us pondering things, but *why?* There was no apparent advantage if all it led to was atomic bombs. Yet we were the only ones who thought, who prayed, who feared, and who wondered. It was our curse and our blessing.

Some teens said we were around to know God. And others that we were around to come up with better explanations than God.

The thing about the stars that first night, I remembered, wasn't just that they were cold, vast, and awesome. It was that I actually *knew* something about them, such as how many there were, and how far they stretched. I didn't know as an astronomer knows, but I knew a little because astronomers had figured it out.

To everything else, the stars were backdrop. To humans, the stars were a door. What humans did, collectively, was learn. We built knowledge.

Leading… where? We didn't know yet. Maybe to where the Xu were. And maybe that's why the Xu had created this cruel and diabolical Judgment: Not to qualify us for membership in some galactic fellowship, but to eliminate the one group that could eventually share their star knowledge. Us. People. They wanted humans not just to be less human, they wanted us not to speculate, not to measure, and above all not to go.

They wanted us to end on the plains of Africa, serene, untroubled, hunting without excess, cohabitating without cruelty, and turning away from the stars.

Trusting that Ellie and Nick would do the dirty deed: species suicide.

I couldn't do that. Wonder was cooked into my DNA. As was excess, ruthlessness, and desire, all the things that made us people. So eventually the Xu would murder us too, even if Ellie and I tried to sustain our Eden.

That was my hunch, anyway.

If she killed Adam and Eve, the Xu would have to kill us. Otherwise, the murder of Adam and Eve wouldn't be a Reset, it would be a Repetition. The more we tried to fix things, the more we'd flunk their Judgment.

I had to stop her, because saving Adam and Eve was the only way to keep her and me alive. Once Click and Foxy were gone, we were the next threat. We would have eliminated our usefulness.

I had to stop her – even if it meant forever alienating the first girl I'd ever loved. I had to risk her disapproval, and even hate.

I had to find her, and give her up.

I set out on a loping run even as threads of energy leaked from my sinews and veins. I was so damned tired. But I was going to save them all: Click, Foxy, the People, and especially Ellie. Here we humans were hunting each other again, but we didn't have to. We just needed to cooperate, escape, and learn, to be what we were destined to become.

I saw Africa through a fever. My head buzzed. Weariness hazed the landscape and turned it more golden than ever, but also more dreamlike. I ran alone through waving wheat—colored grass, animals lifting their necks to watch my passing. None feared me. They hadn't learned to yet. None chased me. Maybe they sensed my mission. The sun bent my shoulders. Mirages on far horizons shimmered like receding water.

I'd developed a hunter's eye and could occasionally detect the trampled wake of the People's passage in this grassy sea. When the trail dipped into muddy swales fringed with green, I twice found Ellie's boot print.

So I ran harder, chest heaving, out of breath and in pain, my pulse pounding as it had when I first approached Goat Island. Mile after mile, up one gentle grassy swell and down the other, like a little boat on a rolling sea. Beyond pain! I ran until I burst into that peculiar zone where an athlete leaves the body, and watched myself from a distance. I was a tiny ant in the cinnamon dust of Africa, the continent and the future swelling into infinity like an expanding universe. I dimly thought how easily a lion or leopard could hunt me down, their jaws snapping my neck as if made of glass. Yet when I spotted a pride once, sunning on rocks less than a quarter mile away, an old male stood and nodded as if to wish me well, his black–tipped mane blowing in the wind.

Or wish me farewell.

The day was late when I saw a smudge of smoke far ahead. It marked the latest camp of the People, still migrating north. I slowed to catch my gasping breath and make a plan. I'd find Ellie, explain how humans were here to understand the stars, and talk her out of her madness once and for all. We wouldn't replace Adam and Eve, we'd shepherd them. We, not Gabriel, would play guardian angel.

And with that we would win this crazy game by judging our kind worthy.

I walked the last few hundred yards with a side ache, lungs heaving, heart pounding, head throbbing, dehydrated and utterly dizzy with worry and weariness. I couldn't see well. Spots fluttered in my vision like butterflies. Something stood from the grass and I startled, but when I approached I saw it was only Boy, serving as sentry. Rather than run to greet me he watched solemnly as I limped toward him. The sun had gone down and the sky was deepening from orange to purple, storks winging down to roost in the trees. The People would be tired and bed down soon. Ellie and I would have a chance to talk and make up.

"Aie–ee?" I asked Boy. He looked puzzled, looking past me to the hills I'd come from as if wondering where I'd left her. There was concern in his eyes. Maybe he thought she'd died.

I felt again that sense of doom.

Boy held up a bracelet he'd made. He'd taken small blue savanna flowers and woven them into a grassy wristband. "Aie–ee." He'd made it for her. His voice was sad.

Only humans weave flowers into decoration. We didn't just appreciate the world's beauty; we used it and added to it. No beast did that. No beast gardened. And I'd noticed that while in my time this would be a project for girls, in the primitive prehistoric we men appreciated flowers as much as women and used them to brighten the brown and ochre of everyday life. Guys wore flowers as women did. So I put out my hand, asking for his gift to Ellie.

He solemnly gave it to me.

I slipped the bracelet on and felt a new surge of certainty. "Thank you."

I walked past where Boy stood sentry and entered the ring of people. Some were still sitting companionably by a low fire, but the youngest and oldest had already crawled off to sleep. The sky was a bruised plum, and I could see clouds mounding where the sun had set. It was muggy again, and rain was coming. Mothers were slipping skins over children.

Where was Ellie?

Had I passed her on the savanna without knowing? Had she simply gone off by herself in another direction? If so, how could I find her?

There was a lightning flash in the distance that gave

a moment of lurid illumination. And well beyond the camp, creeping in high grass, was a glint that could only be Ellie's ragged white T–shirt. She was sneaking up on something under a particularly high and lonely acacia tree. I watched as thunder rumbled. She was carrying a spear.

I physically jerked with anger and despair. She hadn't approached the friendly campfire, or let her presence be known. She'd stolen a weapon to stalk her prey. She was a huntress, stealthy as a lion, creeping up on an innocent Adam and Eve like a serpent in the Garden. Click and Foxy had bedded down by themselves this night, and Eleanor Terrell had a perfect opportunity to slay them without interference.

I almost cried warning. But then Ellie might have rushed the resting couple, or bolted from the camp. So instead I trotted silently and urgently toward her, my own spear clutched. A few adults turned their heads curiously as I passed.

"Aie–ee," I heard Boy say in surprise from behind me.

Another flash, and more thunder. I shook to the sound of it.

It felt as if I were trapped in molasses those last hundred yards. It took forever to close the gap, almost as if the girl was receding from me. When I finally neared I saw her ghostly form rise to full height, her spear arm high, one leg back and the other forward as she poised to hurl her weapon. The primeval couple must already be asleep.

"Ellie!"

She looked to the sound of my shout, not entirely surprised, and shook her head. "Too late, Nick!"

How I longed for her. How I hated the grim conviction she'd come to.

A head came up in the grass, his look questioning. Click. He rolled.

His move forced Ellie to adjust her aim. That gave me the instant I needed to make my own dread decision. I didn't really think so much as act. In that last second of choice and responsibility, I hurled my spear with desperate strength. The point struck Ellie's back, knocking her to her knees. I could hear the shocked gasp.

The pain must be incredible.

Now Foxy sat up too, crying out. Ellie's suspended spear wavered in her fist, still pointed at the two. Then it fell, harmlessly, into the grass.

"No!"

I realized it was me who had shouted.

Ellie remained kneeling, chest heaving, staring at the cave people in wonder. The trio had frozen into a tableau. Foxy held an antelope skin protectively up to her neck. Click had his arm raised in defense. And Eleanor Terrell was white with shock. To my horror my spearhead stuck out the front of her body. The power of my throw surprised me.

I'd speared the girl I loved to save two savages whose

importance I took on faith. I'd lost my chance at happiness to sustain our wretched human history.

"I'm so sorry."

Had she said it, or had I?

I could see the flint tip jutting beyond her chest. The rear of the shaft stuck out her back as sturdy as a peg. It was horrible.

But there was no blood. Anywhere.

Ellie slowly stood, wincing, turning to me as lightning flashed. She seemed weirdly translucent, as if she were a ghost or made of ice. I could see the shadow of the wooden shaft sticking through her body as if looking at an X–ray. A tear ran down her cheek. She wanly smiled.

"You won the game, Nick."

"I threw in desperation, but you can't murder…"

"You had to persuade us, Nick. The Xu never decide. An intelligent species must decide its worth for itself. You were chosen to be the judge even as you chose yourself, and were doomed to make a choice between humankind and me. You had to really care. You had to be certain." Another tear slid down her cheek. "I'm proud of you."

I was shocked at my own deed. "I've killed you."

She staggered to one side, fighting to keep her balance. "You sacrificed me."

My own eyes filled until I could barely see. Lightning slashed, and thunder boomed. "I came to tell you about the stars."

She coughed, weakly. "I know about the stars."

And then she vanished in a rain of golden sparks.

CHAPTER 30

HOME

BIRDCALL. SHRILL, PIPING.

It penetrated my consciousness like annoying pricks of sound, lilting yet insistent. *Chirpadee–chirp–chirp–chirp.* The calls were different than Africa.

My eyes opened. Instead of a thunderous storm in the African twilight, I was looking up at the branches of Douglas fir trees. The sky was its habitual Northwest gray. How?

I groaned and sat up. My body felt pummeled, and my mind was clenched with sorrow so vast, and loss so overwhelming, that I had to work to breathe.

I had stabbed Eleanor Terrell, and she hadn't just died, she'd vanished. No blood. No corpse. No explanation. Poof!

And I was back on Goat Island.

You won the game, Nick. I'm proud of you.

I was vacuumed empty, and crushed with utter defeat. I'd destroyed the first girl I ever loved. Given her up for what? The grim present? I shook my head, trying to locate reality. I could feel the prick of under-brush, smell the forest duff, and hear lapping saltwater. Had the Africa adventure been some kind of hallucino-genic dream inhaled from mold I'd breathed in the Fort Whitman tunnels? A brain trick fostered by the diaboli-cal Xu?

The problem was that Africa felt all too real. Ellie felt real, those piercing eyes and her last sad smile. There was none of that evaporating haze of memory you get in waking from a dream. The prehistoric seemed urgently recent, and more tangible than home or high school. My head pounded, my thirst was thick, and my hand calloused from holding a spear.

I took inventory. My pack was bloody and empty. My clothes were in shreds. My arms were dark brown from sun. I was covered with dry dust. I pulled up my jeans leg. There they were, two pocks of scar from the snakebite, my calf still bruised. I could smell campfire smoke, and my boots were battered and filthy.

There was a circlet of dried flowers on my wrist.

"It really happened." My own raspy croak made me jump. The conviction horrified me.

So I cried. From exhaustion, from survival, from bitterness, and from loss. I hadn't cried in years, but I sure did there in the Pacific Northwest underbrush. I'd survived, but some part of me – the innocent part – was irrevocably gone.

Responsibility sucks.

While Africa was real, nothing Ellie had told me about herself was true. She wasn't from California. She hadn't been kidnapped by space creatures. She wasn't human. This girl I'd loved and kissed was a hallucination, a bizarre trick, still as vivid as my own trembling hands.

I should have been angry. All I could muster was heartbreak.

There was a roar of anguish, and as birds flew up in alarm I realized it had come from me. It left me panting and numb.

I stank, even to me. So I waded into shockingly brisk Skagit Bay, temperature about fifty degrees, and clenched my gut long enough to dive under and use my fingers to comb the worst grit out of my hair. The saltwater stung a hundred scrapes and scratches, and my muscles tightened in protest. Then I surged back out, wheezing from the cold, and stood on the barnacled cobbles to shiver and peer about.

Everything looked normal, if I knew what normal was anymore. The fog had lifted. A gillnetter was thrumming towards Deception Pass. A pleasure boat had its sails up, and a power yacht was cruising toward La Conner. There was even a sonic growl. I looked up. Jets from the Navy base on Whidbey Island were sliding by. Same humans, same militaries, same culture, same world. I'd murdered one Eve to save another, and save this.

So nothing had really happened. And yet, despite

wanting to deny it, I knew in my soul of souls that all of it really had. I had prevented a Reset, and a Consequence. For better or worse it was still us, puzzling about the stars.

I dragged my kayak back down to the water and clambered wearily aboard. I didn't care anymore if someone saw me trespassing and yelled. Such a challenge seemed utterly trivial. I drifted away from Goat Island, getting the feel of my paddle. It seemed a hundred years since I'd touched it. There were no thick throngs of silvery fish, no slapping salmon. Wildlife was back to its depleted norm. This time the tide was running as I'd calculated, back towards the open sea, so I slowly paddled with it back through Deception Pass, under that high green bridge, and worked my long way home.

"You're late," my mother said. She was changing clothes in order to barmaid, and Carl was watching TV on the couch. "Lasagna in the fridge."

My stomach growled. An ordinary meal would be ambrosia. But I had something to say first. "Mom, we can do better."

"What?"

Then I told Carl that he couldn't smoke or drink in or around our house. Ever.

He looked at me with wary surprise, and huffed something about not giving a shit.

"What happened to your clothes?" Mom asked to try to divert the showdown, looking at me for the first time. She wrinkled her nose. "You smell like seawater."

I took Carl's beer from the end table and poured it down the sink. He jumped up, blustering, but stopped when he saw my eyes. The man was confused.

"Carl, you don't do anything for us but take up the couch."

"Listen, you little…" But he looked beyond me to the expression in Mom's eyes gone wide, her look of fear and agreement as cutting as a slap.

I braced for an explosion, but even Carl knew he'd invested nothing in the relationship.

He left that evening and never came back.

And my flustered Mom, I could tell, was glad to have him gone.

The rest of my homecoming stuff isn't too important. I did notice that apprentice hood Seth Rutledge took a surprised look at me in the school hallways and stayed out of my way. I stayed out of his, too, until I thought about it for a while and finally went up to him because no one else would. "Hey, Rutledge, you ever hiked to the bat caves in the woods?"

He looked at me warily. "What?"

"We should hang out some time, go up there."

He was confused. "With you?"

"Think about it." He needed friends, too.

Coach Springer evaluated my leather–lean profile and asked, "You ever consider the wrestling team, Brynner?"

Another thing: I asked Andrea Martinez to the prom. I didn't care that Shane Wagner had already done so, and it turned out his invitation was tentative and half–assed and that Andrea, for some inconceivable reason, had always been more interested in me. So after a second in which I registered her pleased surprise that I'd finally had the guts to ask her, she said yes, Shane gave her up, and I decided risking an invitation was better than letting life pass you by. So that was different.

What wasn't different was that I hadn't missed a day of school or a single homework assignment, if you can believe it. I had a math test the next morning. Time travel sucks.

My History Day project was toast. There was no way anyone would believe what I had to say about Fort Whitman and beside, I couldn't let anyone go out there. Not to mention that a caveman named Click had my cell phone.

It has probably rusted away after fifty thousand years, but what a hoot if an archeologist ever finds it!

My baseball cap hung in my room as souvenir, along with the key to that cave padlock. I found the key in my pocket when I got back.

The flowers I pressed into an old copy of *The Wizard of Oz*.

I went to confront Mr. Faunus, and wasn't particularly surprised that he wasn't there. Seems he'd been called to a family emergency and wouldn't be completing the school year after all. A substitute for the substitute would be found.

Two days later a letter came that had been mailed

with a local postmark. I rarely get letters – who does, anymore? – and this one was hand addressed, with the return address our high school. The penmanship was abnormally neat, like the kind that people were taught a hundred years ago. But then time and history didn't have much meaning in this context.

Here's what it said:

Dear Nick,

What does it mean to be human? Every child explores this when growing up. Part is love. Part is loss. Part is learning, that unquenchable desire to know. Your own exploration was more extreme than most, and you demonstrated considerable courage and determination. Hooah, a jarhead might say.

I know your heart is broken right now, but what happened had to happen for the Judgment to play out. It was utterly real, by the way. And utterly important. Never blame yourself. Ellie was not who you thought she was. This is not the last time you will be disillusioned.

You confirmed my expectation that you are not ordinary, Nick, and in fact are growing into someone quite extraordinary, and remarkably remarkable. Your demonstration of character, particularly your willingness to learn from your choices – and to sacrifice what you loved most for a higher good – was necessary. I promised that you would perform well as a representative of your kind. As your companion said, you passed the test. You may remember that choice is freedom, freedom means responsibility, and responsibility requires faith.

Intelligent species, unlike animals, have the freedom to choose. It's the choices they make that qualify them for membership in a higher fraternity. This was a first step. It mattered that you had faith in your own species. Time will tell if it was justified. We are still watching.

You will not win a History Day scholarship. But you must become a leader in teaching your own kind about stewardship, not fifty thousand years ago but now. My belief that you can do so is represented by a trust fund I've left behind. We've granted you a $100,000 scholarship account to be used at a college of your choice. Consider it fair pay for your recent experiences. Our ability to create such a fund should not surprise you. Future correspondence will inform you how to access the account, and will explain to your mother that it is a gift from a previously unknown relative. Given her circumstances, I doubt she'll want to question too deeply. She is very proud of you, Nick.

This fund can be used for only one investment — education of yourself. Your planet needs wise leaders.

My faith is that your life will repay our investment in your learning.

Sincerely, Peter Faunus.

Sincerely. Well, that was chummy. But then I sensed that the Xu, if that's what they really were, did not fit the Hallmark greeting card standard of warm and fuzzy. Not

Faunus. Not Gabriel. Not even Ellie. Certainly not the hulking caveman I had thrust a spear into and changed into stars. Or a patrolling gort. Someone is looking over us, but not in a cuddly way.

Had Ellie felt anything for me in our journey? Could her kind, whatever they were, feel like we can? Had it been as hard for her to betray me as it was for me to be betrayed?

I'd be left not knowing for all time.

But I had a future. And a prehistoric past unlike any kid on earth.

It was only when I turned the letter over that I felt a thrill of dread.

P.S. Now that you've earned your spurs, we may ask you for additional assistance to help sustain the current Track. There can be rips in time's fabric, short-circuits in cause and effect, and required repairs to history.

Rest assured it will never take much time. (That's a joke.)

When I set the letter down, it dissolved into a puff of golden sparks.

*

THE STORY BEHIND THIS STORY

WAS THERE REALLY a caveman Adam and Eve we can all trace our ancestry to?

The scientific answer is yes, sort of. No, not exactly. And finally, scientists will keep researching that question to provide a fuller understanding of our prehistoric past.

The decoding of DNA has allowed geneticists to contribute to our anthropological understanding of the origins of our species. As explained in this book, following genetic traces backwards leads in theory to a single male and single female whose genes survive in us all. These individuals, however, probably did not live at the same time, or ever meet. Rather their descendants met, reproduced, and their DNA wound up by chance in the group – possibly as small as the one described here – that left Africa to populate other continents. This is the scientific story suggested by the weight of existing evidence.

To put this time–travel tale in context, it's useful to know the planet's history and the outline of human origins.

The age of the earth is estimated at 4.6 billion years. The development of complex life on our planet was very slow, with single–celled algae taking more than two and a half billion years to develop.

Such depths of time are impossible for the human mind to fully grasp, so scientists sometimes compare the earth's history to a twenty–four–hour clock. By that standard, algae don't show up until 2:08 p.m., after more than fourteen hours of our planetary "day" had already elapsed.

Dinosaurs appear at 10:46 p.m., and the reign of mammals occupies just the last twenty–one minutes. Hominids and humans arrive the last minute before midnight.

Let's switch back to years. Hominids, the human ancestors descended from apes, evolved two to three million years ago. (The dinosaurs died out sixty–five million years ago, after a huge comet or asteroid hit the earth near Mexico's Yucatan Peninsula. For tens of millions years after that, mammals dominated the land, but people weren't around yet.)

The appearance of hominids coincides roughly with the advent of the latest series of twenty or so Ice Ages that have transformed the recent earth. Civilization began shortly after the retreat of the last glacial advance some ten thousand years ago. Rapid climate change may have spurred our evolution and technology.

Modern Homo sapiens who looked and thought like us are estimated to be only one hundred thousand to two hundred thousand years old: a blink in geologic time. Near relatives such as Homo erectus and the Neanderthals died out as we flourished. The last Neanderthals disappeared – scientists think – about twenty–five thousand years ago.

Homo sapiens did not have a straight and easy path to planetary dominance. After an early advance from Africa perhaps 175,000 years ago, our species appears to have almost gone extinct, at one time declining to as few as ten thousand people. We disappeared from Europe and Asia, surviving only in East Africa.

Then we expanded again. That's the moment told in this story.

The best recent estimate of a second emergence that populated the world is fifty thousand to seventy thousand years ago, the time in which Nick and Ellie have their adventure.

Scientists are still learning when our species invented objects such as clothing, containers, weapons, tools, shelter, ornaments, and religion. Because many items would be made of wood, bone, or grass, most of what cavemen used has rotted or broken. Caves yield some finds, however, and anthropologists also study the technology and beliefs of modern primitive tribes. The implements the People use in this story are consistent with recent estimates of the technology available then. Much remains to be learned.

This book takes place in modern–day Tanzania and Kenya and is based on real places the author visited.

Nick and Ellie are deposited on Tanzania's Serengeti savanna, now a game reserve, and hike to Ngorongoro Crater, which is visited by tourists today. The People flee northeastward past modern–day Olmoti and Empakaai volcanic craters and skirt Ol Doinyo Lengai volcano and Lake Natron on their way to Kenya. The author walked part of this route. The clan of Click and Foxy will continue north through Ethiopia to the Straits of Bab–el–Mandeb in Eritrea.

Genetic evidence suggests a very small group of humans may have crossed this strait at the southern end of the Red Sea and eventually spread from the Arabian Peninsula to Europe, Asia, and Australia. An alternate idea is that they descended the Nile and crossed the Sinai desert to modern–day Israel and Syria before spreading out. In any event, they got to the Americas much later across the Bering Strait land bridge, created by low sea levels during the most recent Ice Age.

It is fascinating to contemplate that all of humanity's future genetic eggs may have been in one basket.

And that a small throw of fate could have decided our species' future.

*

ABOUT WILLIAM DIETRICH

WILLIAM DIETRICH IS the author of twenty books of fiction and nonfiction. His fiction, including his New York Times bestselling Ethan Gage series of Napoleonic adventures, has sold into thirty–one languages. The author's Pacific Northwest nonfiction has won the Pacific Northwest Booksellers Award and Washington Governor Writers Award. As a career journalist at the *Seattle Times*, Bill shared a Pulitzer Prize for coverage of the Exxon Valdez oil spill. Dietrich has been a Nieman Fellow at Harvard University and the recipient of several National Science Foundation journalism fellowships. He lives in Anacortes, Washington, USA.

The author's website is www.williamdietrich.com.